Broken Justice

THROUGH DARKNESS TALL
VOLUME I

D.W. CRAIGIE

Cover and Interior Art by Alexis Vergara
Cover Design and Interior Layout by Jennifer Tuite

ISBN-10: 1477646728
ISBN-13: 978-1477646724

Dedication

*To Charles Clarence Craigie and Dorothy Alice Craigie.
Both of you, in your own ways, taught me to live
with grace, dignity, and passion.*

Acknowledgements

Thank you to my Mom for showing me the value of hard work and loving me no matter what.

Thank you to my Dad for encouraging me to be an independent thinker and for never once doubting my dream of being a writer.

Jeremy, Zack, Jeanette, and Erin – no man could ask for better brothers or sisters. You've supported me and kept me grounded all at the same time.

Merle, you helped me realize I had my own voice and that my writing didn't have to sound like anyone else's.

Without the skills and knowledge of Casey, Aaron, Pam, Alexis and Jen this project wouldn't have gotten off the ground. Thank you from the bottom of my heart.

Sammy and Ella, you are the reasons I strive to be a better man. Never give up on your dreams.

To my beautiful wife Kathryn, this book wouldn't exist without you. I picked up a pen again because of your love and support. I cannot even begin to express what that means to me. This one is for you, babe.

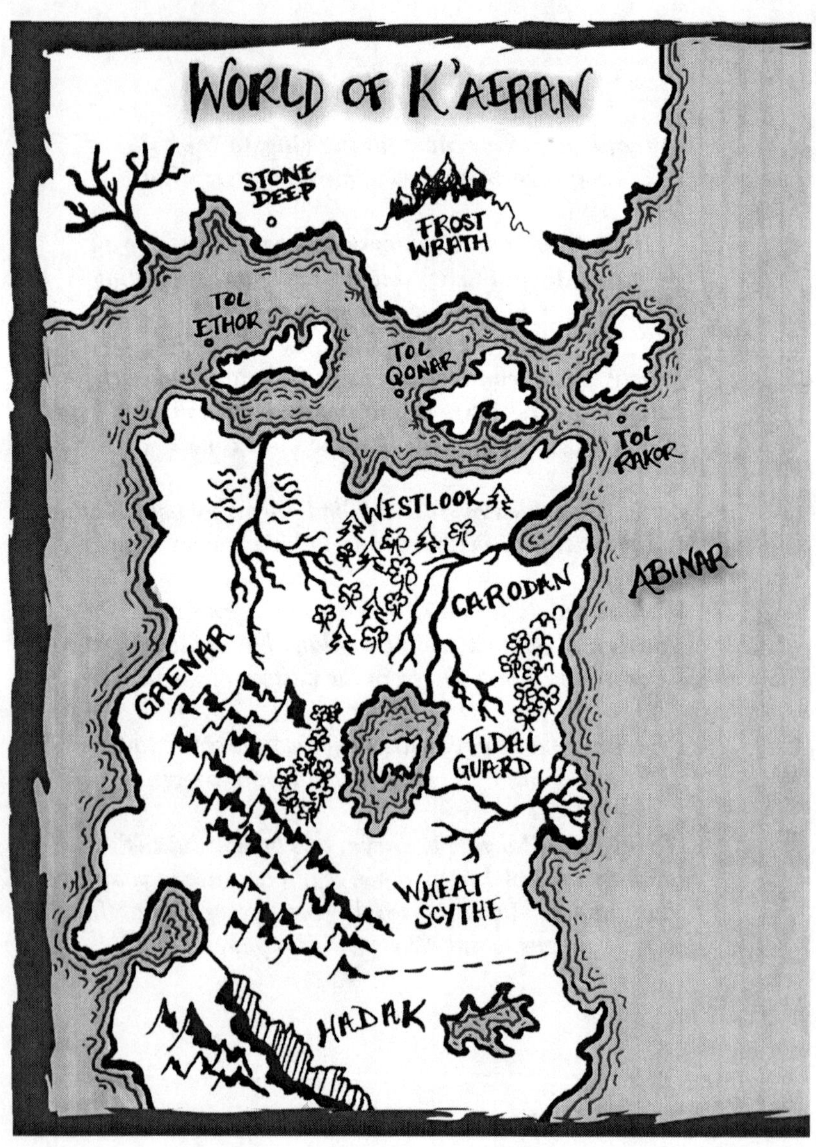
WORLD OF K'AERAN
STONE DEEP
FROST WRATH
TOL ETHOR
TOL QONAR
TOL RAKOR
WESTLOOK
ABINAR
CARODAN
GRENAR
TIDAL GUARD
WHEAT SCYTHE
HADAK

ICE DAGGER BAY
STONESTRIKER LUMBERCAMP
WINTER PINE FOREST
FROST CREST OCEAN
FRIDINIKAR
PLAINS OF THIQOK
GRANIKAR
NORISTAR
SONISTAR
NORIZARAD SEA
BAY OF CAROTHAK
EBON SEA
TANGAN'LAR

MAP OF CARODAN
SHARK BAY
MEANDER VALE
TWIST REED
LITTLE TOP
GRENFEL MARSHES
IRON BARK WOODS
GREY ROCK
ANGLER'S COVE
WESTLOOK
THE HIGHTOWER
SANCTUARY BAY
WHITEBREAK
BRONZE CAST LAKE
HEDGE TOP
VINEHOLD
THE FRIGID MANSE
VINE BASIN
BLACK TREE
EVERWATCH
Amen'Kar
The Meander
Upper Karneden
The East Kar
The Karneden
THE KAR DARK
LAKEMOUTH
THE GREEN KEEP
LAKE AZURERON
CITADEL
JADE FOREST
TRUESHORE
THE TRUE DEEP
TIDAL GUARD
THE FORLORN RAMPARTS
Solitary Course
LONG HOLD
Teratawn Flow
CROSSROAD
WHEAT SCYTHE
SUNMANSE
ALONE LAKE
BARLETON
HORNSTONE
DARKHOME
SOUTH HAWK
ANTAUNNA'S DIVIDE

Blessing of Antaunna

I am only one
And the world is great
I know not where my road takes me
I know not how long it is.

The trials are many
And the pain is great
I will be shaken
I will be torn.

But in all life there is reason
There is Balance
For everything I lose
There is something gained.

Antaunna is my strength
Her hand my guide
From her I have the will to stand
Through the darkness tall.

Chapter 1
BROKEN JUSTICE

The late afternoon sun set on Kailen Tidespinner as he darted across the forest floor, slipping from shadow to shadow. The soft soles of his boots did not betray his step. His clothes, darkened green and brown, matched the foliage around him. Quiet as a ghost, he stalked his prey. Those he followed were not as silent.

He knelt and inspected the tracks of four men. All were weighed down with armor and weapons. One set of prints, long and deep, had been made by someone big, very big. Using the undergrowth as cover, Kailen followed them. In this remote corner of the Ironbark Woods, close to the Grenfel Marshes and on the very border of Carodan, the path was kept open only by light foot traffic. Kailen guessed the raiders had been using the area for several months.

A mile down the path, the snapping of a strong fire and an echo of voices peppered the air. The first traces of smoke, flavored with cooking meat, caressed his nostrils. His mouth watered. Once finished, he would have his first hot supper in days. It smelled like actual beef, not horse.

He slowed. Night would soon lend him cover. The trees here were not as closely packed, and fingers of sunset lit the forest in amber light. Kailen kept to the deep shadows between these slivers. Named Darogo's Touch, after the Father Dragon that formed the sun, the evening twilight could expose him and spell his death. Alert to all threats, the breeze roared in his ears like the Upper Karneden after the spring thaw. Just over the next ridge the now-visible smoke of his quarry's fire drifted through the branches of the surrounding ironbarks and pine trees. Kailen looked to the sky. Half an hour until sunset. He would wait.

Concealed within the gnarled branches of a jade berry thicket, Kailen checked his gear. His leathers and harnesses were tightly strapped with no loose ends to snag or flap about. The oiled ironwood of his bow flexed comfortably under his draw. His gull-fletched arrows, secure in their quiver, were ready to pull. The two daggers strapped to his boots slid easily from their sheathes. Lastly, he held the hilt of his father's sword, the leather worn to his grip. The bronze pommel was worn and pitted, the steel crossbar marked with dings and scratches, but the blade's balance was perfect. He trailed a finger along the cold metal already knowing every spot of wear.

Kailen sat cross-legged on the forest floor with his bow balanced on his knees and his hands folded over its center. He closed his eyes and focused on his pounding heart. A single, flowing breath threaded over his lips. The air filled his lungs, its crisp sting a shock to his body. Evening's chill fingers seeped through his chest. His heart beat slightly slower. The first breath left him.

He took another breath, this time picturing himself slipping through the darkened underbrush with perfect body control, his prey unaware. The forest would shield him. It would give him the power to judge and sentence. The second breath left him.

He inhaled once more, thinking of the four-wagon caravan he had found three days ago. The family of a peat-farmer, they had been returning from town, their load of peat sold and fresh supplies filling the wagons. Kailen wondered how many people were still waiting for those supplies. No clues revealed the caravan's destination. The oxen had been slaughtered, and everything of value was taken. Only the bodies, and their bog-stained clothes, were left; three men, two boys, and three women. The men had been killed quickly, but not the women. Their skirts were torn, the flesh between their legs a bruised and bloody mess. Kailen had at first thought this the work of bandits. Then he found the blonde girl. Carved into her forehead was a glyph. No Cardanan, bandit or not, would ever trace the Mark of Galantaegan.

The attackers were Noriziem.

There was no way to know how the sons of bitches had made it this far inland, away from the safety of their longships, but it didn't really matter. Eight Cardanans, dead at the hands of Noriziem, had nothing more than simple cairns and a brief prayer from Kailen to honor them. If he were able, he would kill every last Noriziem. The world of K'aeran would be better for it.

The third breath left him.

His thundering heart calmed and the jittery heat of nervousness cooled to hardened resolve. He opened his eyes to the failing light and let them adjust. It was the time of a Warden of Carodan. The branches of the thicket whispered with his light-footed departure.

He froze, turned, and peered through the growth behind him. The only light was the pale mist of moon and stars. The hairs stood on the back of his neck. The sensation was the same as when a mountain lion had once stalked him. He studied the forest, saw nothing, and shook it off.

Fog puffed from his mouth. He closed on the encampment and scaled the small rise. Reaching the crest, he peered through the branches at the small hollow below.

Kailen studied the encampment. The hollow was wide and well hidden, a deep bowl carved from the top of the hill. Several lean-tos and tents ringed its center. A spiked earthen berm formed the camp's perimeter, but Kailen saw only two sentries, one close to him, the other on the opposite side. At the camp's center six men sat around the bonfire, hunched over their food and drink. Their laughs and jests floated to him in pieces over the crack of the fire. The language was harsh and old. Lording over it all, nailed to a stripped sapling trunk, was a simple banner marked with the silhouette of a black dragon.

Kailen picked his path down the hill. He chose his footing carefully and avoided the loose stones and arced roots that dotted the downward slope. He trusted the twisting fire-shadows to hide him. The nearest guard stared back at the camp with an expression of hunger and irritation combined. He never heard Kailen slip beside him. There was no chance to cry out as a long dagger was driven below his jaw and into his brain. Kailen removed the dagger, wiped it off on the sentry's shirt, and sheathed it. He pulled the body away from the camp and laid it beneath a large fern. None of the other men noticed the guard's disappearance.

Drawing his dagger again, Kailen circled to the opposite side of the camp. This guard, more diligent, stared out into the forest. He had no reason to look back at the camp. Kailen snuck from under one of the sharpened barricade logs, right behind the man, and slid his steel cleanly between the man's skull and first vertebra. The Noriziem could only gurgle on his choking blood. Kailen tucked this one's body down into the encircling ditch. The men around the fire still drank and ate.

Over the berm he climbed, landing lightly on his feet behind one of the tents. The Noriziems' conversation was now easy to hear. Peering around the edge of the tent, he watched a bear of a man, clad in tattered leathers and rusting chain mail, stagger to his feet with a splashing mug still in hand. The brute made pumping motions with his arms. Kailen was able to understand most of what he said.

"Now the blonde was a real joy. She fought and kicked, but you could tell she loved it. I haven't had a woman like that in months."

The man next to him, in furs that Kailen could smell from twenty paces away, chimed in, "And you won't again anytime soon. You cut her deep."

"Well," the big man held a hand to his chest as if indignant, "the bitch did try to kick my cock in. She deserved it."

"Aye, a true believer of justice you are!"

They roared with laughter, and the raiders slapped each other on the back, buried their faces in their joints of oxen, and poured beer down their throats. They did not hear Kailen draw his bow. They did not hear his bowstring creak. They did hear the man in stinking furs scream when an arrow sprouted from his eye. He fell back, dead before he hit the ground. The others stared, stupid surprise their only expression. Before they could turn to see where the arrow came from, a second shaft found its mark in the throat of a pot-bellied oaf sitting to the left of the man in rusted mail. The rest stood, drawing axe and sword, but Kailen was already moving.

He rushed between two tents and closed on the man nearest to him, a Noriziem of average build and wearing boiled leather armor. He wielded a mace in one hand and a dagger in the other. Clouded by ale, he took a clumsy swing at Kailen. The Warden side-stepped and gutted the man on the first hit and opened his throat on the second. The raider collapsed trying to hold his entrails in with one hand and staunch the flow of blood from his neck with the other. Kailen could have driven his sword through the man's heart and ended his suffering quickly. He didn't.

Two Noriziem charged him at the same time. One held his sword high over his head and screamed. Spittle flew from his mouth. The scream turned to a gasp of surprise when Kailen's sword pierced the Noriziem's stomach and its point punched clear through his back. The second man almost on him, Kailen tried to pull his sword out of the Noriziem, but it was lodged in his ribs and would not budge. He dumped the body in front of the other Noriziem. The man tripped, sprawling on the dirt, but he was quick and regained his footing. Kailen drew his daggers and parried the Noriziem's clumsy swings. The man was using a short, heavy sword and Kailen's arms numbed from the impact. The Noriziem swung at his head. Kailen ducked the sword and slashed the man's thigh. His attacker cursed in Norzaat and was thrown off balance. Kailen drove one dagger into the man's side and the other up through his jaw. He collapsed, his blood staining the forest floor. The giant in chain was the only one left. The brute held a great axe in both hands, but he hung back. Just the slightest quiver of uncertainty lurked behind the anger in his eyes.

"Shu tack au? Vaut kay au toqeth?"

Who are you? What do you want?

Kailen said nothing. He wanted his sword back. He walked, with exaggerated calm, to the formerly screaming berserker and braced his foot on the man's chest, grabbed the hilt, and pulled. The sword came out with a wet, grinding hiss, the blade smeared with blood. Kailen held the weapon ready and kept one of his daggers in his offhand. He approached the big Noriziem. Grunting, the barbaric foreigner charged and swung his axe. Kailen sidestepped, the battleaxe whirring past his left shoulder. He slashed with his sword and felt it skip off the man's chain mail. Kailen circled to the right, dodging another chop from the axe. He came in low, distracting the Noriziem with a feint from his sword and then burying his dagger in the man's thigh. The Noriziem screamed and almost dropped his axe. He held on though, and brought the butt of it down on Kailen's shoulder.

His left arm numb, Kailen struggled to hold on to his dagger. His fingers wouldn't respond and the small blade was suddenly heavy. He dropped it and swung wildly with his sword, pushing the bigger man back.

Trying to shake his arm back to life, Kailen circled again. The Noriziem couldn't put any weight on his injured leg, and his arms sagged with fatigue. Kailen had had enough of this. He switched his sword to his left hand, consciously willing each finger to wrap around the hilt. With his right he drew his other dagger and threw it straight at the Noriziem. Cold, tempered steel sunk into the man's groin. The giant dropped his axe, falling to his knees and clutching his crotch. Kailen kicked the man in the face, laying him out. Bracing his boot against the pommel of the dagger, he ground it in deeper. The man screamed so pitifully that Kailen almost felt sorry for him.

He finally answered the Noriziem's question. "I am Kailen Tidespinner, a Warden of Carodan. What I want is to find every Noriziem who steps onto our shores and kill him."

Looking into the man's tearing, panic-filled eyes, Kailen pulled out his dagger. The man whimpered but couldn't scream. His skin was fast turning white and beads of perspiration dotted his pitted and scarred face. Kailen smelled the filth that filled his enemy's pants. The Noriziem tried to speak but had no breath left in his shaking body. Kailen placed the dagger under the man's chin and said, "You'd ask mercy of me, wouldn't you? You don't want to die."

With a spastic jerk the man nodded.

"That blonde girl, with your bastard god carved into her forehead, did she ask you for mercy? You had none for her. I have none for you."

Kailen flipped his dagger down, its point to the man's heart. He punched the knife into the Noriziem's flesh and pulled it out while twisting. A puncture in the man's chest, visible through his torn armor, oozed crimson with a steady, slowing beat. The man gasped at first. Desperately he clung to life, but as the minutes passed even his lungs began to whisper. His body relaxed.

Kailen wiped his blade off on the Noriziem's shirt. "It'll be a clean death, but as you bleed out it will be slow. You can feel death coming, can't you? Remtagast's cold breath is working its way down your spine. Your last moments in this world are going to be spent lying on your ass, shit in your pants, fear stinking your breath. You will greet the White Dragon as a wretch. Covered in filth and pitiful."

With his remaining strength, in broken Cardanan, the Noriziem said, "Galantaegan will burn you. Carodan will burn. The Noriziem carry his will."

Kailen didn't respond. He didn't want the Noriziem to think his words affected him. He watched the man's last breath escape. An odd sharpness tainted the air. It felt like the temperature dropped, and Kailen imagined the sound of great, leathery wings beating. He glanced around but saw nothing. He thought of the White Dragon Remtagast, god of ice and death. The moment passed, and he felt warmer. There had been no sound of beating wings, only his imagination dwelling on old legends. Kailen ignored the goose pimples covering his arms.

The hungry roar of the fire was the only sound. Soon it would burn higher, fueled by the bodies of the eight Noriziem. Kailen walked to the fire, still shaking his tingling arm. A cut of meat still roasted on the spit, and a mostly-full cask of ale sat open by a log. As the strength of battle left him, Kailen's stomach rumbled and his limbs trembled. His arms ached terribly. He sat down on one of the logs, his body jarring as his knees wobbled from the dissipating battle-rush. He picked up the spit and gnawed on the crackling flesh. It burned his mouth but tasted so good he didn't care. A rusted and dented mug lay in the dirt before him. With it he drank a healthy portion of ale that helped to cool his scorched palate.

His eyes, blue and cold, trailed across the dead men strewn around him. He took another draught of ale then set the pewter mug and joint of beef on the log beside him. He kneeled before the fire, crossing his arms over his chest and gazed into the flames. He prayed. "By the edge of steel and the light of flame I send these souls to you for trial, Antaunna. They have darkened the world with their deeds, and I pray that the souls they stole from life will now find peace and satisfaction. May your brother Remtagast find a just sentence for them in the Hereafter. I pray that you will watch over us, as you always have, and keep Carodan strong. Keep me strong. Lady of the Azure, Lady of the Deep Seas, I offer this prayer to you."

With his sword he traced an angled glyph of his own in the

loose soil, its lines evoking the shape of waves; the Mark of Antaunna. He sat back on the log, picked up his drink, and took another bite of meat. Looking over at the dead man in chain and tattered leathers, he again wondered what these Noriziem were doing so far inland. The more he thought of that, the less he thought of the dead blonde girl.

With a full belly and the comfortable buzz of ale tickling the back of his eyes, Kailen destroyed the bandits' camp. He collapsed the tents and knocked down the lean-tos. The fire climbed high as he fed it debris. He sifted through the bandits' loot, still searching for some sign of where the caravan had been heading. In a pile of almost empty leather satchels he found it. A writ of sale, dated recently, to the Twistreed Settlement. A very small village on the border of Carodan and the Grenfel Marshes, it was two days west.

He would make the journey. With the writ he found some of the homesteaders' belongings: a few necklaces, a dagger, and a ring. The necklaces were gold and silver, the emblem of their sept engraved on the front. The Twistreed sigil was several stalks of reed, caught in the gentle pull of a stream. The dagger was well cared for, but the date inscribed on its pommel, 1203, showed it to be over a century old. It may have been the only real weapon that family had, passed down from father to son. Lastly, the ring, a band of twisted gold, held a small, dingy sapphire secured in a dragon-claw setting. It was an engagement ring, most likely also handed from generation to generation. It could have belonged to the blonde girl; she had been the right age. He slipped them into his rucksack. Buried beneath the empty leather bags, he found a full one. Bulging with gold and silver coins, the satchel weighed against his palm. He ran his fingers over the top layer of coins and threw that into his rucksack too. Many Cardanans had died to furnish the Noriziem with that large a sum.

Anything he couldn't carry went into the fire. It grew tall and cast a vivid light into the forest night. When all the wood, leather, and cloth were aflame, Kailen threw in the bodies of the eight men. He had already extracted one tooth from each. Proof of fulfilled duty. The smell of burning human flesh stung his nose and eyes, the way it had when Noriziem raiders sacked his town eighteen years ago. He forced those thoughts away, instead thinking of turning the Noriziem into cinders, appropriate, since

Galantaegan, their god, was the Lord of Ash and Chaos.

To ensure the fire didn't spread, he stayed until the flames gave way to embers. Kailen slung his rucksack and bow across his back, gave his sword one last wipe with a cloth, and sheathed it. He knew he should sleep and not travel at night, but he couldn't. There would be no sleep until he reached Twistreed. At least he could do that much for the families of the dead. He climbed out of the hollow and looked back at the fire. Only a few scattered timbers, too heavy to lift, remained of the camp. A good night's work. Far from the dying fire, the blue light of the stars and moon cast its gentle touch upon his skin. He looked at the moon, round like the blonde girl's face, and wondered what her laugh may have sounded like.

He left the hollow, slipped between the trees, and melted into the shadows. He was far distant when another shape moved down into the encampment. With the exception of the tingling on the back of his neck, Kailen had never even known he was being followed. This creature was made to move in the forest.

Two heads taller than an average man and twice as wide, the Grenar possessed a silence and grace that did not fit his size. His iron gray skin blended into the forest without the need of camouflage; his senses functioned as well at night as they did in the day. The muscles bulging beneath his dark skin were tensed and powerful. He wore only some boiled leather and cloth but was otherwise unencumbered. The only thing of real weight the brute carried was a great halberd, seven feet long tipped with a two foot blade of hammered steel.

The Grenar came to the edge of the ember pit, drawn to the stench of burning human. He knelt in the dirt, surveying the drying pools of blood and the wrecked camp. He had followed the Warden for three days and had been impressed with the little man's speed and stealth. Watching the battle, his respect for the human had increased greatly. This Cardanan knew how to fight.

Another scent caught his attention. He found the keg of ale and the joint of meat by the log the human had sat on. He had never eaten their food, but after watching the tiny man in action, he was curious to experience things as the Warden had. The meat was sweet and parted easily under his long, sharp canines. The beer was a new taste, but not unpleasant. It was very different from the mead the shamans of his tribe made.

Having watched the Warden bury the people from the ambushed caravan, the Grenar realized these were the men who had been responsible for that slaughter. Their smell, different from a Cardanan's, had been all over the slain people and their ruined wagons. The Warden had been impressive in his tracking and handling of the men. Having observed Wardens before, the Grenar knew they were skilled fighters and woodsmen, but this one possessed an admirable fierceness. Even outnumbering the Warden, the raiders never stood a chance. This man had strength and honor. So many of his people thought the humans completely lacked these traits. While often true, it was a misplaced and short-sighted prejudice. A quiet unease, crouching in the back of his mind, urged him to continue tracking the Warden.

He couldn't ignore last night's dream. Most Grenar did not experience visions when they slept, but he had, and vivid pictures of the Warden, encircled by flames and clouds of ash, had haunted his sleep. The fire consumed everything, leaving nothing but char and desolation in its wake.

Chapter 2
IN STONE

"Dora, my cloak."

"Yes, my Lord."

Morrikii Stonestriker wondered when he'd become so old. The man staring back from the silver mirror was a stranger. Beneath the lines that traced his brow and cheeks he saw the young man that used to be. A man who had made history. A man who dared defy the ruling elite of Carodan. A man willing to stand and fight for his convictions. A man who'd lost that fight. His hair, more silver than black now, was still long and full, but more of his forehead showed than it used to. He didn't look at his hands much anymore. The age spots were obvious. Which cloak did he want? "The seal pelt with ermine trim."

Dora, already holding the cloak in her vein-laced hands, clucked and grunted with well-practiced irritation and said, "This is the only cloak you wear. Even during what passes for summer in this wasteland."

Morrikii grinned as she shook her head in frustration. Her silver hair, bound in a bun so tight that not a single strand escaped, seemed to glow orange in the firelight. "It's my favorite."

The weight of the cloak spread over his shoulders. Dora stood on a stool to fix the clasp and ensure that the cloak fell smoothly over the warhammer strapped to Morrikii's back. She tugged at the edges, searching for a perfection she never managed to find. "It looks as good on you as it did your father, my Lord. He was a good man, as are you."

"Thank you, Dora."

Morrikii looked again to the mirror. What would his father think of him now? Maekor Stonestriker had hated the corruption and power struggles that plagued the elite of Carodan, and had passed that disgust down to his son. After assuming the patronage of House Stonestriker at too young an age, Morrikii sparked a revolution to change all that. That grand campaign of righteousness ended with his disgrace and exile to the northern wasteland of Fridinikar. He felt pride tainted with guilt when most of his House, and the septs and high septs that fell under his rule, accompanied him. Dora had been his nanny when he was a lad, and his Matron-of-Care when he reached adulthood. She knew nothing else but love and devotion to Morrikii, but if his parents could see where he'd led their House would they still love him?

"Are you going to the Pinnacle today?"

The question surprised him. "I am. I have not spoken to Him since the last moon."

It was not often he ascended the long, winding stairs to the Pinnacle. On the days he did, his fingers always lacked strength and his stomach could not hold food. But he had no choice. He needed to go.

"You will do well, as always, Morrikii. You do what you must. Even if it means following Him," Dora said.

Morrikii could not ignore the tone of her last sentence. It was the same tone his father would have taken. "You would do well, woman, to remember that because of Him we are still alive and prospering. He will guide us to victory and restitution. All our loyalties, yours included, belong to him."

She stopped smoothing the cloak, stepped down, and turned her back. "Of course, my Lord. You had best go. You should not be late."

He wanted to apologize, but couldn't. She was still his servant and needed to remember her place. He turned from the mirror, looked to the left side of the study at a door that lead to an ascending staircase, and asked, "How is Mella?"

Over her shoulder Dora said, "Your wife is resting well. Last night was a good one."

"Very well. I shall return this evening."

"I'll have dinner ready, my Lord."

"Of course."

She busied herself dusting one of his bookshelves, even though she had cleaned not three days ago. She refused to meet his eyes. If his father were alive to see what was in the Pinnacle, and knew Morrikii was involved with it, he would have disowned his son. There was no question in Morrikii's mind about this. He would take the long way today and tour the city before making his ascent. He closed the door behind him, leaving Dora to her chores.

***

The cold saturated Morrikii. Even in the depths of the mountain he was never really warm. Striding through the torch-lit tunnel, wrapped under the fur cloak and several layers of wool, he did his best not to shiver. The cold draped the edges of the air, clung to the heart of the stone, and slowly worked its way into his bones. The smooth, black granite walls locked the cold in tight, and even the braziers set every ten feet into the walls could not heat the air. Carved to resemble snarling dragons, they were grand things, but their fires were too weak against the cold of the north.

He heard voices, echoed and jumbled, ahead. Soon he would be among his people. Squaring his shoulders and looking straight ahead, he loosed his grip on the ermine-trimmed cloak and let it fall from his shivering body. It was a posture his father had taught him. Leaders of men needed to project a certain confidence. The tunnel widened and the flagstones, etched with smoky patterns, broadened and flattened. He entered a large intersection. Six tunnels converged into a star-shaped junction. A wrought-iron chandelier hung in the center of the vaulted ceiling. Its sunset glow gave false warmth to the ashen stone. Morrikii pretended not to feel cold.

Pairs of guards, clad in black plate and mail, flanked each tunnel mouth. The arms of House Stonestriker, a steel warhammer embossed over a pale silver field with a four-peaked mountain at its base, adorned the tabard of each soldier. The guards snapped to attention and raised their hands in salute as Morrikii passed. He acknowledged them with the smallest nod. In front of the soldiers he always held a hard face.

He crossed the junction and entered the Tunnel-Galant. Dragon torches and iron chandeliers lit the passage in uneven, amber shadows. Statues of great warriors, covered in complicated, ornate armor stood silent guard along the walls. Unsure of who they had been, Morrikii always wondered how he measured up to their past deeds. Had they been afraid to ascend the Pinnacle? Had they been good men? Did they fall prey to same greed that plagued Carodan?

It was warmer here and Morrikii's legs relaxed; his step quick. The muscles in his shoulders loosened, and the lines of his face softened as he walked among his people. Old men, housewives, and children went about their business, crossing from one side of the city to the other. The choices he'd made, the compromises he'd accepted, had all been done for their sake.

He nodded, smiling to all he passed. Be gracious. Be magnanimous. Be their lord. The mantra helped him not think of his destination. In front of all his people, here in the center of this great city, he stood tall and proud.

He neared the end of the road and was almost to Cavern Centre, the heart of Frostwrath, when his name was called. Oily and sweet, the voice chased after him. Looking over his shoulder, Stonestriker saw a mop of greasy hair pushing its way between the shoulders of the crowd. He stopped, rubbed his nose, and mumbled, "The man never leaves me alone."

Short and plump, Jamon Brokesaw reminded Morrikii of a badger. The man's stomping run strengthened the comparison. He pushed aside two merchants, who looked at the Councilor with contempt, but knew better than to say anything. Brokesaw reached Morrikii's side and bowed with regal practice. Morrikii nodded, casting a disapproving eye over the man's daintily trimmed beard and velvet robes. Brokesaw acted as a noble but wasn't. His family was a very wealthy high sept, but strip away the gold and they were still only commoners. The man's presumptions irritated Morrikii, but he was a shrewd Councilor and expert organizer. The man reveled in processing details. Brokesaw's eyes darted and shifted more than normal.

"What brings you down here, Councilor?"

"My Lord, we received a falcon this morning from the Frozen Claw garrison. The first wave of Noriziem ships has been sighted on the Eastern Shore."

"How many?"

"Several hundred."

"How many different clan banners were seen?"

"Four."

"Outstanding. Their ambassadors did not lie. How long until they reach us?"

"The storms off Cape Tower are intense this time of year. Three weeks."

Morrikii rubbed his chin. Allying with the Noriziem, another sin for which his father would have killed him. "Ready the southern wing. It's empty and should house their troops comfortably."

"Yes, my Lord," Brokesaw said and bowed.

As Morrikii stepped past the little man, he said, "I'm on my way to the barracks, I'll inform Axehaft myself of their arrival."

His advisor twitched, swallowed a gulp, and said, "Are you sure, my Lord? I could deliver the news for you."

Morrikii faced him fully. Staring evenly at Brokesaw, and trying not to think of badgers, Lord Stonestriker brooked no argument. "I am quite able of communicating with my own generals. Let the Noriziem ambassadors know their people are arriving in a matter of weeks. We'll have dinner tonight."

"Of course, my Lord, I just thought to spare you the distance--"

"I am also quite capable of walking through my own city. Now go see to the southern wing. Immediately."

Brokesaw bowed quickly and turned away, running from Morrikii almost as fast as he had run to him. Morrikii shook his head and sighed. "Twit."

He continued into Cavern Centre, thinking of the Noriziem's arrival. There had been no outcry from his people when he'd announced the alliance. They trusted him, but Cardanan and Noriziem blood did not mix well. Perhaps their time living in the north had softened their prejudices. Survival required a certain brutal practicality.

The sprawling hall dwarfed him with its looming columns of black granite that stretched from a white marble floor to the matching ceiling. Hundreds of his people milled about the cavern. Erected between the columns, stalls and shops pushed their wares and formed focal points of hollering and heckling. Word spread quickly of his presence in the hall, and even though none ever dared crowd Morrikii, he felt everyone's eyes fall on him. He loved this part of the city. It reminded him of

Whitebreak, the oldest stronghold in Carodan and the former seat of his House. He hadn't seen the sprawling city in a quarter of a century, since his banishment, but he could still remember the reaching towers of the palace and the broad avenues of the town center. He and his father would walk together every afternoon. His family had ruled the city for two centuries, and they were welcomed wherever they tread.

Morrikii strode into the throng, trying not to think of the white city. The people parted way before him. Morrikii exchanged smiles with young merchants, vibrant young women, and aged laborers. Here in the market, they were all from common families, or septs. It didn't matter. They needed to see him strong. Confident.

At the center of the hall, in a hearth unlike any other, burned a great fire. Rising from the white marble, carved of the purest black granite, a dragon head opened its maw towards the ceiling above. The height of a siege tower, it dwarfed all those near. Every scale and ridge was precisely carved into the surface of the stone, and two clusters of garnet served as eyes. The two horns, much like those of a ram, were made of the same white marble as the floor and swept back from the dragon's brow, curling into wicked points. The teeth may have been white as well once, but had long been stained black by the fire burning in the great wyrm's throat. Fueled by a deep cistern hidden within the floor, the heat given off by the dragon was constant and intense, so through the days and nights it always cast its light and warmth on Cavern Centre.

As companions to the great head, two immense claws reached up from the floor, their talons long and curved. Within the palms of each hand were smaller fires that also burned constantly. The Black Dragon watched over them, as it had since that day Morrikii first led his people to this strange, ancient city. Always He watched them.

A cold itch formed at the base of Morrikii's skull. He felt the Presence. The same sensation had awoken him last night: it was how he knew to climb the Pinnacle. There was no ignoring it. He dared not.

At the end of the hall he ascended a spiral stair. He climbed five stories, and at the top entered yet another tunnel. A short passage, it opened onto the city's main barracks, Marshal's Cairn. Carved into the walls of the cave, the entries and balconies of the barracks reached far over Morrikii's head. The entire center floor of the cave was cleared for battle drills.

He exited on to one such balcony and watched a battalion practice close combat. Pairs of soldiers faced each other with sword and shield. An officer stood in front of the drilling soldiers, all eight hundred of them, shouting the count. With his every bark the men swung, parried, and blocked their partner's strokes.

Morrikii was reminded of all those years ago, when he had stood in front of soldiers wearing the silver and blue of Carodan. He had sat high on the wall of the Legion fort in Whitebreak, looking down at the parading regiments. Trumpets had called and drums filled the air with aggression. The blinding pride it engendered had been intoxicating.

He descended another spiral staircase and approached the drill master. From under the bristle of his faded brow, the grizzled man caught the flick of the Stonestriker's cloak, and without even looking at Morrikii, bellowed, "Battalion, form ranks!"

The soldiers halted their drills and fell in. Before him, eight hundred men flowed into two perfect rectangles. Shields held directly before their chests, their sword arms perpendicular to their bodies, the three-foot ribbons of steel contrasted against the black of their chain mail. The officer pivoted smartly on his heel and saluted Morrikii. "My Lord Stonestriker, I present the 1st Battalion, 3rd Brigade, of the 5th Legion for your review."

"Excellent, General Axehaft. Are they coming along?"

Morrikii walked past the front rank, looking each man over. Not one flinched. All stared ahead. They looked proud, battle-ready, and completely unaware of combat's reality. They would have to be perfect for when the Noriziem arrived. He wanted the barbarians to see what a real army looked like. With a voice of gravel, Axehaft answered, "They can march and form up into pretty rows, but they're still holding their swords like scared little girls. They're not men yet."

Morrikii smiled. The tone in Adeus Axehaft's voice betrayed his pleasure with the troops' progress. An experienced veteran, the general had been with Morrikii since the beginning, and would accept nothing less than perfection from these men. He always spent at least four hours a day training the men personally -- Not something all of Morrikii's generals did.

Stopping in front of a tall soldier, who's upright spine and raised chin screamed pride, and a bit of arrogance, Morrikii asked, "Infantryman, what is your name?"

With chest puffed out and a smirk teasing his lips the young soldier said, "Kaeven Windcatcher, my Lord."

"Ahhh, son of Darnen Windcatcher?"

"Yes, my Lord, the Master Smith."

"I know your father. Excellent craftsman. Tell me, did he make the sword you are now holding?"

"He did, my Lord."

"May I see it?"

Kaeven presented his sword pommel-first to Morrikii. The weapon looked like a soldier's standard issue blade, but Morrikii felt the difference in its balance immediately. The blade was three feet in length, with a diamond cross-section. It was unfullered, so as to increase its weight and the force of the blow. The crossbar was smooth steel and given the slight upward curve of all Legion swords. However, there was a small inscription along the crossbar that was not commonplace. It appeared to be sept Windcatcher's words. *Reach Always High.* The pommel was also of regulation shape, an oblong globe of steel to counterbalance the blade. However, on two sides of the pommel were etched the sigil of Windcatcher, the leaf of an ironbark tree caught in the grasp of an autumn breeze.

Morrikii made three quick cuts and a thrust with the sword, and he felt how it traced through the air with smooth lines. Grunting and nodding slightly, he handed it back to Kaeven. "Growing up as the Master Smith's son, you've known how to use a sword long before you came here?"

"My father had a sword in my hands as soon as I could walk, my Lord."

"Did he? Do you feel confident in your abilities, young Kaeven?"

"I do. The sword is a natural extension of my arm. With it in my hand and the shield and armor protecting me, I will defeat your enemies."

"Sounds like you've remembered well what General Axehaft has taught you. I want you to defeat me."

Morrikii had somehow made the quiet even more still. The only noise was from the sputtering torches and the slight howl of wind in the ceiling, where the vents brought in outside air. Axehaft grunted, scratching the corner of his mouth. Morrikii strode to a sparring ring a few yards in front of the first rank. "Come, Kaeven, let us duel. I want to see the true quality of your blade."

Kaeven, a mixture of fear and excitement churning in his eyes, marched smartly into the circle. The two were of roughly the same build and height. Kaeven was fully armored; Morrikii only wore was a mail hauberk under his robes. The General stepped beside Morrikii and presented a sword. "Thank you, Adeus, but no need for that," Morrikii said as he reached up behind his neck. "It has been a while since Sunder danced."

Morrikii reached for the shaft of his warhammer. With a slight tug and flip of the wrist it came loose of its harness, and with a precise motion he pulled the weapon out from under his cloak. Huge and ornate, the hammer was covered in glyphs of the old language. The top of the hammer had a single marking, the silhouette of a black dragon. The leather wrap around the shaft was smooth and worn and fit perfectly into his hands. Sunder had been his since turning fifteen, passed on by a father who had grown too old to wield it. The mark of the Black Dragon had been added only after Morrikii's exile.

Fear almost replaced the arrogance in Kaeven's eyes. It was not often one saw a weapon of this quality, and even rarer to face it. He hefted sword and shield. Morrikii gave no warning.

The lord's first stroke, a slow down cut from the right, was easily deflected by the younger man's shield. Kaeven responded with a quick thrust aimed at Morrikii's shoulder. The older man twisted his torso and the blade slipped past. Morrikii brought his hammer back up in the opposite direction, retracing his path. He caught the edge of the shield this time and put more force into the blow. The shock jerked Kaeven's arm aside, and a split appeared in the iron band that trimmed his shield. Stunned, he waited too long, and Morrikii brought Sunder in for an overhand cut. The shield was there to block, but splintered under the hammer. Kaeven unsuccessfully stifled a cry of pain. Morrikii imagined the lad's arm was quite numb from that impact. Kaeven backed off and circled. Within moments he had lost his main defense and the use of his left arm. Anger and frustration replaced the hesitance in his stance. He came in thrusting low, but it was a feint, and as Morrikii moved to parry, Kaeven quickly changed the sword's course and brought it up for a slash at Morrikii's arm. He found his target, but the mail held against the sword and its edge skittered off the armor. *That will be a nasty bruise*, thought Morrikii.

He allowed Kaeven the small victory. He wasn't looking to humiliate the boy. Well, not completely. The next attack was predictable, a thrust to his upper chest. With the head of his hammer, Morrikii turned the blade. As Kaeven's momentum brought him closer, Morrikii stepped forward and brought the butt of Sunder up and cracked Kaeven on the side of his helmet. He pulled the brass knob back towards him and brought the hammer down onto Kaeven's armored shoulder. The crunch of armor, followed by the ring of steel, echoed through the chamber as Kaeven's sword slipped from useless fingers. Morrikii stepped back and then brought the hammer back in low, sweeping Kaeven's legs from under him. The young man landed hard, the wind knocked completely out of him. He looked dumbly at Morrikii as the older man, his lord, brought the hammer up high over his head and back down at Kaeven with all possible force. Every soldier in the room reflexively tensed, waiting for the wet crunching sound of Kaeven's skull shattering. Instead, they all jumped at the sharp tone of Sunder slamming into the floor beside Kaeven's head, spraying stone chips in every direction. The boy's face was bone-white, his eyes fixed on his lord. Morrikii picked up Sunder and turned to address the other soldiers.

"I do this not to embarrass Windcatcher or any of you. You are all young. You have not seen the same battles as I or General Axehaft. Feel pride in how we train you, but do not let it blind you. Trust in your armor but," he paused as he picked up a shard of Kaeven's shield, "always remember you are not invulnerable. Never be so consumed by your own abilities that you assume your opponent is less than you. If you temper your hubris with humility, you will achieve the same balance as your swords. And if you do that, you may just stand a chance against graying, old men."

There was a hushed, nervous laugh, and Morrikii turned back to Kaeven, who was still on the floor. Pain paled the boy's features. Setting Sunder on its head, Morrikii kneeled next to Kaeven. He motioned for Axehaft to summon the healers.

Placing his hands underneath Kaeven's shoulders, he lifted him to a sitting position and spoke once again to the battalion. "This is my final advice to you. While on the field against our enemies, you will be frightened. Men will die all around you. Blood will flow and gore will fill your nostrils with a stench like nothing else. There is one true thing, and only one true thing you can rely upon while on the field."

Morrikii stood, helping Kaeven to his feet as he did. He steadied the young man and said, "We fight for each other. The man next to you is your greatest protection. We, the exiles of the North, have only ourselves to turn to. As individuals we fall, but together we stand firm. I am proud of the progress you're making. You will be a living avalanche on the field."

The battalion lowered their heads in unison, a traditional response to praise from a noble. Then, also as one, they raised their swords in salute. Morrikii bowed in return and smiled. He nodded to Axehaft, who dismissed the men, ordering them to their drills. The healers approached and Morrikii turned back to Kaeven. The lad had a mixture of shame, agony, and excitement on his face. "Well fought, Kaeven. Your father would be proud."

"Thank you, my Lord. You are a great fighter, and Sunder is truly as magnificent as I'd heard."

"She is a fine weapon," said Morrikii as he bent down and picked Kaeven's sword of the stone floor. It was undamaged, but would need to be sharpened where it had hit his chain mail. "But so is this sword, young one. Does it have a name?"

Kaeven flushed a bit and said, "Not yet, my Lord. I've been trying to think of one but nothing has fit."

The bruise on Morrikii's arm started to ache. "Young Windcatcher, would you allow me to name your sword?"

"I- I would be honored, sir."

"If it weren't for this mail, I might be short an arm right now. From now on this sword will be known as Stonehew. Treat it well, lad, and it will always be part of you."

Kaeven tried to take his sword as Morrikii offered him the hilt, but winced in pain when he tried to move either arm. Without a word Morrikii shifted to the young man's side and slid the sword into Kaeven's scabbard. The clerics had reached them by this point, and their amusement at the sight of the battered soldier was clear.

"Take good care of him," Morrikii said, "I want him back into training as soon as possible."

"Of course, my Lord."

Morrikii turned to leave, but Kaeven asked, "My Lord, did anyone ever teach you this lesson?"

"Yes. My father," Morrikii said.

Motioning for Axehaft to follow him, Morrikii left the young man and crossed to the opposite end of the cavern. The exiting tunnel was guarded by a gatehouse and a full line of soldiers. It was quiet as a crypt. He told Axehaft about the Noriziem. The general made a sound in his throat and spit on the floor. Morrikii sighed and said, "I agree, old friend, but we need to do this."

"Working with one clan is bad enough, but all four? You're entering a viper's den, Morrikii."

"You might be right, General, but right now we need their help."

Axehaft spit again.

"Adeus, I need you."

"All the troops will be fully geared by the time the Noriziem arrive, and I'll have them arrayed outside the gates in parade formation. We'll show the inbred bastards what a proper army looks like."

"Thank you, Adeus," Morrikii grabbed Adeus' shoulder and squeezed. "Now, I climb."

Axehaft raised his eyebrows and moved off, grumbling under his breath. Morrikii rubbed his arm and walked past the line of soldiers, entering the gatehouse. The tunnel sloped up, slight at first, but as he continued, the grade increased. The air was once again crisp, but didn't feel quite so cold here. Some of his men thought it was caused by heat escaping from the lower levels, or maybe the ground was a little less frozen this far up. Morrikii let the men speculate.

The tunnel flowed into a set of spiraling stairs. On and on he climbed. Halfway up, he stopped at a small landing to sit on a bench he'd had placed in a corner. The older he became, the harder it was to keep his breath. Two thousand steps still lay ahead.

In spite of the cold weight growing in his stomach, he rose and continued. The dark beauty of this passage could not be denied. Each step was inscribed with an ancient, flowing, yet indecipherable, text. As companion to the writing, the walls were covered in sprawling carvings painted with a dye that had not faded. They depicted epic scenes of armies marching upon castles, kings dying in their beds from mortal wounds, the great hunt of a mighty sea leviathan, and over them all was the silhouette of a black dragon. He was always there. Morrikii passed the image of a young girl. She stood on the edge of a cliff with tears welling from her eyes. In the distance, behind her, one could see the grave of her fallen love. The cliff, with its river of ice waiting to embrace her from below, seemed to stretch up towards her like a great wing. Overhead, floating above the clouds, was the black dragon. Morrikii had never been able to tell if the great beast was weeping for the girl or laughing at her.

He passed the final carving that crowned the top of the long stair. It was of a great four-peaked mountain. There were battlements carved into its slopes, and at its base was a gate of steel and stone that even the mightiest ram could not breach. Perched on its peak, pouring forth flame, was the black dragon.

It was Morrikii's mountain, Frostwrath, the great stone protector that cradled his city and his people. The room he now entered was its Pinnacle. Perfectly circular, the stone here was unadorned by carving or statue. The floor, walls and ceiling were polished obsidian. A bow shot, fired from one end of the room, would just barely reach the other. The ceiling disappeared into darkness. Morrikii felt small, even smaller than when he passed through Cavern Centre. The flagstones of the floor formed concentric rings that drew one to the center were the room's only decoration lay. Carved from pure volcanic glass was a statue of The Black Dragon. It was the same black dragon seen in the paintings; the same dragon whose head and face were carved as sconces in the tunnel walls, and the same dragon that lorded as the great fire pit in Cavern Centre. It stood on all fours, its wings stretched into the heavy air of the room. Precisely carved, every surface shimmered like silk. The room's only light emanated from a circular channel set into the floor around the dragon. Flames, two feet high and brilliant orange, licked at the legs of the great statue. When Morrikii had first crept into this room twenty-five years ago, the ring had burned even then. It never went out. Nothing fueled the inferno. It came from the stone.

The welcomed heat enveloped him as he neared. Intense but

subtle, it was this that warmed these upper levels. Next to the fire Morrikii did not feel the oppressive weight of a normal blaze. Instead, it worked its way into his bones and banished the last of his chill. There were no sparks to sting flesh or fumes to choke on. It was completely inviting, secure, and seductive.

At the edge of the fire, Morrikii drew Sunder from his back and kneeled. With the head of his hammer against the stone he grasped the handle with both hands and rested his forehead against the butt end. Morrikii chanted, *"Cantanaa thri cor. Logreth enaa dricoo. Froqouth en toomeya Galantaegan."*

He raised Sunder and slammed its head into the floor. A flash of black light, and the air thickened. The hairs on his neck stood. The fire in its ring intensified and the flames changed direction. Instead of flowing up, as fires tend to do, the flames angled in towards the statue. They grew until the statue was brushed by flame on all sides. In spite of their intensity the flames did not roar or hiss. They made no sound as all energy within the room was drawn towards the statue. Morrikii kept his eyes locked on the floor, bracing himself against his hammer. The cold returned, clawing even deeper for his core. He tried not to shiver, to not show any weakness, but the cold was strong and unforgiving. Tremors shook his legs, and he was certain he would fall. Then the warmth returned, and all feelings of winter were pushed away by a gentle glow. Morrikii looked up into the statue's face, which now looked back at him. The obsidian scales shimmered with an inner fire, and the wings beat once. The eyes, large saucers on either side of the reptilian head, glowed a soft blue, and Morrikii could feel them looking into him. A grumble rolled from its stone jaws, and Morrikii felt the floor vibrate beneath him. After a deep breath, Morrikii said, "Great One, I am yours to command."

A chuckle thundered from the beast's chest. Its lips parted, and a voice as deep as the earth and smooth as silver came forth.

"My dear friend Morrikii, you serve no one. Come, stand, there is no need of kneeling between equals."

"I am flattered, Great One," Morrikii said while standing. "I am not sure if I would consider myself the equal of a god."

"A god? I would not call myself so. You know my name, and may use it as such."

"Of course. My apologies, Galantaegan," Morrikii said.

"Good. Now, what have you done for me today?"
Morrikii was grateful his father had not lived to see this.

Chapter 3
TWISTREED

"Did you bury them properly?"

Kailen didn't know how to answer. What was proper? Standing in the middle of the Twistreed settlement, a ragged collection of two dozen houses surrounded by a sagging and weather-worn palisade, the warden searched for the right words. Before him, waiting for an answer, was Town Steward Antonidas Granitehand. The man, middle-aged and sagging, wore red velvet and furs. His hair was mostly gone and at least two of his chins jiggled when he spoke. Like all towns in Carodan, this settlement was ruled by a member of the House that controlled the lands upon which it was built. The Twistreed sept owed fealty to House Granitehand. Kailen wondered what misdeed the man before him had committed to have been given stewardship of this shithole.

Hair silvered with age, back bent by work, the man next to the steward was the one who truly concerned Kailen. Patriarch of the Twistreed sept, Rankin Twistreed still projected the confidence that had led his large, yet destitute family through the years. One of the men killed in the caravan had been his son. It was he Kailen addressed. "I did what I could. I built rock cairns for all of them using the largest stones I could find. I had no shovel or spade."

"Did you pray for them?" Twistreed asked.

"I did."

"Which passage?"

"Antaunna's Prayer for the Dead," Kailen answered.

The patriarch nodded, seemingly pleased by this. Kailen adjusted the placement of his feet, but then shifted again looking for the balance between appearing commanding and humble. He wanted these people to know he had done everything he could to carry out justice for their loss, and that he had done it well, but still acknowledge their loved ones were gone. That, he could not change.

"I have something to give you," said Kailen. He slipped his rucksack from his shoulders. Half the town's population ringed him, the Steward, and the patriarch. Most of them had likely been related to those in the caravan. Rummaging through the sack, he produced the recovered jewelry and dagger. "The Noriziem had these in their camp."

Twistreed took the items, making sure he had a firm grip on each. His eyes lingered on the dagger, the thumb of his right hand tracing the worn leather of the hilt. "I gave this to him when he turned fifteen. It had been my father's and his father's before him."

"It was stained with blood when I found it," Kailen lied. "Your son fought well before he died."

The patriarch nodded, his chin moving left to right with the quiet grinding of his remaining teeth. A lump threatened to form in Kailen's throat. It wasn't his place to cry though. This was their loss, their pain. He was a Warden. Their protection.

"Where are they? I'd like to bring them home and bury them in our sept's graveyard."

"Of course. They are just off of Stengraff's Road, right after the crossing of Ice Finger Stream. Not far from the Grenar ruins," Kailen said.

"I know the place. We'll find them. Thank you, Warden, for bringing peace to their souls and for bringing safety to our area. Who knows what else the Noriziem could have done?"

Kailen looked at the dirty faces surrounding him. Sorrow weighed heavily on their gaunt features. Tears cleared little paths of white through the peat-grime on the cheeks of one small family. Their clothes were more dirt than linen, their shoes tattered strips of hide. All except Granitehand. The man had said little, more interested in a broken nail on his left hand than the events taking place right before him. A few dots of mud marred his soft leather boots, but he was otherwise unsullied.

Guilt lurked beneath Kailen's façade. He was clad in fine wool and cloth, protected by boiled leather and strong steel. He had so much compared to them. Kneeling, he pushed his hand deep into his bag. He pulled out the satchel of coins he'd found and handed it to Twistreed. The patriarch, wearing robes of somewhat better condition than the clothing of his townspeople, tucked the dagger and jewelry away in several pockets. He took the satchel and examined the contents. With eyes wide he said, "It's been a long time since I've served, but last I knew all coins found by a Legion soldier are to be turned into his commanding officer, and then in turn deposited to the Legion treasury."

Kailen shrugged. "What they don't know won't upset them. It will go to better use here. Replace the supplies the Noriziem stole. Buy your people what they need."

The patriarch's hazel eyes watered and he rubbed them. Stroking his short beard a couple of times, the sept's leader cleared his throat, but before he could speak a suddenly interested Granitehand reached over and scooped the satchel from Twistreed's arthritic hands.

"I will safeguard this, Warden Tidespinner. I'll ensure it reaches the proper coffers."

Twistreed's shoulders sagged. The townspeople murmured and frowned, but none seemed inclined to speak up. It took little imagination for Kailen to understand the Steward's intentions, but he could not challenge the man. House Granitehand ruled the northwestern third of Westlook, and this disgusting oaf held authority over the town. It was his.

"I'm sure the gold will be well spent," said an aged voice from the crowd. Both Kailen and Twistreed turned their heads to the speaker. The crowd parted for a woman even older than the patriarch. A cloud of silver curls crowned her wrinkled face. Her cane slipped on the muddy and shifting ground, but she remained sure in her footing. Even the tremors that disturbed her hands and head did not shake her focus.

"Warden," said Granitehand, "may I introduce Dorthea Twistreed, grandmother to one of the girls in the caravan."

Dorthea treated the Steward with a corrosive glare. "She was my blood. Our blood. At least pretend to be saddened."

Steward Granitehand shifted his feet and looked at the ground. Kailen's eyes grew. For a commoner, a feeble sept-crone, to berate a noble was unheard of. But, the fat lord simply accepted the verbal lashing. Dorthea turned back to him.

"You, my young one, may call me Dorthea. I ask you walk with me. Tell me about my granddaughter."

"What did she look like?" he asked. The faces of the three women still burned his memory.

"Hair golden as a spring sunrise and eyes as blue as Antaunna's sea. She was beautiful."

The blonde one. By Antaunna, thought Kailen, how do I tell her? "I shall walk with you, ma'am. Steward, if I may take my leave for now?"

"Of course," the man mumbled. Remembering the hospitality typically extended towards visiting wardens, he asked, "Will you stay with us for the night?"

"If it is not too much trouble. I'll leave tomorrow. I have a two week journey to Angler's Cove, and it is time I go home."

The Steward nodded, pocketed the satchel, and turned away. Rankin Twistreed stepped forward and grasped Kailen's hand with gnarled fingers. "You've earned your rest, my friend."

The crowd dispersed. Before he left, Patriarch Twistreed gave Dorthea the sapphire engagement ring. So it had belonged to the blonde girl. The old woman rubbed it between her fingers and raised it to her mouth, kissing the stone with life-worn lips. Staring into the sky, she said to Kailen, "Her parents died when she was only seven. Killed by Noriziem. They had gone to the coast for their wedding anniversary. She was in my care while they were gone. I raised her after that."

"What was her name?" Kailen couldn't think of anything else to say or ask.

"Auerel. She could light up the night with her laughter and smile. She had so much joy. Now, I pray, she shares it with Antaunna."

Kailen looked at the town. The water stained homes. The haphazard pig fences. The stacks of crates that held dried peat. On a hill stood a solid cabin with freshly stained timbers, the Steward's abode. Anywhere but this woman's face. He couldn't tell her about the blood and bruises between her granddaughter's legs or the profane mark carved into her forehead.

Dorthea looped her arm through his and pointed with her cane to the town's excuse of a gate. "It has been awhile since I've seen outside the palisade. Will you escort me?"

"Of course, ma'am."

She waved her hand and laughed. "I'm too old for that foolishness. Dorthea is just fine."

Outside the walls it didn't smell like human and animal waste mixed together, but instead the age-old creep of the Grenfel Marshes permeated the air. It was disgusting. Kailen didn't understand how anyone could live here, but he knew it was how these people eked out an existence. At least the sun shone. They walked to the edge of the swamp, and even Kailen saw that with the blue sky reflecting off the pools of water it was almost beautiful. Green was starting to creep into the brown patches of weeds. Dorthea looked over the dead waters nodding, or what Kailen thought was a nod. He could feel the tremors running through her entire body.

"Will you tell me how my granddaughter died?"

Kailen thought about the blood. His stomach clenched with the memory of the girl's violation. Auerel was her name, he reminded himself. "She died as well as she could have. I can say no more."

"Don't I have the right to know?" Dorthea asked.

"You do, but I don't know if I have the words."

"Was her honor at least intact?"

Kailen rubbed the bridge of his nose and pulled in several deep breaths. "No."

Again Dorthea nodded. She pursed her lips and seemed to be gazing at something far away. Very quietly, she asked, "Would you let me tell you about her life?"

"Of course."

The labyrinth of wrinkles painting Dorthea's face deepened with her smile. A smile meant to hide pain. Patting Kailen on the hand she said, "She's really not dead, as long as we remember her."

Chapter 4
AN EBON SUN

Kailen stood at the edge of a cliff, kicking stones into the ocean below. The sun rose far in the east. Bands of clouds, stretched across the sky, caught the light in a cloak of amber and garnet. The salt air filled his lungs, burning and soothing at the same time. Every time he came home he stood here. The dizzying drop to the waves of the Ebon Sea, the endless horizon, and the simple openness of it helped to push back the shadows of the forest. Here, he did not have to be the Warden.

Stepping back from the precipice, he turned east. He jogged over a small hill and down into a grove of stunted, weather-beaten trees. Anemic compared to the leviathans of the Iron Bark Woods, they still pressed in close and limited his view.

He stopped. The hairs on his neck tingled and a shiver rattled his spine. Gripping the hilt of his sword, he scanned the trees and scant undergrowth. It was the same feeling he'd had back in the woods, just before attacking the Noriziem camp. But, just as then, there was nothing to be seen. He spit on a nearby stump and continued down the path.

The trees gave way to a field of green-brown grass. Beyond that, the granite wall of Angler's Cove stood high. Kailen slowed his jog to a walk. Running towards a heavily guarded wall was generally considered unwise. The morning sun glinted off the sentries' steel helms as they walked the battlements.

Yawning wide, the West Gate stood unbarred, its massive wood and iron doors thrown open and its portcullis raised. Four sentries stood to either side of the gate. A soldier to the right of the gate, proud and tall in his mail, approached Kailen. The warden slowed and dipped his head. "Sword Corporal."

"Sir. May I ask your business in the city?"

Kailen didn't know this soldier. He didn't feel like getting to know him. The sigil pin adorning the sentry's left shoulder was that of sept Stoneshore. That was enough for him.

Holding out his right arm, he pushed up his woolen sleeve. On the inside of his forearm, close to his elbow, was a tattoo. No larger than a coin, it was a blue dragon's eye framed by two curved daggers. The guard's eyes widened. "My apologies, Warden, I did not know."

"You're not supposed to."

"Did your patrol go well, sir?"

"Well enough."

"Kill any Noriziem bastards?"

"A few. I have to report to the General."

The corporal frowned. "Good luck to you, sir. I heard he was in a foul mood today."

"When isn't he?" Kailen responded.

On the other side of the wall, beyond the inner gate, Angler's Cove's thatched-roof houses and cobbled lanes stretched before him. The sun was higher now, and it illuminated the smoke twisting lazily from the chimneys. Around the harbor the town curved like a tremendous horseshoe. From the wall down to the shoreline the land sloped gently. The houses and buildings of the town were carved into its sides like steps. The sound of banging pots and crying babies mixed with the steady rhythm of the distant waves. Kailen smiled, loving the sound of Angler's Cove waking up.

Walking down the main street, he reminded himself he did not have to keep looking over his back. The road felt wide and open. There were no trees to hem him in. No Noriziem waiting beyond the next bend. He forced his muscles to relax, but, try as he might, was unable to remove his left hand from the hilt of his sword. His index finger played against the runes inscribed on the pommel, and his grip was loose, but he just couldn't let the weapon go.

His route took him to the high, southern part of town. The buildings here were stonewalled and roofed with fresh thatch.

Swept clean, the streets were lined by homes with freshly stained wood trim. The people Kailen passed were finely dressed and bedecked. They were of the high septs, common families that had made their fortunes and risen to comfort and luxury. They acted like nobility, even if they quite weren't.

Many gave him a wide birth. He smelled. His hair was greasy and tangled, his beard thick and matted. The fabric of his shirt and hose were stained with mud and old blood, and his leathers creaked their need to be cleaned and oiled.

Measuring each as they passed, he could not stop from thinking they all owed him. They owed every warden and every soldier in the Legion. It was men like him who kept them safe, allowed them to run their shops and trade in peace and prosperity. The jiggling stomachs of the men and their matching jowls turned Kailen's stomach. They were weak and complacent. Strength to them was bargaining power. Happiness was making another gold piece by fleecing fishermen's wives from the lower quarters.

The women didn't even look at Kailen. Wrapped in silk and gold, with their hair arranged into perfect curls or elaborate, sweeping braids, they flared their nostrils and curled their upper lips as he passed. He tried not to notice. Tried to not think of all the hard working women he had seen battered and bruised. Raped and dead. Most of these women hadn't worked a day in their lives. They had come here with their wealthy merchant husbands and fathers. Men like Kailen were an unwelcome necessity.

It was not the first time he had felt this way in the upper quarter. He hated it here. He planned to finish quickly with the General and then head down to the Harbor District, where the men were dirtier than him, but just as proud, and the women were not afraid of honest work. Carra was there.

The street turned sharply left, and the fine houses gave way to a wide parade ground paved with smooth flagstones of gold granite. It stretched to the town's wall. At its center was the Legion's stronghold. A squat, thick collection of towers and walls, it was the Fourth Legion's headquarters in Angler's Cove and their main base of operations in northern Westlook. At the top of the highest towers flew Carodan's flag. The blue compass rose, embossed on a silver field, flew brazenly in the morning breeze.

He strode across the parade ground with shoulders held back and eyes straight ahead, passing a century of troops performing drills in formation. Multiple pairs of eyes followed him, but he paid them little heed. He reached the stronghold's main gate quickly, rolling up his right sleeve as he neared the guard. The guard challenged him, but let him pass when he saw the warden's mark.

Inside the stonehold, ordered bustle was the norm. Legionnaires stood in lines outside the cook shacks awaiting the day's first meal. Others drilled in the courtyard, practicing small group tactics. Still more sat on benches outside of the long barrack houses, sharpening swords and oiling their armor. A few glanced at him, saw he was a warden, and continued on with their work. Crossing the yard, he approached the inner gate to the squat, simple keep. After showing his mark to the guard, he asked, "Is General Bronzehide available?"

"May I ask who requests his audience, sir?"

"Warden Tidespinner."

The soldier's eyes glinted with recognition, and he bowed his head and dashed inside the keep to find the general. He returned a few minutes later. "Sir, you will find the General waiting for you in his study."

"Thank you, Swordarm."

Beyond this other set of heavy gates was a cool stone corridor. It was dim, lit only by several wall sconces. The flames danced in the drafty hall. Some looked ready to go out. Kailen walked to the very end of the corridor, found the spiral stair, and started to climb. The sun poured in through the arrow slits set into the outer wall, lighting the stairs with dust-filled shafts of gold.

Reaching the top floor, Kailen found his way through the maze of passages to the General's study. He paused to even his breathing. Wiping his clammy hands on his trousers, he took a moment to arrange his gear. A cold flutter always invaded his innards when meeting with the General.

He knocked and was bade to enter. Tall shelves of books lined the room. On the far wall, a giant map of Carodan was painted on yellowed canvas, and in the center of the room a massive, circular table of oak was heaped with smaller maps that detailed the greater world of K'aeran and local provinces alike. The room was bright, with an iron chandelier overhead and leaded glass windows that allowed a clear view of the inner courtyard. The General stood at the table, his back to Kailen, broad shoulders hunched in concentration over the maps.

Tandar Bronzehide was a thirty-year Legion veteran with skin of leather and a grizzled brow. Thick hair, more silver than blond, framed a face traced with lines of laughter and worry. The light was still quick in his jade eyes, and his solid frame was heavy with muscle. His armor was burnished to a flawless shine, the steel of his breastplate mirror-perfect. His cloak was a deep blue and lined with gold slashes and silver twists, each one marking a battle fought or a campaign he had led. A son of House Bronzehide, the man could have bought his commission and rank like so many other nobles. However, he had entered the Legion as a youth at the rank of Line Commander and ascended through merit and skill. Technically, Kailen's sept of Tidespinner owed fealty to House Bronzehide, since it controlled this portion of Westlook, but in the Legion all feudal ties were supposed to be forgotten and superseded by rank. General Bronzehide adhered to this principle and never acknowledged Kailen as anything but a warden. Not that it mattered much, the warden was the last of his sept. Unless he produced a male child, the name Tidespinner would die with Kailen.

Staring at the greatsword slung across the general's back, Kailen still fought the flutter in his stomach. He felt like an errant pupil reporting to the headmaster. "Legion General Bronzehide, Warden Tidespinner reporting."

The General stood straight and turned away from his maps. Looking Kailen over, taking in the dirt and bloodstains, the torn clothing, and undoubtedly the smell, he frowned. "Warden, you need a bath."

Remember, thought Kailen, don't lose your composure. "Yes, sir, I believe I do. I am afraid there are few baths between here and the wilds, and the spring run-off is still damned cold."

The General raised an eyebrow. "No matter. Did you encounter anything on your patrol?"

Kailen reached into a pouch on his belt and pulled out eight yellowed teeth, dried blood still caked to their roots. He tossed them on the table, the enamel skittering across the hard oak surface. Bronzehide nudged a few with his meaty index finger.

"Eight?"

"Noriziem. Twelve leagues from the coast."

Bronzehide looked sharply at him. "Twelve? That far in?"

"I've never seen it. They always stay close to the shore."

Bronzehide turned to the world map on the wall. The continent of Abinar was a stretched piece of land, taller than it was wide. The Kingdom of Carodan took up most of its top half. It was divided into three regions. The oldest province, Tidal Guard, lay in the east. Wheat Scythe, the breadbasket, was the entire southern portion of the realm. And in the west, filled with mostly old forests and rocky hills, was Westlook. Of all the nations in the world of K'aeran, Carodan was still the youngest. Founded only a few centuries ago by their ancestors, who'd fled the old world of Granikar and the hatred of the Noriziem, the upstart nation had quickly grown in stature and power.

The general squinted and said, "They could have come from the raid on Shark Bay. It was a month ago and the town was hit hard. Half the population gone. Some of them must have stayed behind and pushed inland."

"Sir, have there been any more attacks since?" Kailen asked. He had been in the deep woods for two months.

"Yes." Bronzehide picked up a roll of parchment, its seal freshly broken. "A courier hawk brought this today from Citadel. One raid along the coast of Tidal Guard, two on the East Shore of Wheat Scythe, and five more in Westlook."

"Counting Shark Bay, sir?"

"In addition to Shark Bay," Bronzehide said.

"By Antaunna."

"Aye, and the navy can't keep up with them. We've managed to capture and destroy a few groups of longships, but most get past us. They slip ashore, burn and kill, then slink back off into the night."

"I don't remember them attacking this much over the past few years."

"They haven't."

Kailen was still at attention. His beard itched terribly, but he dared not scratch it. "Is the legion doing anything about it, sir?"

Bronzehide treated Kailen with a look that expressed his dislike of being questioned. "What do you think, soldier? All legions are being readied, and the reserves and militias are being called up, especially here in Westlook. It seems to be a favorite of theirs."

Kailen could guess why. Westlook was the youngest province, only eighty years old, and sparsely populated compared to the other two. People were slow to settle here. This used to be the land of the Grenar. Great beasts of muscle and anger, they had warred with the Cardanans for over two centuries, until King Binar Ironheart led a great invasion into the Grenar homeland. The brutes had been pushed out of their homes and slaughtered. Those who survived had fled across the river Amen'kar and into a narrow stretch of wild land along the western coast. The Amen'kar was now the border between the Grenar and the Cardanans. They had not been seen since the end of the war. Some said they had died out. However, the memory of them, and their fierceness, made it hard to find people who would brave Westlook's wilderness. No one wanted to be here if the Grenar ever returned.

Bronzehide tapped the parchment against his lips, his eyes focused on a distant thought. When he felt Kailen's slight impatience, he shook his head and said, "Well, enough of this talk. You get two weeks rest before reporting back to me. Find a warm bed, a soft woman, and for the love of Antaunna, find a bath."

Surprised, Kailen said, "Not that I'm complaining, sir, but why so long?"

"You'll see when you report in."

The general rustled though some papers on a side table and produced a leather pouch that jingled when handled. Kailen took it and looped it onto his belt. "Thank you, General."

"Yes, yes." Bronzehide was already bent over his maps. The wave of his hand was more of a dismissal than a farewell.

Kailen saluted, didn't dare not to, then spun sharply on his heel. He left the stronghold and burned up the distance of the parade ground. He wanted to leave the upper district as quickly as possible, but still felt he had to maintain some sort of dignity. He took a street that went straight down to the waterfront with no twists or turns or distractions. Passing through the merchant district, he skirted around the Hadari quarter. His senses were assaulted by the aromas of foreign cooking and alien dialect. He caught glimpses of the Hadari in the alleys between their homes.

Black-skinned and tall, the immigrants had been here for two generations in search of new opportunity. They were tolerated, but the memories of the Slave Wars were still too fresh in many a Cardanan's mind for them to be truly accepted.

He reached the lower district. Here the timbers of the homes were not freshly varnished. The people wore clothing of wool and linen. The streets were crowded. Most of the men strolled towards the harbor and their waiting fishing boats. The women moved in the opposite direction towards Market Lane to buy what they needed for the dinner their husbands would expect when they came in from the fishing grounds. Here and there groups of children ran about laughing and chasing each other. The familiar smell of humanity was all around him, and in spite of his desire to rush, he enjoyed it. This was real. *The way people should be*, he thought. This is what he fought to protect.

Even with the crowded streets it didn't take Kailen long to reach the waterfront. Angler's Cove was a large settlement for Westlook, but far from the size of a true city. Here, at the water's edge, was the lifeblood of the town. Crews of both great fishing sloops and smaller skiffs readied their ships for the day's work. Many of them recognized Kailen and bellowed their greetings as he rushed past. He happily returned each one.

Passing the buildings on the waterfront, Kailen always noticed the sea-inflicted scars they carried. Their wooden beams sagged and splintered, the thatch of the roofs was dark brown and sodden, and the plaster cracked and flaked. The buildings leaned to each other at crazy angles, and the alleyways between were filled with people bustling to the docks or women doing their wash with the neighbors. Several small children ran past Kailen, naked except for the mud splashed over them. Their laughter bounced down the streets ahead of them, and then disappeared out over the harbor. There was more than enough money in the upper district to give these people better housing, but no one could be bothered. It angered Kailen every time he came home.

Kailen had been walking an automatic route, east along the waterfront. Quickly he reached his destination, a large building that hugged the shore, its rear hanging out over the sea wall and supported by warped pylons. Except for the freshly thatched roof it was as worn and sea-tired as its neighbors. Kailen looked at the sign hanging over the door. Swinging in the morning breeze, the new sign of the Nightsong's Hearth displayed twin half-moons, one waxing and one waning, over a bare-breasted beauty playing a harp and laughing. Chuckling, he stepped up to the oak door, lifted its latch, and pushed it open. The smell of frying eggs and bacon set his stomach grumbling. This early in the day the tavern was quiet, with only a few old sailors sitting scattered amongst the tables. It was dark but comforting. Light came in through the small windows, but the few lanterns hanging from the low ceiling cast an even glow over the room. His lingering distaste of the upper district was forgotten, as was his residual nervousness from reporting to Bronzehide. Kailen wound his way through the tables, minding the uneven floorboards. Several bits of old, unidentified food crunched under his boots, and a couple of the sailors looked up at him. Some nodded hello, but then returned to their ale.

His cousin, Beth, was serving the seamen and when she saw him her eyes widened and she grinned. Holding up a hand and putting his finger to his mouth, Kailen returned the smile. Understanding his intent, Beth bit her lips and hung back. She was a sweet girl, good of heart, barely a woman. Their mothers had been sisters, but Beth's had married into sept Rainforge. They were a small family, but respectable and hard working.

Along the tavern's back wall was a long bar of once-polished oak. From the kitchens Kailen heard the laughter of several women mixed with the clatter of cast iron pans. Behind the bar, facing away from Kailen was a woman wearing a simple cotton dress, secured around the waist with a belt of tooled leather. She was bent over, reaching underneath a cupboard for some clean mugs. The shift did little to hide the curve of her bottom.

"Now that is a beautiful sight," Kailen said.

The woman set the mugs back and stood. Her hands on her hips, she faced Kailen. Auburn hair framed sea-green eyes capable of piercing the hardest heart. "If you were any other man, Kailen Tidespinner, you'd be on your ass out in the street."

"But I'm not, so what does that mean Mistress Nightsong?"

Carra rolled her eyes and said, "Keep talking like that and you'll definitely be out on your ass." She stepped to the bar, leaned over its worn top and came nose to nose with Kailen. "You smell."

"As do you."

"Like lavender and bath soaps. You smell like shit."

Kailen shook his head. "To think I was actually looking forward to coming here and seeing you."

Carra's lips pursed, quivered and then relented, stretching back into a radiant smile. "It's good to see you. You've been out a long time."

"Tough one this time. Noriziem. They hit a caravan on its way to Twistreed."

"And?"

"And, it was the same as it always is."

Kailen broke eye contact.

Carra reached over the bar, taking his grizzled chin between her finger and thumb. "It's okay. You're home."

"I certainly am."

She reached over the bar, grabbed him by his belt, and pulled him closer. She brushed her lips against his. He smiled, forgetting the forest. She tapped him on the end of his nose with a slender finger. "You must be starved. I'll have the girls prepare a plate. We can sit out on the back pier, over the water."

"I'm getting special treatment today? I'm impressed."

Keeping her face mostly straight Carra said, "Not really. I'm just going to sit with you, and I want a fresh breeze to blow away that lovely aroma. Head on out, I'll meet you." She winked, her lips still curled into a cat's grin. Nodding to someone behind him, she said, "I think someone wants to say hello first."

Kailen turned and was almost bowled over by Beth's flying hug. Returning the embrace, he tried not to think of how much the young girl resembled his mother. "How've you been, little one?"

"Good, Kailen. I'm glad your back. We missed you this time."

"This time only? Is that flatlander boy still hanging around you?"

Beth blushed and didn't seem to know how to respond. Carra rescued her. "Kailen, leave her be. He's a good lad."

"He's from Wheat Scythe," Kailen said and frowned.

"Behave. Beth, come help me get Kailen's breakfast. You," she pointed at Kailen, "get your ass outside. I'll meet you."

Smiling, he watched them go back to the kitchen, his attention mostly on Carra's swaying hips. The blood rushed through his body. It was good to be home.

He went to the back door, but the latch was stiff, crusted with rust and sea salt. As Kailen pulled hard to open the door, the hinges groaned. It hadn't been used all winter.

On the other side of the door was an old fishing pier that Carra's father had rebuilt and made into a broad patio with benches and tables. Breathtaking and unobstructed, the view never failed to impress. Kailen leaned against the rail and watched the sun-laced water lap against the docks and rocky shore. The fishing fleet was off, cutting its way across the bay and making for the channel that connected it to the North Ebon Sea. Kailen looked back at the town. Bathed in the morning light, everything could have been made of gold. Smoke rose from all the chimneys, haloing the town in a gray-yellow haze. People filled the streets, and even here on the far side of town Kailen heard the hum of voices. So far removed from the shadow of the forest, from the sweat of fear and the stain of blood, Kailen allowed a smile. *This is why I do it*, he thought. All the blood spilt keeps this safe. It's the right thing to be done, isn't it?

Kailen left the railing and sat at a table close to the water. Now was not the time for such thoughts. Carra carried out a platter of food and two steins. His stomach growled at the sweet smell of ham and biscuits. Kailen tore into the food, barely giving Carra time to get her hands clear after setting down the plate. Handing him one of the mugs, she kept the other for herself. She raised it with both hands to her mouth and took a sip. Kailen felt her watching him, her mug held loosely and resting just below her chin. He knew he should eat more politely, but, by Antaunna, he was hungry.

"If you're not careful, your gut will ache for hours," Carra said.

"It'll be worth it. Tilda outdid herself this morning. Send my compliments."

"I'll let her know you approve."

Kailen felt her eyes. He knew she wanted him to talk about what he had seen, to share it with her and get it out of his mind, but he wasn't going to place that upon her shoulders.

Carra broke the silence. "I'm amazed you haven't touched the ale yet. You always go for that first."

"Like I said, great food."

That had come out more gruffly than intended. Swallowing the last bite, Kailen grabbed the pewter stein and drank. The amber liquid spread its cool caress through his chest. Carra sipped her drink, a mulled wine, and watched him over its rim.

"Do you need anything else?"

"No, thank you."

His plate was clean, the stein dry. Sighing, he stretched back and said, "I feel almost human again."

"You don't smell it. Let's get you a bath."

Carra grabbed his hand and led him back inside. They turned down a corridor to the left, away from the bar and its few patrons. Only a couple of candles lit the hall, and the floorboards creaked a song of aged wood. The air was dusty, laced with the aromas of stale beer and unwashed sailor. They passed the common baths and Kailen raised an eyebrow. The right side of her mouth curled up, and she said, "I have something special for you. It's better than a pine tub."

They were at the end of the hall, in front of a door Kailen had never been behind. Pushing it open, Carra said nothing, giving him only that smile. Kailen smelled bath salts and steam mixed with a bit of wood smoke. The room was lit by thick, yellowed candles placed in each corner. At the center of the room was a long basin made of black, polished marble. Kailen walked to its side and set his hand on the edge.

"The stone is warm to the touch. How?"

"Something I've saved for, straight from the artisans in Whitebreak. Any visiting ship captain, or anyone with enough coin, can bathe here in water that stays heated."

Kailen dipped his fingers into the still pool. It was quite warm. "How does this work?"

Pointing towards the base of the tub, at a cast iron box fitted smoothly to the marble, Carra said, "I keep that hopper full of hot embers from the fire. The stone heats up, helping to keep the water warm."

"This must have cost you."

Carra looked at her own reflection. "My father wanted the Nightsong to grow. Now that it's just me, I'm not letting him down." She flicked the surface of the water, breaking her mirror image, and said, "I figure this is a luxury ship-weary sailors will spend a little extra on."

Carra shook her head and treated Kailen again with that smile. "Enough talk. Drop your gear over there. The girls will wash your clothes. I'll get the bath soaps."

Stepping into the corner, Kailen undid his belt and harness. His sword and scabbard he hung on the wall. He heaped his clothing on the floor, the bits of leather armor thumping dully against the wood. Wearing only a film of grime and sweat, Kailen walked to the basin, threw his legs over the stone lip, and slipped into the water's gentle grip. He leaned back, eyes closed. The tension seeped from his muscles and he uncurled his fingers. The fists became hands. His guard was down; there was no sword to hold here.

"Kailen, take this." Carra handed him another stein of ale.

"Are you trying to get me drunk?"

"Me? Never." The candle light danced in her eyes.

Nodding his thanks, Kailen took the stein and swallowed a quarter of it. Carra, soap in hand, lathered Kailen's chest. "I can wash myself, you know."

"I know, but this is more fun. Shut up and relax."

"Yes, m'lady."

Carra splashed water in his face and stuck out her tongue. Kailen laughed and set his head back. He watched her hands move across his skin. They were callused and cracked. Grease burns discolored her wrists and scars from slipped knives lined her fingers. Somehow, they still felt soft, and Kailen couldn't imagine any other hands on him.

Carra rinsed his hair with a pitcher of warm water and then worked his scalp with scented oils. Kailen sniffed and asked, "Is that vanilla?"

"Too feminine for you?"

"I smell like a whore."

"You smell better than you did before."

"Can't argue with that."

Carra rinsed his hair once more and stepped back from the tub. The whisper of falling cotton mixed with the rhythm of rippling water. Two slender legs arched over the edge of the basin, followed by a body sculpted through hard work and labor. Straddling him, she rested her head against his chest. Rocking her hips, she rubbed against him. He kissed her hard and grabbed her bottom, guiding them together. She buried her face against his neck and gasped. His fingers gnarled in her hair, Kailen whispered, “I’ve missed you.”

“I know.”

Chapter 5
GHOSTS AND DEMONS

On a large, rolling hill east of the town and outside its walls, Kailen knelt before two gravestones. The granite was pitted and water-stained, but the names etched into the hard surface were still clear. Kailen read those names over and over, almost as if he did it enough the two people would come back. A welcome breeze broke the unusually hot air. No leaves rustled though, and even the dust on the paths did not stir. There was very little sound in the graveyard.

That made it easy to hear Carra before seeing her. The scuffing of her sandals against the dirt path scratched and echoed over the graves. The hairs on his neck were standing again, and his skin goose pimpled. When she reached him, she squeezed his shoulder and knelt beside him. He shook away the tingling sensation, dismissing it as an instinctive response to her approach. Auburn hair framed her oval face, and in the sun her eyes blazed green. *By Antaunna*, thought Kailen, *she is beautiful.*

Carra tipped her head down, placing her hands over her heart. She prayed. He knew the prayer and recited it with her, but only in his head. She looked to the north when finished, towards the sea. Quietly, she said, "You know they'd be proud of you."

"Maybe."

"I know they would be. I am."

"Thank you. It doesn't bring them back though."

"As long as you keep them in your thought, they'll never be truly dead."

Kailen stared ahead, avoiding her eyes. "I hear that a lot lately.

I was so young. What do I truly remember? Are the memories real?"

"They're as real as they can be. Are you all right?"

Looking at the gravestones of Laina and Ka'leb Tidespinner, Kailen tried to ignore the hollow space in his gut. "I always am."

Kailen looked at her again and noticed a worn cord hanging around her neck. Dangling from it was a small clay disc that rested between her breasts. An intricate pattern was etched into its surface. "I can't believe you still have that."

Carra lifted the medallion. "I found it in my wardrobe this morning, tucked in a drawer and wrapped in oil cloth."

"I was nine when I made that."

Kailen took the disc between his thumb and index finger. The lines carved into the clay were clean and even. Nestled between those lines, with painstaking symmetry, were six glyphs. The center glyph was the Mark of Antaunna, but the other five were not often seen in Cardanan life. "I remember us sneaking into the temple library."

Carra smiled and said, "We could barely even read. I think I was seven."

"My little shadow."

"My parents had little love for you, and even less for the trouble you got me into."

Kailen laughed. "Especially at temple lessons. The clerics never could keep track of us. This was worth it, though," he said, holding up the medallion, "I still remember the scroll we found this on. It was old, very old."

He thought back to the two of them, with dirty faces and grubby hands, tip-toeing between the towering, dusty shelves of the temple's library. Iron chandeliers had given the cavernous room a warm, but uneven light, and they had used the shadows to hide. He could still remember the great scroll, lying open on a low, wide table. The parchment had been thick and yellow, bordered with ancient runes, from the time when their people had been known as Clan Carothak. There had been no way that they couldn't touch it. "To think when that scroll was written we were part of the Norizaad Empire. I've killed more Noriziem than I can count."

Kailen rubbed his thumb over the etching again. "The time of the Pantheon, when all six dragons were worshipped together.

Antaunna was just a piece of the puzzle."

Carra took the medallion and said the name that belonged to each glyph. "Daranayta, Galantaegan, Antaunna, Syltankaran, Oaukenterra, and Remtagast. I wonder what Carodan would be like if we had held to the old ways."

"Complicated. More so than it already is. Besides, one god is enough to me, and I like what she stands for. Balance. For everything we take, something is given in return." Kailen paused, cocked his head to one side and asked, "How, by Antaunna, did we end up talking religion?"

"I don't know, but you've stopped dwelling on things you can't change, haven't you?"

"I have."

He held her chin and kissed her. She smiled and said, "Good. You should come back to the inn with me. I'm sure you noticed the Hadari galley that hauled into the harbor this morning."

Standing, and offering Carra a hand, Kailen looked down to the harbor. "They're hard to miss."

Riding at anchor, in the deep water, a large galleass lorded over the smaller craft around it. Three times as long as any of the fishing ships, its hull was a dark wood. The gunwales were painted in twisting patterns and gilded in bronze, and the sails were a deep purple. Each mast was topped by a white flag emblazoned with a crescent moon surrounding a blazing sun that was pierced by a black scimitar. The standard of Hadak.

Hands on her hips, Carra looked at the galleass with narrowed eyes. "Thanks to a little bird, the captain and crew of the *Desa'sta* know the Nightsong's Hearth is offering half off all food and beverage tonight."

"A little bird?"

"A well-paid little bird. And with the crew in town you can be sure some of the immigrants from the Hadari Quarter will be there to hear news from the homeland."

"Wouldn't the crew just go there instead of your tavern? What's that place called? The Desert's Rose? It would probably feel more like home."

"It probably would, but I heard the oddest thing happened to their beer supply. The whole thing turned sour - completely undrinkable. Strange, isn't it?"

"Extremely," Kailen said and cocked an eyebrow. She was

smirking. "You do not play fair."

"I'm the only woman shop owner in town. I can't afford to. Come on, you. Let's have some fun. These sand-faeries throw a damned good party."

Carra took Kailen's hand and led him down the hill. Looking over his shoulder, Kailen said goodbye to his mother and father.

Once they were down the slope and out of sight, the Grenar moved from behind several large tombs. He was taking a risk by coming into the open this close to the town. The voice of his grandsire, scolding yet affectionate, echoed through his memories. "Rend'arr, your curiosity will be the end of you." He'd always ignored the old warrior. The stupid arrogance that came with being the chieftain's son had plagued him during most of his youth.

Stepping into the open was dangerous, but Rend'arr wanted to kneel before the same two stones as the warden. The man had spent a great deal of time here. Reaching out, the brute ran a thick finger along the grooves of the left stone's inscription. His nail scratched against the granite and the sound crept across the cemetery. The Grenar remembered the dead in his own past. He thought about the dream. Each night it persisted and came with increasing clarity. Now, he saw the blood of Grenar and Cardanan intermixed, staining the land.

* * *

The Nightsong was filled with the black-skinned, hairless sailors. Kailen stood at the bar, one foot resting on the bottom rung of a stool, a pint in one hand and a pipe in the other. He drank and smoked, watching the foreigners. Tall and trim, their ivory smiles and amber eyes seemed odd and alien. Their voices were deep and rich, their laughter contagious to the few Cardanans still in the tavern. Dressed in rich fabric of bright yellows and blues, the Hadari looked like royalty when compared to the rough-spun wool of the Cardanan fishermen. Only the diehard regulars were in tonight, and he hadn't seen Paedar Swiftstream. That suited him just fine. He didn't like the way the snot-nosed brat looked at Carra. The kid wasn't much younger than Kailen, and always respectful, but the smile he'd give Carra always lingered and hinted at more. The boy thought his family's gold, Swiftstream was a high sept, made him Antaunna's Gift to all the town's women. Many of them fell for it.

The desert men had taken over Carra's tavern, their mirth mixing with the sound of banging tankards and shifting bench legs. Smoke from their water pipes hung thick as fog, and the light from the hearth and lanterns danced wildly in the haze. Kailen could smell only sweat, beer, and pipe weed. And a bit of urine.

Ale, wine, and liquor flowed constantly. Platters of beef, fish, and fowl were piled high and served with loaves of fresh bread and turnip stew. As quick as the food poured out, the coin poured in. Cardanan silvers and Hadari ducats jingled together and the girls never stopped. They went from table to bar, carrying their loads, taking money, and always flashing a smile, sometimes kneeling in close with their cleavage straining over the tops of their bodices. Kailen chuckled whenever the trick worked, and they received a larger tip. Beth tried it once and he'd scowled at her. She stopped after that, and it was a good thing. If any of these men laid a hand on her, the offender would soon find that hand separated from his arm. Kailen was fairly certain dealing with that type of mess was the last thing Carra wanted.

Kailen drained the mug and pulled deep from his pipe. He blew a smoke ring and let the rest of the sweet cloud drift slowly out of his mouth. No sooner was the empty mug set on the bar than it was replaced with one full, the foam overflowing its rim. Carra winked at him from behind the bar, wearing a burgundy silk dress. The neckline plunged and was bordered in gold thread. A sash, also gold, hung on her hips at just the right angle. "You look good."

"Why thank you. The dress was a gift. A quiet, handsome Warden gave it to me."

"He has good taste."

"He does, but he never told me how much it cost him."

"Smart man."

Carra leaned across the bar and kissed him. Kailen asked, "You sure I can't pay for the ale?"

"Your money is no good here, Tidespinner. Now shut up and enjoy yourself."

Winking and cocking her hips, she walked along the bar and refilled the empty mug of a young Cardanan smithy. Kailen picked up his mug and went to drink, but paused when he sensed someone step behind him. Turning slowly, Kailen encountered the whitest grin he had ever seen. Pin points of perspiration covered the Hadari's skin, and his amber eyes seemed unable to fully focus. When he spoke, Kailen's nose curled at the mixed aroma of beer and hashish. "If my ears do not deceive me, I believe I heard our lovely hostess call you a Warden."

Even though his voice was low and warm, with that odd, rolling accent that gave his words a musical cadence, Kailen tensed and responded evenly, "I am."

The Hadari bellowed, his laughter startling Kailen, and he put his arm around the warden's shoulders. "Come, my friend! My crewmates and I wish for you to sit with us and share stories of the Westlook frontier. My name is Ishbal."

Kailen hesitated, trying to think of some reason not to sit with the Hadari. Before he could say anything though, a gigantic pitcher of ale was being held across the bar right in front of them. The Hadari slapped some coins onto the bar with his free hand and then snatched the pitcher. Behind the bar, her lips pulled back in that smile, Carra said, "Have fun."

Kailen let the Hadari lead him to a table in the back, where seven of his crewmates sat around a collection of tipped-over mugs, empty platters, and several glass water pipes. Ishbal slapped Kailen on the back and said, "My friends, I have found a special guest. A Warden!"

Kailen sat slowly on a bench that wobbled under his weight. He drank from his mug, using the movement to buy time. He had nothing in particular against the Hadari - their two nations had been at peace for over a century - but he wasn't fond of them either. It was still quite common for slaver raids to take place across the border between Hadak and Wheat Scythe. Even though officially condemned by the Hadari shahs, they did little to stop the raids. Kailen knew several Legion soldiers who had fought hard in some of those border skirmishes. They were good men.

"So," said Ishbal, "We have often wondered what it is like to fight in a land so overgrown and restrictive. The forest is an odd thing to us. The trees seem to close in around you, claw at you. And there is so much green!"

Kailen swallowed more beer. "If you use the forest to your advantage, it can be a great ally. The enemy doesn't know you're there until your sword is in his throat. I've spent most of my adult life in the wilderness."

One of the Hadari shook his head and drank from his goblet an amber fluid that curled his lips. "I could not do it. I grew up in the port of Auronak. I have either lived in the city or on the waves. The trees, I do not understand them."

Kailen shrugged. He had little to say to a city-dweller. Ishbal reached in front of Kailen and took a chicken leg from a platter that was mostly bones and scraps of skin. "So, have you fought many Noriziem? We know they are like a plague here in the north."

"I have fought many."

"Killed many?" asked another Hadari.

"Yes."

Ishbal poured Kailen a glass of the amber liquid and moved the water pipe between them. The Hadari inhaled from the mouth piece and said to Kailen, "Enjoy yourself my friend, and tell us your stories."

***

It was well into the small hours when Kailen stumbled up to his room. He couldn't feel his legs, and the walls spun. He fumbled with his clothes, pulling them half off and trying to make it to the small cot across the room. Halfway there he planted his face into the floorboards. They were the most comfortable floorboards ever. As unconsciousness reached its inky arms wide, he imagined himself melting into the floor, sliding through the cracks, and slipping into darkness. In the blackness there was quiet and peace; welcomed solitude.

The floorboards were above him now. Cold, hard-packed dirt pressed against his back. His body was tiny and weak. Instead of wearing armor and carrying steel, he was clad in a woolen tunic and hose. Small leather boots covered his feet. He was seven, a boy. Wanting to break free, to be big again, he willed himself to be strong. He remained frozen still and useless. There was little light and nothing to see, but noise assaulted his ears.

He heard his father standing at the door, telling his mother to stay back. His father's sword was drawn, and the firelight it reflected darted here and there through the gaps in the floor. Kailen imagined him standing tall, sword held ready with both hands. Kailen told himself that no one would hurt them. Who could possibly make it past his father?

Someone kicked in the door. Heavy boots slammed into the house, and the cries of a harsh tongue filled the air. He heard his father's sword swing through the air, and the shocked grunt of a man taking the hit. Before the sword could whistle again, there was a wet crunch; the sound of a mace caving in his father's head.

He still couldn't move. He was still useless. He heard the men move into the house. Heard them jesting with each other in what vaguely resembled Cardanan. There was the crack of a punch, followed by the tearing of a dress. Kailen heard laughter and grunts. He heard the slapping of skin against skin. He heard the roaring of distant fires, the clash of steel, and screaming. Screaming all around.

His mother never cried out; never begged for mercy. She did not ask to be spared. Kailen only heard her spit. Just once, and it produced a string of curses from the Noriziem assaulting her. Again, the wet crunch punched the air and the invaders left house. Their footfalls echoed away. He was alone, all alone. He did not move. Not even when drops of blood found their way through the floor and spattered warm on his face. He was weak.

***

Carra entered his room quietly. The downstairs was finally cleared of patrons. She knew he had come up, but was shocked to see him tangled in his own clothes and stained with vomit. She felt guilty for pushing him to sit with them, but told herself it was fine. He had been laughing and animated, obviously enjoying his audience. It might take him a day or two to recover, but it would be worth it. He spent too much time behind his own walls.

He was dead weight and too heavy for her to lift. Random muttering stumbled from his lips, but Carra couldn't understand it. She grabbed him by the armpits and hauled him towards the bed. His muttering increased, and she felt his muscles tense, but she paid it no attention. Her head hurt and her back ached. She was going to dump him into bed, get him out of his stinking clothes, and then take a bath and sleep. She imagined her over-stuffed pillows cradling her head.

Kailen's hand darted out and grabbed her by the neck. He twisted out of her grasp and pulled her to the floor. Carra tried to pry his hand off, but it wouldn't move. She struggled to breathe. Only rage shone in Kailen's eyes. He looked through her, seeing something that wasn't there. He raised his arm and aimed a white-knuckled fist at her. Carra looked at him evenly, green eyes trying to connect with blue. He wasn't there though. Everything was swallowed by hatred. "Don't you dare hit me," she said.

Kailen's fist slammed into her face. She tasted iron and saw stars. His grip loosened, and she fell back, her head cracking against the bedpost. She forced herself back up, spitting blood and trying to ignore the clenching of her stomach. He reached for her again, but she pushed his sluggish arm aside and punched him hard enough that his head bounced against the floor. Kailen lay on the floor with mouth open and eyes half-closed. She stood, grabbed him again, and hauled him into the bed. Pulling off the last of his clothes, she covered him with a quilt. She blew out the candle on his nightstand and left, closing the door behind her.

Out in the hall, with only the dying lanterns bearing witness, Carra reached up and felt the growing welt on her cheek. She spit blood on the floor and held in the tears.

***

No matter how deep he buried his head into the pillow he could not escape the sound of morning crows. Kailen's head hurt. It really hurt. Stale sweat soaked his sheets, and his mouth was dry and pasty. The alcohol still exuded from his pores, mixing with his body odor. He didn't dare open his eyes. Sunlight leaked through the shutters, the rays finding his eyes no matter how he turned his head.

Kailen eased himself up, scanning the room. The floor was freshly scrubbed, which was odd, but nothing seemed out of place. On the nightstand was a pitcher of water and a cup. He didn't bother with the cup, draining the pitcher and wanting more. His body felt desiccated.

Rubbing his eyes, he tried to push the fog away. The flesh of his left cheek was tender, and his hand was sore. Looking at it he noticed bruising on his knuckles. "How did I do that?"

The door opened, the creaking hinges startling him. Carra came in, wearing a simple linen dress. Her hair was down and brushed to cover the left side of her face. She never wore her hair like that. Without smiling she asked, "How are you feeling?"

"Like shit. I think a battalion is marching through my head. I don't know why I'm even awake this early."

"It's not early. You've been passed out for over a day."

Kailen's eyes snapped to hers. "That long?"

"Aye, you barely stirred yesterday. Don't think I could have woke you if I tried."

"What did I drink?"

"The men you sat with bought the last bottle of Hadari Cactus Amber I had in. Paid a huge amount for it. You drank most of it."

"Still, I've never been out that long."

"You had a lot of their pipeweed. That's what finally got you."

"And that's why my mouth tastes like cat shit."

Carra offered a half-smile and laid his folded clothes on the foot of his bed.

"Thank you, you didn't have to wash them."

"Who said I washed them? That's what I pay the girls for."

Kailen stood, his legs wobbling only slightly. He walked to Carra and went to brush the hair from her face, saying, "You take good care of me. What would I…"

He stopped. There, on her left cheekbone, was a large bruise. Dark purple and peppered with the red flecks of broken skin, the mark looked raw and painful. It went down to her jaw line, where the skin was yellow-green and puffy. Kailen's insides turned cold. "Who did this to you?"

He raised her chin to look better at the bruise, and saw the five smaller bruises on her neck. "Where you attacked?"

Carra shrugged. She stepped back and crossed her arms over her chest. "It was some idiot down in the tavern. He got so drunk I don't think he even knew where he was anymore."

"Why you? Why did he touch you?"

Her eyes came to rest on the corner of Kailen's bed. "I was in the wrong place at the wrong time. I was walking by him with some empty pitchers when he came out of nowhere and hit me. Some of the boys grabbed him, beat him up a bit, and threw him out. He won't bother anyone else."

Kailen let go of her, gathered his fresh clothes, and took his sword off the wall mount. Carra grabbed him by the shoulder. "What are you doing?"

"I'm taking care of this. No one hurts you."

Carra looped her hand over his elbow. Her mouth set in a grim line, the level gaze of her eyes brooked no argument. She reached up and brushed the matted hair back from his face. "You need to rest. What's done is done. And I know you've been having the dreams the last couple of nights."

"How?"

"You talk in your sleep." Carra let go of his elbow and went to the window. She rubbed her temples with her right hand.

Kailen wished the liquor had erased the memories of his dreams, but it hadn't.

"I saw Angler's Cove burn."

"I know. Did you dream about your parents?"

Kailen looked down to the floor.

Carra nodded, stretched her back, and took a deep breath. "I'm not telling you who it was, as will no one else."

"Carra, he's not getting away with this."

"He's been taken care of. I don't want you getting in trouble with the Legion."

Kailen stepped behind her and held her shoulders. She looked up at him, tears threatening to wash away her normally unshakable determination. She did not cry often. "Are you okay?"

She whispered, "I always am."

He hugged her and kissed the top of her head. Every one of her muscles was taut, and it felt as if she were leaning slightly away from Kailen. Pulling her closer, he said, "If I find out who did this, I will kill him."

"I know."

Chapter 6
IN GOOD COMPANY

Do not sit in front of the Noriziem, thought Morrikii. *Keep your back straight, look them in the eyes, and never show weakness.* The mantra helped to keep his mind off the weight of his burnished plate armor. At the base of his throne, arms behind his back and chin held even, the Stonestriker stood tall and faced the khans of the four great Noriziem clans. They stood in line, wearing their clan's colors and their most impressive attire. No two of them were alike.

Logarsh of Clan Wathiem was a short, wiry man with eyes that never stopped moving. His chain and leather armor clinked whenever his weight shifted.

Markan, leader of Clan Nathikan, looked more bear than man. He stood at ease, his corded arms resting against the haft of his great-axe. A beard of amber and gray spilled down his chest, somewhat hiding a belly that sagged with ale and age. Morrikii had found the brute on the coast of Fridinikar over seventeen years ago. He and his crew washed ashore, their longship blown off course and battered by winter storms. Morrikii believed Galantaegan's will had led him to the khan's rescue. The man had been fighting for House Stonestriker ever since. It had been the first step that led to this day.

Clan Thent was led by a man named Toral. He wore no armor, only black robes. His head was shaved and a sliver of bone pierced his nose. Morrikii could not read his face.

Jenaka el' Lebren ruled Clan Lobrenth. She wore the heaviest armor, full plate custom-made to fit her every curve. Her raven eyes, framed by jet-black hair, never left Morrikii. He'd heard she was the most ruthless of the four.

Morrikii bowed, maintaining eye contact. They returned the gesture with measured respect. Morrikii motioned for the servants, who offered goblets of wine to the esteemed visitors. Toral did not accept. He simply stared at Morrikii and held his only weapon, a long and graceful spear.

Morrikii met that gaze and did not flinch. He drank the wine quickly, letting its sweet bitterness calm him. He was still practicing his Norzaat, and now was not the time for mistakes. "I welcome all of you to Frostwrath. This is the first time all of us have gathered. I am sure it pleases Galantaegan."

Hearing the Black Dragon's name, the four Noriziem lowered their heads and turned their eyes downward. Logarsh answered in fairly fluent Cardanan. "We are honored by your invitation. The Black One blessed our journey here, and we are unworthy as guests in these halls."

"You are most worthy. You made the effort to cross the Ebon Sea while the northern ice still lingers in the fog. Your bravery is worthy of Galantaegan," Morrikii responded.

Toral snorted, and not quietly. Morrikii ignored him and turned his attention to Jenaka. "Your presence honors me most of all, Lady of the Lobrenth. The power of your clan is well known, even from across the ocean."

Her face should have been carved from marble. Her pale skin and shining armor were out of place in this hall of black granite and stained wrought iron. Her answer was wrapped in precision and control. "My clerics tell me the Black One favors you. I care little for your cause, only that it gives us a chance to crush Carodan. Clan Nathikan's raids may have hurt them, but it is time for proper force to be used."

Markan's chest puffed and his face flushed to match the red of his beard. "Woman, Nathikan has spent the last seventeen years fighting the Cardanans. While you've hidden in your pretty forest, we've fought the Unbelievers. We've taken their gold, burned their homes, and killed them. What have you done?"

Morrikii stepped between them, placing a hand on Markan's chest. The Noriziem had spent the last three centuries fighting amongst themselves. It would not take much to splinter this lofty alliance. "Old friend, you have fought beside me loyally for many years. No one questions that. It was the Black One's will that brought you and me together. But, if we are to truly win through, we will need the help of all Noriziem. You have set aside your differences. Now, let us move forward."

With a hand on Markan's shoulder, Morrikii led the khans away from his throne. The straight-backed chair, carved from black granite, frowned down on them. He avoided being around it as often as possible. They passed under an archway to a low table of polished pine. A map of their world, K'aeran, stretched across it. In the east was Granikar, the old world. In the west was Abinar, home of Carodan. In the north, lying white and chill, was Fridinikar. Three continents, all separated by the Ebon Sea.

Morrikii waited for the khans to gather around the table before saying, "For some time now Markan and his clansmen have raided the shores of Carodan. They spread terror and panic. Carodan has a strong navy, but Noriziem longships are too swift and silent to be easily tracked. They never know where the strike will fall."

Their eyes were on him. His presence and words would have to be perfect. They had committed their forces based on the negotiations of ambassadors. Now, it was time to prove his worth. He leaned over the table, resting his fingers on the northwest shore of Carodan. The coasts of Westlook. "This is where we have concentrated our attacks. Westlook is the youngest province, and sparsely populated. An easy target. Over the last six months Markan has increased his attacks per my orders. Cardanan villages have burned, Clan Nathikan has profited greatly, and after the attacks they sail north to the protection of my harbors. And these are only raids. Imagine what our more vigorous incursion could gain."

His voice had risen, and he clenched his fists when he spoke. Markan's large chest swelled with pride, and Logarsh's eyes darted over Carodan. Morrikii imagined the gold coins counting up in the skinny khan's mind. Jenaka kept her face and body completely still, but her hips had shifted towards the table without her noticing, and her left eyebrow arched. Toral's face was a stone mask of disdain.

Logarsh gulped his wine and spoke with forced calm. "You have achieved much, Lord Stonestriker. The Noriziem still remember quite well when Clan Carothak fled across the Ebon Sea. To strike them down now, to burn Carodan from the map would finally bring the Noriziem justice, and as such we stand to gain much from this, but what about you?"

Morrikii met the small man's gaze and answered. "For too long has Carodan been under weak rule. Gold, lust, and self-gratification are the driving forces. House Ironheart has sat on the throne for two hundred and fifty years, almost never challenged, and most certainly never questioned. If led by the right man, Carodan could rise to new heights. It needs to be cleansed by fire first, but renewed it could achieve so much. From the ashes comes new life."

"The Galan-Tome. Verse 253. I'm impressed," said Jenaka. Morrikii had made sure to memorize the huge book before the khans' arrival.

"And the man to lead it is you," Toral said.

Morrikii had wondered when the leader of Clan Thent would speak. His voice was low and cool in tone. "You are old, and stranded in this cold, miserable land because you tried to take control of Carodan before. You failed."

They knew his history. He'd made no effort to hide it from them. "You speak the truth."

He took another goblet of wine from an attendant. He drank, swishing the wine in his mouth. Conveying the right amount of hesitation and regret was vital. "I was young and headstrong. I had risen quickly in my House, sped along by my father's untimely death. By twenty-five I was lord of the Stonestrikers; the wealthiest House in Tidal Guard. Some say we owned the old city of Whitebreak. They were only half right."

Their attention was undivided. Even Markan did not know the full details of his past. It was said all cultures shared a love of story, and he hoped his would be the solidifier of this mercurial alliance. He took another sip of wine and continued. "Carodan has grown over the centuries, but slowly. We gained Westlook through the defeat of the Grenar, a race so powerful and vicious that the Legion Command had maintained for decades we would never beat them in open warfare. We drove them from their land, but let them escape into the western wilds. We should have pursued them and pushed them in to the very sea. House Ironheart chose mercy.

"Before that we defended the southern province of Wheat Scythe from the Hadari who wanted it for their own. The sand-faeries needed the fertile lands to feed their people," Morrikii stopped to laugh before adding, "and Cardanans fetched a handsome price on the slave market.

"But we held them off and stood firm. We forced them into a peace with us. A peace! My father talked of it often. The Hadari should have been broken and forced to bend the knee to us and swear fealty. Instead, House Ironheart cut a deal. They ceased hostilities, officially, and we would trade them surplus wheat for silk and spices. A large amount of that gold lines the pockets of both Tidal Guard and Wheat Scythe Houses. Slavers still raid the border and take people from their homes. Cardanans deserve better."

His voice starting to go raw, Morrikii drained the last of his wine. Even Toral could not hide his interest. "I saw my chance three months after taking the rule of my family. The old king died and his son was crowned. A wet-eared whelp of seventeen, I thought Jo'el Ironheart weak and indecisive. I raised my army from the ranks of unhappy commoners throughout Tidal Guard. Two legions joined me. Their commanders had family that lived in either Westlook or Wheat Scythe. The septs and high septs that owed my house fealty mustered as many men as possible. Thirty thousand troops marched to my command, united under the ideal that our country could be something better.

"Whitebreak fell without a fight. The town steward met me at the opened gates with an embrace. After that we swept through Tidal Guard, placing most of the province under our control. I thought the people of Carodan wanted me to rule. It was easy to forget that my family already controlled most of the old province."

Morrikii looked into the bottom of his goblet, watching memories play out in the dregs of his wine. "I met the young king on the Roundstone Fields, not far from the shores of Lake Azureron. I only needed to get by the boy and his soldiers, cross the lake, and take True Tower Isle where the capitol stood. I could so clearly imagine the banners of House Stonestriker waving over the walls of Citadel. I was certain I would win."

Morrikii walked around the table, his fingers tapping out the march of armored boots. "Our two armies met. I still remember the sounds of steel and death. I can smell the blood and filth and fear. My defeat of the little king was certain."

He stopped in front of Toral, staring the khan in his unflinching eyes. "I underestimated him. My army was defeated, I captured, and my House stripped of its lands and titles. He could have beheaded us all, he could have personally flayed and quartered me, but instead he granted us mercy. Banishment to the north, to Fridinikar. The ground never thaws, and if you drop your guard while in the wilds the wolves and bears will make a quick meal of you."

Toral stared back. Morrikii did not see compassion or understanding in his face. Instead, those small, dark eyes measured him. *Well*, thought Morrikii, *let's give him something more to judge.* "By all rights, I was finished. I thought I'd come here with a few followers and die frozen upon the coastal wastes. Fifteen thousand men, women, and children came with me. Most had been septs of House Stonestriker for centuries, but others came because they believed in me." Morrikii turned away from Toral, shaking his head. "To know that so many other people wanted the same change I did, and were willing to come here to this wasteland, honored and humbled me.

"Young Ironheart had not planned on such a mass exodus, but he decided the fewer dissenters in his kingdom the better, so he allowed it. It took all of the Northern Fleet to transport us. We wasted no time building a settlement on the most hospitable land we could find. It didn't matter. We would still die. The cold was inescapable."

Toral interrupted, "Yet still you live. And you squat in the halls of our god."

Morrikii punched Toral in the face. In one fluid move Morrikii reached over his shoulder and drew Sunder. He held the hammer in front of him and shouted, *"Ushtan Galan throll!"*

A cloud of swirling ash materialized around the head of the hammer and filled the room with the smell of heat and char. The khan readied his spear, but with a lazy swing Morrikii brought Sunder down upon it. The wooden shaft of the spear disappeared in a puff of soot, and the steel tip clattered to floor, blackened and curled. Toral blinked at his hands. They were covered in ash, but otherwise untouched. His spear, a weapon that had been his father's, and his grandfather's before that, was simply gone.

Through gritted teeth Morrikii said, "Do not equate my people with beggars. I will not tolerate it. I owe them everything."

The other khans watched, not moving. In all the time Markan had known Morrikii, he had never witnessed such a display. Logarsh hid his fear poorly. The smile that tugged at Jenaka's lips made Morrikii blush slightly.

Toral swallowed. He swallowed again, forcing his hands to rest at his sides. He took a stuttering, deep breath, trying to put his stone mask back together. "Your people are not all you owe. You would not be here if Galantaegan did not wish it."

Morrikii stepped back, and with a twitch of his wrists the cloud of ash disappeared from Sunder. His limbs trembled from the battle-rush. "I've proven I have the Black One's favor. Can any of you summon his Ash?"

None of them answered, and Morrikii laughed. Not a chuckle, or amiable mirth, but outright laughed at them. He breathed deep and turned his back on Toral. "If it weren't for Galantaegan, we would be dead. Of that, Toral is right. However, he spoke to me, showed us the way to safety. He showed us kindness and warmth. He showed me his favor. That's more than I ever had from Antaunna. I see the truth now."

The memory was still crisp. It seemed so long ago, huddled in a blanket, hugging a fire and relying on a crude stone house to shelter him from the unending wind. A voice so kind and warm had whispered into his thoughts. He hadn't really heard it. It was that odd feeling at the base of his neck, but the next day he took a band of his strongest soldiers, led by Adeus Axehaft, to the east. They traveled for three days, crossing fields of frozen mud and hills of tumbled stone towards a lone mountain that dominated the horizon. The four-peaked monstrosity, standing by itself, black against an infinite plain of white rose to command all within its sight. The warm voice had whispered at the edge of his thoughts, telling him this was home.

Morrikii faced Toral and walked up to him, nose to nose. "There is no such thing as balance. Chaos is the only constant. Kingdoms burn, wars rage throughout time, and people die for no reason. I have embraced the Black Dragon, and he has chosen me to lead this war. For those who follow, there are great rewards. We can build something new."

Toral turned from Morrikii, unable to hold his gaze. He walked to the table and looked at the map, squinting in the dim light. "Carodan is strong, and in spite of what you think, the

Blue Dragon does watch over them. Legend tells of the fleets that our clans sent out to pursue them, never to return. They were swallowed by the sea, Antaunna's realm. How would it be any different now?"

Morrikii motioned the other khans close. "Old legends and superstitions. We will have a much shorter distance to travel than your ancestors. When the remainder of your forces arrive, we'll sail south."

Markan and Logarsh grinned. Toral was starting to lower his guard. He stared at the map of Carodan, almost as if he was picking where he would build his summer estate. Only Jenaka expressed doubt. "Carodan is large, and its legions well trained. In Granikar we hear tales of their prowess, rivaling that of the Old Empire. Even with all our numbers I don't know if we can do this."

Morrikii had to be careful with this one. He knew she was hungry for the conquest, but the risk would have to be worth it for the Lobrenth. He moved close to her, but not too close. He looked her in the eye, seeing the black strength that lay there. "You are right. This will not be easy. I have trained my own army in the tactics of Carodan, and I feel confident of their ability to meet them on the field. But, we will have to move carefully. Our first blow will have to come soon, and in the right place."

Morrikii went to the map and placed a finger on Westlook. "Our concentrated attacks have focused the Cardanans' attention on this province. Markan, tell them about our plan to generate too much attention on this backwater."

***

Walking down the empty corridor, towards his quarters, Morrikii was unable to keep the smile from his face. The gathering had gone better than he'd hoped. The rough spots were expected, and he was rather glad for the confrontation with Toral. His display of Galantaegan's power had been quite convincing. Before leaving the throne room, Jenaka lingering gaze had stirred an inner heat long absent.

Morrikii's thoughts kept shifting back to her. The sheen of her hair, the way her armor fit every perfect curve. He laughed. He was too old for such thoughts. It had been so long since he'd been with a woman that he didn't know if his privates even worked anymore.

He pulled his cloak close. It was always cold. This entire wing of the city was his, but the only warmth he found was in his personal chambers. His legs were tired and his back ached from the weight of his armor, and nothing sounded better than lying in his bed with the fire fully stoked.

The two guards flanking the heavy door to his quarters snapped to attention. Morrikii noticed the sleepiness in their eyes but decided not to comment. There was so little activity on this side of the city that it often felt like a tomb.

In his sitting room Dora waited for him. She was silent as she removed Morrikii's armor. Since he had snapped at her a few weeks ago she had been very withdrawn.

He slipped Sunder from his back and rested it on a cradle bolted to the wall. Flanking it were two paintings of Morrikii's home city Whitebreak, a reminder of why he climbed out of bed every morning.

As each piece of armor was unbuckled and removed, the pressure on his back lessened. When the last bit was lifted, his chain hauberk, he rolled his shoulders back and stretched. Pulling his head to the side, his neck and spine popped with loud satisfaction. Dora handed him a goblet of wine. She wouldn't meet his eyes. He motioned towards the spiral staircase on the far side of the room and asked, "How is she?"

Dora looked down at her apron, brushing off non-existent crumbs. "Better today, my Lord. She recognized us and even talked some."

"Good. So she's improving?"

"I think so," said Dora, "She even ate a little. Did you want me to have dinner sent for you, my Lord?"

"No thank you. I'm not hungry."

Dora nodded and shut the thick pine door behind her. He told himself her silence was only a mood and would soon pass. Alone, Morrikii focused on the wine. It had a smoky undertone that lingered on his tongue. Sitting on the cushioned bench in front of the fireplace, he let the quiet wash over him. Here, at the edge of everything, it was peaceful and warm. He closed his eyes feeling only the fire, the soft cushions, and the sweet wine.

He knew he needed to go up the stairs and see her. Finishing the wine he stood, stretching his back. Leaving the goblet on a table, next to an almost-full decanter, he went to the stairs and climbed to the grand bedroom.

Cool and lit by only a few candles, the room whispered with the wind blowing through the vents cut in the ceiling. He walked slowly across the room, his footsteps silenced by the thickly woven rug. A huge bed sprawled across the middle of the room, hidden by sheets of cream-colored silk hung from the ceiling. Breathing, soft and shallow, was the only other sound. It punctuated the wind overhead with weak, strained beats.

Morrikii stopped at the edge of the bed, not wanting to open the curtains. He clenched and unclenched his hands, which were clammy and clumsy. He drew a deep breath and forced a hand to the curtain, pulling it aside. She lay there in the center of the bed, on her back with the covers arranged neatly across her. Her face was pale and hollow. Her hair, once thick and red as the sun was brittle, washed out by age and fatigue. Her eyes were closed.

Morrikii sat on the bed and trailed his fingers down her cheek. She turned her head towards him, a rattling sigh her hello. Keeping his voice calm and even, Morrikii asked, "Mella, can you hear me?"

She opened her eyes. They were clear today. Her voice scratched its way from her mouth. "I was hoping to see you. How was the gathering?"

Good. She remembered, thought Morrikii. "The Noriziem are charming as always. But they all seem convinced. By the beginning of summer we'll sail for Carodan."

She smiled, but before she could speak a cough wracked her body. On the stand next to the bed was a cup of dreammilk. Morrikii brought the cup to her lips and the sweet liquid eased her spasms. He continued, doing his best to pretend nothing had happened. "Soon, we'll be home. I'll take you to the top of Gull Point, and we can look down on Sanctuary Bay, like the night we met. We'll see Whitebreak sprawled across the southern shore and lit by a thousand torches in the evening. It will be warm, with the sun brilliant in the sky."

Tears crept into the corners of Morrikii's eyes. His voice remained steady though, and he forced his smile to stay warm. Still, she knew. She rested a hand against his cheek and wiped away the tears even though it took all her strength just to do so. "I'll be fine 'Kii. Today was good. I think I'm getting stronger."

"You look it. I see fire in your eyes."

Her illness had been progressing for the last five years. For the past three weeks she had gone into spasms whenever he came near, screaming of how a demon surrounded by clouds of ash had come to consume her soul.

He leaned down and brushed his lips against her forehead. "You need to rest. I have plans to review and supply ledgers to check. I'll be back up."

"Promise?"

"I promise. Have the rest of the dreammilk. It'll help you sleep."

She emptied the cup and tried to smile. If she pulled her lips back too far, they cracked and bled. He kissed her gently and stood. She was already asleep by the time he set the curtain into place. Her gentle snores were silenced as he closed the bedroom door behind him. He used to tease her about her snoring, but she had never believed him. In the small bed in his study, it was always quiet, and he missed the sound of her breath.

Back in the sitting room, he helped himself to more wine. He usually had only one glass before bed, but tonight finishing the whole decanter sounded attractive. Tears fought for release, but he pushed them back. He sat down on his bench and stared into the fire trying to think of something other than Mella. The simply brutal and relentless flames calmed him, and he almost didn't hear the knock at his door. He looked up, eyes narrowed, and slammed his goblet down on the table. "Enter."

One of the guards poked his head through the door, his eyes fixed downward. "Pardon the intrusion, my Lord, but a guest requests your audience."

Morrikii arched an eyebrow. "A guest?"

"Yes, my Lord. Lady Jenaka."

His eyebrow went higher. What could she want? "Show her in, Corporal."

Retrieving his goblet he stood and walked to the side table. From the decanter he filled his own glass and a second. He felt more than heard soft footfalls and looked up from the table. The guard mumbled his pardon and closed the door behind him.

She no longer wore her armor. Instead, a woolen gown, dyed black, gray, and red clung to her with measured sweeps and folds. She approached the table and Morrikii handed her the fresh goblet. She smiled and accepted. He met her smile with his own, looking for any sign of nervousness. None. Even here, in his inner sanctum, she was completely confident and in control. Her smile was the most disarming thing. It turned a face hardened and scarred by battle into an invitation. To what, Morrikii wasn't sure. He didn't have time for games. "To what do I owe the honor, my lady?"

She drained the wine in one swallow. An amused grunt sounded from the back of her throat. "There is no need for formality, Stonestriker. Call me Jenaka."

"Well then, Jenaka, what brings you across the city at such a late hour?"

She walked around the room, looking at the paintings and shelves full of books. Bathed in the unreliable light of the fire, she appeared carved from living marble. Morrikii's eyes wandered down to her backside, where the dress accented her curves most precisely. He wondered if he could bounce a silver coin off her rear, and that if he did, how high would it go?

Stopping in front of the fireplace, she considered him with an almost predatory interest and smiled again. "You impress me, Stonestriker. I've heard tales from Nathikan clansmen of your great city and of how you'd earned Galantaegan's favor. I never really believed them."

She walked towards him, her eyes unwavering. "I was wrong. What you offer the Noriziem is amazing; a chance to bring back the Empire a thousand years after its collapse."

She came so close he tasted her breath, mint leaves mixed with wine. She ran a hand down his chest, and with the other hand undid a cord on the front of her dress. Already low-cut, the bust opened even more. "But, every emperor needs an empress."

The vein in Morrikii's neck pulsed. He kept his eyes locked on hers, forbidding them from moving over to the staircase that led to Mella's room. He grabbed her by the waist and pulled her close. She gasped, grinding her pelvis against his. Their lips almost touched but not quite. "So, I take it I have your unwavering support?" asked the Stonestriker.

"Make me your queen, and yes. I can ensure the full cooperation of Logarsh and Toral."

Morrikii kissed her, pressing so hard he tasted blood. He picked her up and she wrapped her legs around him. He moved towards his side room, but changed his mind when he reached the bench. He threw her down and turned her over so that her rear faced him. Jenaka looked back at him, biting her lower lip. She lifted her skirt, revealing no undergarments. Pretending it was Mella in front of him, the way she was before she became sick, Morrikii fumbled with his breeches and noticed that everything did indeed still work.

Chapter 7
THE WOLF, THE SWORD, AND THE SHADOW

Kailen notched his sword belt, setting it over his hips. His armor, cleaned and oiled, was strapped in place. He readjusted his cloak. Outside, sheets of rain danced over Angler's Cove, rattling windowpanes and painting the world gray. Even his room was awash with the faded half-light. The single candle on the dresser did little to pierce it. Carra was still in bed wrapped in the sheets. Her right leg and hip were strategically uncovered. The musk of sex hung in the air. His eyes kept going to the bruise on her face. It was mostly faded, a washed-out green now, and the marks on her neck were pale red spots. Still, she refused to tell him who had done it.

The bed groaned under his added weight as he sat and trailed a hand across her bruised cheek. She pulled away, just a little. Thinking her cheek must still be sore he instead ran his fingers through her hair. "You're awfully quiet this morning."

Carra shrugged. "Just watching you dress. Wanted to make sure the girls cleaned your gear well. Looks good."

Kailen bent down and kissed her, caressing her shoulder, tracing the collarbone and arch of her neck. "You look good. Two weeks isn't long enough."

She walked her fingers up Kailen's arm, staring past him at the wall. Something didn't feel right. Kailen tried to read her eyes but couldn't see them clearly in the dim light. In what Kailen knew to be her best-practiced nonchalant tone, Carra asked, "How long until you're home?"

"I don't know. Bronzehide was sparse on the particulars."

Her fingers stopped at the boiled-leather spaulder covering his left shoulder. She tapped her fingernails against it, the sound blending in with the rain bouncing against the glass. Kailen noticed her hand shaking slightly. He was going to ask her if she was feeling all right when she stopped and bolted upright.

She coughed. Violently. Jumping from the sheets, she snatched a kerchief from the nightstand. Holding the cloth to her mouth, she coughed even harder, so hard her ribs contracted visibly with the force. Even though she was turned away Kailen saw blood stain the kerchief. "Please tell me you've seen the healers."

Carra coughed once more and spit the last of the blood. She nodded yes. "They said I just need more rest. I asked them if it was lung-rot, but they said no. Maybe I'll let Tilda run the bar for the next couple of days. I could use some sleep."

She flashed him a reassuring smile, but Kailen still saw traces of blood between her teeth. "I'm not sure that's it. I've been fatigued. I've gone four days without sleep. I've never coughed blood."

"Maybe I'm just not as strong as you," her tone cut like the edge of his sword.

"Carra, that bleeding isn't right. Are you sure it's not the dreampowder-"

"I'm sure," she said, "I've told you before I only use it occasionally, and I mix it with wine. I'm just worn out. I'll rest the next several days."

Kailen wasn't ready to let it go, but Carra interrupted him. "Take care of yourself out there. I don't know what I'd do if I lost you."

Kailen was caught off guard. Very rarely did she express concern so openly, and her tone was completely different from just a few moments earlier. The gate was shut. She was done with his concern. "I'll be fine. Always am. Besides, if something happened to me, Antaunna knows you'd be okay. There isn't a man in the docks who wouldn't kill to be your husband."

Carra looked down, coughing slightly and dabbing at her lips with the kerchief. More red stains dotted the tightly woven fabric. "I only want you."

Kailen never knew what to say when she brought this up.

"When I can be home more. . ."

"When will that be?" Even she couldn't completely hide the resentment that colored her tone. "I'm sorry, I didn't mean it to come out like that."

Kailen stood and went to the window. "I need to do this. I can't put my sword down. Not yet. Too many people out there still need the Legion's protection."

"The Legion's protection, or yours? Even if you never put that blade down people will die at the hands of others. You will not stop tragedies. You can't bring your parents back."

"Don't you think I know that?" Kailen turned on her. "But it's in my heart and my soul where this echo lurks. I can't leave behind the image of my parents' deaths. What happened and still happens to so many people. Antaunna granted me skill with a blade and a strong body. I know nothing else."

Carra cast aside the sheets and joined him by the window. Naked, she was completely vulnerable next to his armor and steel. She embraced him and kissed his cheek. "You know me. Be with me. Please, make me feel like I matter."

"Carra," he said and pulled her forehead close to rest against his, "You're the only thing that keeps me sane. I fight for you just as much as anyone else. When I've served my time and earn my pension, and my Legion-granted land, it's you I want to build a home with. You I want to have a family with. You give me a reason to keep fighting."

"I need to know one thing." Lifting her head and cupping his cheek in her slender hand she asked, "For me, will you stop fighting?"

"Yes," he said and kissed her. "I can't do this forever, but I can't stop now. Not yet."

The tears she'd held in for so long finally fought their way from her eyes and down the gentle lines of her cheeks. She looked out the window, trying to rebuild her composure. "Remember when we met at our first Temple lessons?"

"I do. We prayed next to each other."

"Pray with me now?"

They joined hands and bowed their heads until they were touching. Neither had to ask which prayer to recite.

I am only one
And the world is great
I know not where my road takes me
I know not how long it is.

The trials are many
And the pain is great
I will be shaken
I will be torn.

But in all life there is reason
There is Balance
For everything I lose
There is something gained.

Antaunna is my strength
Her hand my guide
From her I have the will to stand
Through the darkness tall.

They embraced, Carra standing on her tiptoes to kiss Kailen. Tears gathered at the corners of her eyes, but she refused to let them run. "Take care of yourself out there. Don't die before I do."

"I won't."

***

Wearing only a thick wool robe, Carra saw him off from the front door of the tavern. The air was cold and damp. The downpour had passed, but a thick mist still fell on the sodden rooftops. Kailen pulled his hood tight over his head and held his cloak close. He looked back once wondering how much longer she'd tolerate him leaving. She was leaning against the doorframe, holding the top of her robe closed with one hand. Her crooked smile did little to hide the tears. He turned away, letting the curtain of rain fall shut behind him.

The streets were nearly deserted. Running water streamed across over-full drains and forced mud and waste into the thruways. Climbing the slope of the town was careful work, and Kailen concentrated on every footfall upon the slimy cobblestones. Slipping into the muck was not how he wanted to start this day. Everything passed in a foggy, wet blur. He tried not to think of Carra, with her warm skin and bruised face. Who had done that to her? Was he right to leave her while she was still hurting? What choice was there though? There was a choice, and duty had won out. It was on these days, as he left her behind, that he questioned the cost.

The courtyard of the Legion fort was a rain-soaked bog. The mud sucked at Kailen's boots, almost pulling them off several times. A call from across the courtyard disrupted his navigation of the morass. "Be careful how you step, princess. You might get dirt on your fine clothes."

Kailen smiled as he recognized the heckler. "Rian, where have you been, you tiny bastard? I haven't seen you since the onset of winter."

Rian Direpaw, Warden Captain of Westlook, slogged over to Kailen and hugged him, slapping him on the back. In tow was his direwolf, Nina. She whined and pushed her massive muzzle against Kailen's leg until he knelt down and scratched her neck.

"The Legion had me down in the Southern Reaches, along the Jade Forest. I was exploring the old Grenar ruins. We'd heard rumors of bandits setting up camps down there, but I found nothing. I spent the worst of the winter in Everwatch, staring out across the frozen Amen'kar at the Grenar Wilds. Hoped to see a living one. No luck."

"So," Kailen stood, still scratching Nina behind the ear, "What brings you this far north?"

"Our assignment."

"Our?" asked Kailen. Wardens typically worked alone, and for him to be paired with the commander of the warden forces in Westlook was extremely odd.

"I haven't been told anything. I received a message directly from General Bronzehide a month ago. It said to report here on this date and nothing more. Here I am."

"Well, let's see what this is about."

The two wardens entered the keep. The air was only slightly less damp in the granite corridors. A chill was already setting into Kailen's bones and he hoped the General's study would be warmer. They climbed the spiral stair, the steps slick from the mist blowing in through the arrow slits. The door to the study was open, and indeed it was warmer than the rest of the keep. Bronzehide was waiting for them, along with a Legion officer Kailen did not recognize. The man was tall and broad of shoulder. His hair was oil-black and a beard, neatly trimmed, outlined his face. A long, pale scar traced along his cheek. The two wardens came to attention and saluted.

"At ease. Gentlemen, let's not waste time. This is Line Commander Zaketh Darksteel, one of King Ironheart's military advisors."

Kailen shook his hand. His knuckles popped under Darksteel's grip. He was familiar with the man's name. Darksteel was one the largest Houses in Wheat Scythe, and this particular son of the House had spent his early years in the Legion patrolling the border between southern Carodan and Hadak. Though technically at peace, incursions by the Hadari occurred frequently. Any slavers caught by the Legion were supposed to be brought to trial, unless they resisted, in which case deadly force was permissible. The records had never shown the Hadari not resisting, and in the last century there was not one documented trial of Hadari slavers.

After first joining the Legion, Kailen had heard stories of Darksteel around the cook-fire. They said he nailed Hadari to whatever south-facing surface he could find. Barn walls, fences, road posts, he didn't care as long as any living Hadari coming north encountered his welcome signs. Darksteel had come to the King's attention when it was reported that slaver attacks in his patrol area had been reduced by over three-quarters. Kailen still remembered one story that described the Commander gutting a Hadari with only a sharp rock and his free hand.

Each limb, every muscle, in the Commander's body was wound tight as tempered steel. Aggression radiated from the man. Kailen bowed his head and said, "Commander Darksteel, it's an honor to meet you. Your reputation precedes you, sir."

Darksteel nodded. When he spoke, his mouth moved in tight, controlled bursts. "As does yours, Warden Tidespinner. General Bronzehide showed me the variety of teeth you've collected. Impressive."

"My duty, sir."

Those black eyes bored into Kailen. He shifted his feet and an odd jitter rattled his belly. He had only half believed the stories about Darksteel, but there was something about the man that sat poorly with Kailen. He sensed the violence brewing just below the Commander's self-control. He turned to Bronzehide, needing an excuse to break eye contact with Darksteel. "So, General, why the three of us here? I thought I was going back out into the wild."

"You are," answered Bronzehide, "but you'll have company this time. Direpaw and Darksteel are going with you."

Kailen raised an eyebrow. "Two wardens and a legionnaire is an odd mix."

Bronzehide reached down to the map of Carodan and tapped its center, where Lake Azureron and True Tower Isle lay. "The King is concerned over the increase in Noriziem activity, especially along the shores of Westlook. He wants the Commander to observe the situation and report back to him. You and Direpaw will be his guides."

Bronzehide faced Kailen squarely now. "You're to take him to the locations of the most recent attacks and to survey the defenses of our coasts and the towns close to them. You'll be given horses to make the trip faster."

Kailen was not happy. "So we're sight-seeing instead of fighting?"

"Trust me, Warden, I've never had the opportunity to kill Noriziem, but I'm hoping to change that. If we find any, we will not shy from combat," Darksteel said. The anticipation and excitement in the commander's tone made Kailen's skin ripple with goose pimples.

Rian had been unusually quiet. He was looking down at the table and stroking his goatee so hard it might rub off. Kailen asked him, "Ready for a tour of the countryside?"

The other warden sucked a quick breath through his nose, clearing his throat. "Should be easy. I can think of several towns that will be of particular interest."

Bronzehide looked each man in the eye and said, "This is a serious mission. The king wants to know what's going on out here, and wants his advisor to see it first hand. The Noriziem have had the most success here, in spite of the increase in naval patrols and troop emplacements. He may want to raise another legion, but he needs to justify it to the Council of Lords first. Let Darksteel see everything he needs to and bring him back in one piece. The Noriziem have been slowly bleeding us for too long. It ends.

"I expect you back in seven weeks. May Antaunna speed you home."

They left the general, the three not saying much. Fresh horses awaited them in the courtyard, under the cover of the castle's gate. Kailen's horse stamped its hoof and shook its head. It didn't seem to be happy to have him on its back.

The streets were still quiet, and the wet clopping of their horses echoed off the houses. Nina calmly padded along behind them. The sky resembled a sheet of dark gray cotton soaked in dirty water. Next to Kailen, Darksteel sat tall on his horse, not minding the rain. Kailen wondered how long it would be before his shining breastplate, steel greaves and vambraces started to rust. Armor was crucial when serving in the lines of the Legion, but in the woods it would weigh him down, and its highly polished surface could give away a man's position. Kailen would have to tactfully mention that to the Commander.

Kailen nudged his horse ahead to ride next to Rian. "So, the winter spent in Everwatch? How'd you not go crazy?"

"The place is more fortress than city, so there are huge numbers of soldiers there. You know what that means."

Kailen laughed. "A red light district where the beds are warm and the women warmer?"

"You, my friend, would be correct. There was one girl, I think her name was Steffa, whom I kept going back to. She was up for things I didn't know you were allowed to do to a woman."

"Must have been paradise for you."

Rian grimaced and sniffed. "It was fun but dangerous to my savings, and to other things."

Kailen cocked his head to one side.

Rian rolled his eyes and shifted in his saddle. "My dick got a cold and started dripping green stuff. The healers cleared it up though with some umber weed, owl root, and black moss."

"Did it sneeze at you?" asked Kailen.

"No."

"Then it wasn't a cold."

They approached the Western Gate. The rains seemed to be moving off, and more people walked the streets. Four soldiers stood guard at the massive doors. Taking shelter under the inner arch of the gate was a lone woman. Because of the shawl over her head Kailen didn't realize it was Carra until they were close. He stopped, dismounted, and led the horse behind him. Out here in the dim rain-light the bruise was almost invisible, washed out by the filtered sun. Meeting her eyes, he paused. The pupils were dilated much smaller than they should have been in this low light, and there was a distinctly redder than normal flush to her cheeks. She'd taken the powder after he'd left. Not sure what to say, he just hugged her. She squeezed him back, grabbing so hard her nails dug into his shoulders. "Are you all right?" he asked.

"I don't know much of this world, Kailen, but I know this. We are right, and I don't want to lose it. Nothing can shake that. Nothing," she said and then held up a full drinking skin, "I forgot to give you this when you left the tavern. It's that red ale from Tidal Guard. The one you liked."

"Thank you. I'm much happier saying goodbye like this."

"I hoped you would be." She kissed him on the nose then noticed the other two waiting. "Why are they with you? Is that Rian?" she asked.

"It is. My assignment is a little different this time." he said.

Carra smiled and waved at Rian. She nodded to Zaketh, who bowed in his saddle. Her eyes lingered on the black-haired man before looking back to Kailen. "When will you be back?"

"Two months, give or take."

"A long time."

"I've been gone longer."

"Of course," she said.

He hugged her close, not caring about those who watched. "I'm going to miss you," he said.

"I miss you."

He kissed her once more, let her go, and climbed on his horse. She didn't cry, but her smile was hollow, almost vacant. He rode past, blowing a kiss, hiding his worry. It wasn't like her to take the powder this early in the morning. What was she thinking?

They passed beyond the outer gates and rode quickly through the sodden field. Among the dripping, scraggly pines that clung to the coast Kailen felt closed in. He looked off the road. The hairs on his neck were standing again and a shiver passed through him. It wasn't from the cold though. Kailen started to ask Rian if he felt anything, but Zaketh interrupted him. "She's a pretty girl. You're lucky, Tidespinner."

"Thank you, sir," he said, not really paying attention.

"It's a pity about her face. Do you hit her often?"

Kailen's sword was in his hand and at Zaketh's throat before the commander could draw breath. "If you ever say anything like that again, I will slit you from crotch to gullet."

Zaketh didn't blink, paying the three feet of tempered steel aimed at his windpipe little heed. "I apologize. I saw the bruise and assumed."

"You assumed wrong," Kailen said. In his peripheral he saw Rian's hand resting on the hilt of his kukaran fighting knife, but the senior warden didn't seem sure of whom he should draw on. Nina, who had been following quietly this whole time, growled at Darksteel with laid-back ears and raised hackles. None of it fazed the soldier.

"Again, I apologize. I did not mean to offend you. You wouldn't be the first man to hit his woman. I assumed wrong."

Kailen took a deep breath and sheathed his sword. He breathed again, trying to settle the heat in his veins. "You can charge me with assaulting a superior. Bring me before the Tribunal. Is that my fate after the mission, Commander?"

Zaketh shook his head. He sniffed and cleared his lungs, spitting what came up onto the road. "No. You have backbone. You're not afraid to kill. I like that."

"I kill because it's my duty, not because I like to."

"Of course," said the legionnaire.

"Do you doubt me, Darksteel?"

"Commander Darksteel. Remember that, Warden. We all kill for our own reasons. In the end I don't care what drives you. If your blade serves Carodan, I respect you."

Kailen nodded. He would waste no more words on Darksteel. He boiled inside, hunching on his horse and thinking of finding the man who had struck Carra. He imagined his sword sliding into her attacker's belly, stealing the bastard's life away inch by inch. He could see the body lying on the floor, its life spreading away in crimson pools. If only there was a face to go with the body.

Hiding between the shaggy pine trees off the path, the gray-skinned Grenar watched the three men. Rend'arr kept his halberd low, so the metal would not cast a reflection. He had remained hidden for all this time outside the human town. To betray himself now would be unforgivable.

He had not expected others to be with the human, but he would still follow. Last night the dream had fully revealed itself. The land was engulfed in flames and clouds of ash. The blood of his people mixed with that of the Cardanans, staining the ground red and black. Over it all flew standards bearing the silhouette of a black dragon, but through the clouds and fire the Grenar had seen the Warden walk towards him. In the wake of the human's step the grass grew back and the fires died. The air cleared and the ash was pushed aside. Stepping right in front of him, the human bowed, and for the first time the dream completed. The human had smiled and offered his hand.

Rend'arr thought himself addled, but knew he could not lose track of this human. He didn't understand it, but his heart and instincts told him it was crucial. Why was he dreaming? Only shamans did so, not warriors. Something greater than him was at work here, of that he was certain. His dreaming went against the cultural history of his people. Doubt did linger though. What he was doing made no sense. Why was the Cardanan so important, and if he knew he was being followed, how would he react? Most likely he would try to kill Rend'arr, thinking him just a dirty beast. Wasn't that the way all humans thought?

Chapter 8
ALE BY MOONLIGHT

The next two weeks were a blur of spring rains, damp forests, burnt-out homes, and unmarked graves. They visited three towns, all sacked by the Noriziem in the last few months. The first two had mostly recovered, but not Shark Bay. Half the village was reduced to ash, and its people lay in shallow graves. Echoes from the night Angler's Cove burned haunted Kailen whenever he slept. A century of Legion troops and a cohort of Legion engineers had been assigned to rebuild the town. However, the hollow, washed-out faces of the townspeople spoke of damage that could not be repaired by hammer and saw.

Now, two days south of Shark Bay, the three men had traveled several leagues inland. Their next stop was a fairly large town called Littletop. An adamantite vein had been discovered there thirty years ago, quite by accident, in the side of a small hill. A mine, settlement, and a thick stone wall, had sprung up around the vein in the course of a few years. The adamantite was used in the forging of incredibly strong steel, making Littletop one of the wealthiest towns in the far west and a busy trading center. They had not yet been attacked by Noriziem, but Zaketh felt they were a good target and wanted to observe their defenses. It was an excellent place to resupply, Kailen knew, and Rian was looking forward to seeing a miner's daughter he had met there the previous spring.

Littletop remained a day's travel distant, and night still came early. They had set up camp next to a stream. Rian built a fire as Kailen constructed a simple lean-to in case the rains returned. Zaketh gathered firewood, and had thought of hunting, but Nina beat him to it, dragging a fully grown deer into camp, its throat ripped out. Getting a haunch away from her hadn't been easy, but after Rian had cut off a rear quarter she had been happy with the rest.

Now, several strips of venison roasted on a spit, cracking and popping with hot fat. Rian sat cross legged in front of the fire, a wooden bowl cradled between his legs. From his pack he had produced several clay vials, each holding a different spice or herb. He had mixed them together with some water from the stream and now a thick, red paste stuck to the bowl and the stick he was using to stir. Kailen, sitting on the ground next to him, drank from the skin Carra had given him and asked, "What, by all that's holy, are you making?"

Rian dipped his finger into the concoction and tasted a small amount. "Something I learned from a Hadari merchant in Everwatch. A fellow winter prisoner. The spices from Hadak are amazing. Even out here, in the middle of nowhere, we can have a fine meal." Using a horse-hair brush, Rian spread his creation over the roasting venison.

Zaketh, sitting on the stump of a fallen tree, ran a whetstone over the length of his greatsword. He had already removed and meticulously polished each piece of his plate armor. He did so every night and polished every piece in the same order and with the same method. When finished, he wrapped them in oilcloth and kept them under the lean-to. And every night he ran the whetstone over his sword, even though he had not yet drawn it in anger. "What if I don't like Hadari food?"

"Well, it's not actually a Hadari recipe. I came up with my own combination. The merchant simply taught me and I took it from there," Rian said. He looked over at Kailen and shrugged.

"What if I still don't like it?" Zaketh asked and once again the scrape of the whetstone wheezed over their camp.

"Haven't met anyone yet who dislikes it, and besides, it'll put hair on your chest," Rian said. The Commander, whose black hair and beard were thick and full, paused his sharpening and treated Rian with a raised eyebrow. "Well, maybe that's not the best expression for you. It'll clean your insides out."

"Didn't you do that earlier today?" Kailen asked.

"I did," Rian said, "Think it was that cheese I had at Shark Bay. Felt like I passed a small Hadari child."

The two laughed. Rian, done spreading the sauce, sat next to Kailen and took the ale skin. He handed it back to Kailen, who swallowed another pull. Against his better judgment he offered the ale to Zaketh. "You always say no, but as always, you're more than welcome to some."

The stone scraped down the blade again. Kailen's fingers quivered with a cold that was not in the air. Zaketh blew the grit from his blade and said, "Thank you, but no. I appreciate the offer though."

"Do you ever drink?" asked Rian.

Zaketh worked his stone along the other side of the blade. Not bothering to look up, he replied, "Not for many years."

"Why?" Rian asked.

Scrape. "No one benefits when I do."

Kailen smacked Rian in the leg and glared at him. Rian shrugged and grabbed the skin back. Kailen shook his head and checked the meat. Across from him, at the edge of the firelight, Nina chewed on her prize, working every bit of meat off the bone. He knew that after all the meat was gone, she would crack open the bones and lick out the marrow, leaving nothing to waste.

The meat was done and Rian's sauce did smell good. He handed his companions each a cut and took one for himself. They ate in silence, tearing the meat off the bone and staring at the fire. Spicy and sweet, the venison was the best thing Kailen had eaten in days. The smoked pork and dried bread in his rations were quickly becoming boring. Zaketh sheathed his sword, and the night seemed strangely quiet. The two wardens continued to share the ale while Zaketh washed his meat down with cold stream water, drinking from a simple pewter mug he carried.

None felt the pair of eyes that watched them from the tree line, several dozen yards distant. Not the men, not the horses. Not even Nina.

When the men finished, they gave their bones to Nina, who wasted no time in cracking them open. With full bellies they sat back. Kailen took a pull from the skin, thinking how nothing tasted sweeter than a fine North Shore ale. He was not expecting Zaketh to ask, "Where are you from, Tidespinner?"

Kailen paused, the ale-skin halfway up to his lips. Conversation with Zaketh for the whole journey had so far entailed geographic details, town defenses, frequency of Noriziem attacks, and sometimes what to have for dinner. He drank and handed the skin to Rian. "I was born in Angler's Cove. My father served in the Legion for ten years, mustered out, and used his stipend to buy a house and a small fishing boat. He met my mother shortly after, then I came along."

"Where are your parents now?"

"They were killed in the Noriziem raid of 1295." Kailen kept his voice level.

"The first recorded attack by the Noriziem. I'm surprised you survived. Most of your town burned."

"I'm well aware. Why do you ask?"

"I like to know the men I fight beside."

Kailen and Rian looked at each other. Rian said, "We're only on a survey mission."

Zaketh sipped his water, staring into the fire. "I pray to Antaunna every night before I fall asleep, and she tells me we'll fight before we return to Angler's Cove."

"She tells you?" said Kailen, knowing how poorly he kept the doubt from his words.

"It's true."

"Well," Rian couldn't keep his mouth shut, "Does she tell you if I'll be bedded in Littletop?"

Kailen elbowed him hard in the ribs. "You never learn. That's how you got dick-rot last time. I'm simple, Darksteel. I fight to protect Westlook. It's my home, and the people here are struggling to build a livelihood. I fight for their safety."

Darksteel picked his teeth with a sliver of bone. Still holding it between his lips he said, "You're telling a half-truth."

"What's that supposed to mean?"

"You do not fight for duty alone. You fight out of anger. To avenge your parents."

Kailen shifted, looking into the fire, then over to the moon-reflecting stream, then up to the stars. Zaketh's dark eyes bore into him. The man was right.

"What about you, Darksteel?" Rian asked, "I know your House, and that you're from Wheat Scythe, but nothing beyond that."

"My House's seat is just outside of Southhawk. Mine was one

of the city's founding families."

Kailen had never been there, but he knew Southhawk was another fortress city, like Everwatch, that had been built along the Cardanan/Hadari border as the lynch-pin of a long line of defenses. It was a century older than Everwatch and renowned for its military families.

"Were you born in the city?" asked Rian.

"No, I grew up on our estate, Darkhome. From the time I could walk I was trained to hold a sword. Every man in my family has served in the Legion since the founding of Wheat Scythe."

Kailen looked away from the fire, met Zaketh's black eyes, and asked him, "Is that why you fight? Family tradition?"

Zaketh drew his greatsword and held it before him, the blade casting a fire-warped shadow over his face. "This sword has been in my family for ten generations and its name, Darksteel, is what my House is founded upon. My forefathers carried it in the Old World and used it to fight against the Noriziem before the Exodus. In Carodan, it has spilt the blood of Hadari, Grenar, outlaws, and even some of the Stonestriker rebels. I am only its most recent wielder, and when I have a son, it will go to him."

Looking at it closely, Kailen appreciated the weapon's beauty. Made from steel that was darker than usual, the blade was covered in whirling, smoky patterns that seemed to dance and shift in the steel itself. The four Runes of Balance were engraved along the length of the blade, with more ancient words of protection inscribed along the steel and bronze hilt. "Do you fight for only your name then?" asked Kailen, "To bring honor and fame to the Great House Darksteel?"

"No. To protect Carodan and ensure the safety of Antaunna and her people is our honor-bound duty. Every Darksteel lad swears to do so during his tenth birthday. It's who we are. It's all we know."

"Now it is you telling only partial truth. As you look at that sword of yours, I can see memories playing themselves out behind your eyes. What is your pain?"

Zaketh ran a finger along the edge of Darksteel and then sheathed the sword. "My pain is my own, and no concern of yours. I fight because it's all I know."

"Have you ever wondered," Kailen asked, "if there's another way?"

"What do you mean?" asked Rian. He had been quiet this whole time.

"Well, I think about all the Noriziem I've killed in my service, and I think about all the Cardanans who have died in spite of that. It doesn't seem to make any difference. Is there another way that doesn't involve wasting the blood of so many people?"

Rian raised an eyebrow, not sure of how to respond. Zaketh said, "Even if we chose not to fight, how can we stop the others from attacking us? We've only asked to exist in this world and practice our ways. But the Noriziem, Grenar, and Hadari have not let that be. They hurt us, we hurt them back. It's that simple. I leave the questioning and philosophizing to the scholars and priests."

Kailen did not respond. There was truth to what Zaketh said, but he was unsure if he wanted to acknowledge it. Instead, he punched Rian in the shoulder and grabbed the beer skin from him. There wasn't much left. "What about you, Direpaw? Why do you fight?"

Rian shrugged and yawned. The half-frown/half-sneer on his face spoke of his dislike of probing questions. "My father died when I was young. He was from a humble sept, but married a girl from the Vinecast family. They're not quite a high sept, but almost. Part of House Vineweaver. He was a natural vinter and became master of one of the largest vineyards in Tidal Guard. A savvy man, the vineyard flourished under his guidance.

"The other winemakers resented him as an upstart. Supposedly, his death was an accident. I never understood how a man could catch his head in a grape press accidentally. But, I think enough gold exchanged hands that it made perfect sense to the investigating Steward and militia commander.

"My mother was a good woman. Did the best she could to raise me after that, but she never recovered from my father's death. A string of men frequented her bed chambers. Drowning pain with hollow ecstasy never works, but that didn't stop her from trying. My uncle took over the vineyard, and it has done well enough since."

"And you?" asked Kailen.

"I'm here, aren't I? Kept my father's surname, joined the Legion, saw the world, met new people, killed a few of them. Well, a lot of them. It was better than staying on the vineyard."

The dying fire sputtered and the stream continued to murmur. He shrugged again, stood, and stretched, "Well, I'm going to bed."

He stumbled past Nina, his legs a bit wobbly from the ale, and scratched her behind the ear. Neither of the other men would have gone near her while she was still gnawing on the carcass. She stopped eating long enough to rub her bloody muzzle against his leg. He patted her head and said, "Keep the bears away, girl, and anything else that might wander by."

Rian plopped down under the lean-to, wrapped himself in his blanket and started snoring as soon as his head hit the ground. Kailen stood, speaking to Zaketh but not meeting his eyes. He knew a little of Rian's past, but this was the most detailed account the older Warden had ever shared. He felt genuine sadness for his friend. "Sleep is a good idea. We should get to Littletop quickly. We still have a lot of ground to cover after our visit there."

"Agreed. I do feel odd without one of us sitting watch, though."

"And I've told you, don't worry. Nina will take care of us. Anything comes in, she'll kill it before we can even wipe the sleep from our eyes."

He said no more, not really caring if Zaketh followed. He settled down under the lean-to and could hear Darksteel doing so as well. He wrapped his arms around his chest, willing sleep to come and trying not to picture the faces of the different Noriziem he had killed over the years.

Nina was not ready to sleep. She continued to strip meat from the carcass. She would eat her fill and not have to feed for days. The warm blood and soft flesh disappeared into the dire wolf's persistent jaws. She only stopped when an odd smell drifted in on the wind. She stopped eating, looking back at the tree line. She rose from the carcass, and padded towards the branches. Her head was low, her ears pressed back, her tail straight out behind her. Lips curled, she bared her four-inch fangs. Nosing into the branches, she found a gray-skinned creature sitting cross-legged, with a long piece of wood and steel laid across its lap.

Rend'arr whispered to the wolf a string of low, rumbling, and guttural half-words. She raised her head, more curious now than aggressive. She inched forward and the Grenar held his hand out, palm up. She sniffed and moved closer, letting him stroke her neck and back. He whispered more to her, and she ran back to the fire. She tore a strip of muscle from the deer's neck and carried it back to the Grenar. He took it, bowed his head and gave the wolf a short grunt of thanks. The Grenar usually preferred cooked meat, but was too hungry to care. His long canines tore the flesh apart, and his stomach rumbled in appreciation. Nina rested her head on his knee, letting him scratch her behind the ears.

Chapter 9
AND I REACHED TO THE HEAVENS

"Cantanaa thri cor. Logreth enaa dricoo. Froqouth en toomeya Galantaegan." The words were second nature to Morrikii. He raised Sunder and slammed it into the stone floor. The flash of light, the growth of the flames in their circular pit, the heat being drained from the room, all happened as they should. The force that now emanated from the statue of Galantaegan stood his hairs on end. The scales, shimmering with inner fire, bathed him with comfort and warmth. The eyes of Galantaegan, glowing blue and filled with gentle wisdom, looked down at him but he never felt looked down upon. "My Lord, Galantaegan, I have answered your summons."

"Thank you, my friend. Your promptness pleases me greatly." The voice, resonant yet gentle, was the same that had woken him from his sleep early this morning. Through his dreams it had called to him, demanding his attention.

"I am at your service."

"Come, stand, my friend."

Morrikii rose, using the haft of Sunder to help him up. His knees ached from climbing the twisting stair and his back was laced with fleeting stabs of pain. Jenaka set a pace difficult for him to maintain at his age. She had wanted to come with him this morning, to see the Pinnacle and actually speak to Galantaegan, but his refusal had been unyielding. He alone was permitted in this room. The Black One spoke only to him. Here, in the emptiness and darkness of the great chamber, he could be one with his god. "What do you desire, My Lord?"

"Morrikii, you have done well." The statue sat on its hind legs, curling its tail around its feet. As Galantaegan spoke, he used his hands to punctuate every word, "You've brought my children together. Ever since Clan Carothak left the shores of Granikar, and defied me, the four other clans only squabbled and fought each other. You are giving them purpose again, unity. They are finally realizing their potential for greatness!" Morrikii felt his bones vibrate with the force of the god's voice. He instinctively ducked his head. In the periphery of his vision the statue looked as if it had never moved, as if his spell had made no change, but when he looked directly at Galantaegan the statue was still animated.

"I did not think it would be this easy, My Lord. Shortly, the Noriziems' full force will be gathered and we'll muster out."

"How long?"

"Three months, at most. The second half of their fleet should be departing Granikar as we speak. They've spent so long fighting each other it took little time to organize their armies. They'll resupply here, we'll load my own troops, and then we sail for Carodan. It will be summer there."

"Good, good. Too long have those who worship my sister been left untouched. I don't understand their weakness. I've seen such strength in you humans. We will help them see their error and purge any who resist."

"Of course. We will convert the populace to your worship. They are good people and do not deserve to die."

"Of course," said Galantaegan. He rubbed an obsidian talon against his horned chin and said, "You do realize that many people will die. They will fight you and consider you an even greater traitor for returning to their shores with an army of Noriziem."

Morrikii had long known this. He wasn't entirely comfortable trusting that the Noriziem would follow his orders or command, but he didn't have an option. Without them he simply did not have the strength to return to Carodan. "Sacrifices have to be made for the greater good. When all is finished and I rebuild Carodan, the five clans will be reunited. The Norizaad Empire will rise again. The people will flourish, and we will spread our strength across the surface of K'aeran," Morrikii paced in front of Galantaegan, his own excitement increasing the volume of his voice, “I know this is the best course for the world. I will govern for the people and ensure they are not victims to the avarice of the elite. Granikar, Abinar, Fridinikar, all the continents will be under one banner, one rule.”

“And one god.”

Morrikii stopped his pacing. In his excitement he had stopped looking at Galantaegan, and again from the corner of his eye it looked as if the statue had never moved. However, when he again faced the stone dragon it was very much alive. “Of course, My Lord. One god.”

“Good. Good, good,” said Galantaegan. Now he seemed to be the one preoccupied. “The peoples of the world have already forgotten about my other brothers and sisters. With Antaunna gone it will be as it should. The world needs only one god.”

“Most certainly, My Lord,” said Morrikii. While sometimes brutal, the concept of chaos was the only true constant he had learned. Nothing stayed the same and all things eventually came to an end. Why deny what was so true when embracing it could make him so much stronger?

“Have you begun the next phase of your plans, my friend?”

“Yes, Great One. Markan has sent seventy of his largest long ships to the shore of Westlook. They should make landfall anytime now.”

“And you are still sure this will benefit you?”

“I am certain of it,” Morrikii spoke with confidence in each word. While he had doubts about his plan, he would never show that doubt in front of Galantaegan. “This will be no small raid and the severity of it, combined with our latest attacks on that backwater province, will prompt the king to shift forces from Tidal Guard and Wheat Scythe. What other choice will he have?”

“Indeed. I hope for your sake that it does work,” said Galantaegan. Morrikii’s insides flashed cold as the statement’s implication sunk in.

“It will work, My Lord,” Morrikii again said, mustering the sum of his confidence.

“Your assuredness comforts me, my friend. Now, it is time I take my leave. You are pleasing me, Stonestriker. Continue to do so.”

“It is my honor to, My Lord,” Morrikii bowed deeply. When

he stood straight the statue was back to its original pose. No light shone from within and every detail was the way it had been before he had cast the summons, almost as if it had never moved in the first place.

***

Morrikii's study was a mess of parchments, scrolls, and ledgers. A small room located off his main quarters, its bare stone walls were lined with piles of teetering books. The only decoration was an oil painting of him and Mella, done shortly after their wedding. He had to beg, actually beg, the Cardanan captain that had transported him to Fridinikar to let him bring it aboard. It reminded him of when Mella felt full and alive under his touch.

He spread a map of Westlook over his desk and squinted in the dim light. The wrought-iron chandelier cast poor light. Moving an oil lamp from his nightstand to the desk, he brightened the flame. The route of Markan's fleet was traced in fine pen strokes and Morrikii followed it with his finger. He thought of all the contingencies, for the tenth time that morning, and pushed aside the words of Galantaegan. He would not fail the Black One.

A knock on his door startled him. "Enter."

Dora carried in a tray laden with fried fish, flatbread, and sliced fruit. "Your breakfast, my Lord."

"Thank you, Dora. Set it on the table."

Hands shaking only slightly, she pushed aside several scrolls and a book to make space for the tray on a carved stone table that filled the center of the room. "Will we be seeing you at services this morning?" she asked.

Morrikii looked up from the map and scratched the stubble on his cheek. He had forgotten to shave before going to the Pinnacle. "I'm supposed to speak today, aren't I?"

"Yes, my Lord."

"I suppose I'll be there then. I'd better clean up and practice my verses."

"Eat first. You're pale and moving slowly."

Morrikii raised an eyebrow. "Pale? Dora, we live under a mountain."

Her wrinkled face crinkled with a smile. She tisked Morrikii and gently swatted him on the shoulder. He was glad to see her smile. The tension between them had eased. Whatever had been troubling her before seemed to have passed. "I will eat. Thank you for bringing it. I'd forgotten my hunger."

"What did you do this morning?"

Morrikii, who had gone to the table and was enjoying a slice of apple, said, "I went to the Pinnacle. He summoned me."

Even though his back was to her, he felt her tension return.

"Did it go well?"

"It did. He's pleased with what I've done."

"Good," said Dora, "You've worked hard to keep us safe and bring us home."

Morrikii thought of Galantaegan's words and the implied consequence of his failure. "It is my duty."

He was surprised at the slight weight of her hand on his shoulder. He looked back at her and even though she was smiling he could see the tears in her eyes.

"You are a good man," she said, "and I've been proud to see you grow."

"Not proud of me accepting Galantaegan, though," he said to his own surprise. She had never admitted it, but he knew she had converted grudgingly.

"You've done what you've had to do to keep us safe," she replied, not quite able to look him in the eye.

"Am I doing the right thing, Dora?"

She chewed on her lower lip with teeth that were yellowed but still mostly intact. "It is not my place to answer that. Our dark days will fall behind us, and it is you that will have led us through them."

"Have I led well?" He thought of the Noriziem khans, of casting aside his own beliefs for those of a new and powerful god, and of bedding a woman for his own gain while his wife wasted away in their bedroom. He thought of his father, a man ever proud to be Cardanan in spite of his nation's shortcomings.

"You've made the choices you had to. It's not my place to say anything else. You've always put your people first," she said.

Have I? Morrikii thought as he looked at the painting of him and Mella.

Chapter 10
KELEBRA DE'AL VERDAN

Baked bread and roasted meat flavored the air around Littletop. The sun was setting as Kailen and his two companions slowly approached the town's North Gate. Nina trotted silently behind them. Strains of music drifted through the twilight, a pipe here, a flute there, a drum hit every now and then. "I wonder what's going on?" asked Kailen.

Rian laughed, prodding his horse between Kailen and Zaketh, and slapped their shoulders. Zaketh raised an eyebrow and looked down at the offending hand. Not noticing Zaketh's irritation, Rian grinned and said, "Kailen, my lad, you need to keep better track of time. They're preparing for the Kelebra de'al Verdan."

Kailen shook his head and rubbed his brow. Was it time for the spring celebration already? He had been in Angler's Cove for it last year. He remembered, vaguely, being with Carra after all the patrons had been kicked out of her tavern. They hadn't bothered with a bed and had woken on the bar the next day with their backs sticking to the wood and slivers in their asses. It had been a good night.

The sun was almost hidden below the horizon when they reached the gate. Six guards and an officer stood waiting at the massive doors. Two solid gold bands on the officer's pauldrons marked him as one rank higher than Zaketh, a Group Commander. The officer stepped out to meet them, almost as if he had been waiting for them, and the three men dismounted. They all saluted, which the Group Commander returned with a crisp, precise snap. Kailen was impressed. Higher ranking officers tended to return salutes only out of obligation.

"Sirs, I am Theodric Cragrunner, commander of the Legion battalion stationed here."

"An honor to meet you, sir," said Zaketh, "Were you expecting us?"

Cragrunner pointed to the wilderness behind them. "We have eyes in the trees, Commander. Not much comes to our gates without our knowledge. You are, of course, more than welcome to join us for the celebration, but I am curious. It's not common for a line soldier to travel with wardens."

"Thank you for your hospitality, sir. King Ironheart has tasked me with observing the defenses along the coast of Westlook," said Zaketh, "I'm very interested in the preparations you've made for the town, and your troop strength."

"Of course, join me at the festival. We'll have all night to talk."

Rian leaned over and whispered in Kailen's ear, "Talk all you want. I'm getting into the beer."

"That's not all you're getting into," Kailen said.

"Good point."

"Just don't give some nice girl that crotch-rot of yours."

Rian frowned. "I told you that's cleared up."

Zaketh looked back at them. "Was there something you needed to say, Direpaw?"

Trying not to smile, Rian replied, "Not at all, Commander. Just looking forward to the festival."

Rian winked at Kailen as the men led their horses into the town. The gates swung shut for the night behind them, the muffled thump adding a one-off beat to the drums that were now a constant echo in the night air. Kailen admired the neat little houses lined up perfectly along the cobblestone roads. No refuse or waste lay in the streets, and aside from the occasional whiff of the horse barns or the community latrines, the air was pristine and smelled of trees. After a quick stop at the legion barracks, where they dropped their gear and stabled their horses, they walked to the town square. Vendors lined the main street. One could buy everything from fine furs to Hadari love oils. The merchants stood in the streets trying to out-yell their competitors. Most of the townspeople humored them and spent some of their gold on items they'd never really use. Kailen watched the people as he walked by, amused and disturbed at the same time. If he wanted to buy something, he'd approach a seller and express interest. To have someone yelling at him, trying to convince him to buy something he really didn't want, generated thoughts of reaching for his sword instead of his coin purse.

Past the town hall, a sturdy building of stone walls and shingled roofs, the press lessened. Here one side of the road abutted the rocky hill that Littletop was built around. The mine was closed for the evening, the yawning entrance blocked by heavy wooden doors. Colored lanterns, strung above the streets and over the buildings, lit the town in shades of red, green, orange, and of course blue.

People already filled the town square. Torches and lanterns lined the perimeter. Several large fire pits dominated the center of the square, each one with a pig or a huge side of beef roasting over its hungry flames. Kailen's stomach rumbled at the smell of the simmering meat. The laughter of the people, and the ease with which they embraced the evening, helped Kailen forget his annoyance at the vendors and smile. Since last night's conversation with Zaketh he had dwelled on the lives ended by his hands and the supposed justification of his actions. Knowing he had some part in keeping these people safe, knowing he fought for their lives, reaffirmed that duty and obligation were not simply excuses for what he did. Not completely.

Zaketh spotted Cragrunner, who had left them at the barracks so he could officiate the opening of the festival alongside the town Steward. The Group Commander waved them over. Their armor was discarded and stored in the barracks, but all three still carried their swords. People eyed them as they walked by, parting quickly, and then backing off even more when they spotted the dire wolf following Rian. Zaketh sat closest to Cragrunner, Kailen the furthest away. Strategy did not interest him tonight. A foaming mug of ale appeared before him, which he took and looked up to thank the server. It was a blonde girl, a few years younger than him, with sky-blue eyes. She winked and said, "If ye' want any more, just flag me. I'll take care of ye'."

She walked away, carrying an oversized tray above her head. Kailen watched her, pretending he didn't notice how her bottom swayed beneath her skirts. Zaketh and Cragrunner discussed what the Legion troops had done to fortify the town since their arrival. Kailen pretended interest for a short while, but abandoned the pretense when a platter of cut apples and goat-cheese was set before him. He sucked down several helpings and drained his ale, hungrier than he'd realized. Loaves of bread came next, slathered with fresh-churned butter and honey. He reached for his mug, wondering how he'd signal a server for a fresh helping, but found it already full. Walking away from him was the blonde girl. She looked over her shoulder and winked.

The chair beside him, empty to that point, was pulled back and an older man with a bald head and cleanly shaven face sat next to Kailen. The rich, black velvet robes and the silver chain of interlinked dragon heads around his neck marked him as the Town Steward. "Good evening, young warden," said the man, "Barial Granitehand, Steward of Littletop."

Kailen bowed his head. "It is an honor, Lord Steward. Kailen Tidespinner."

The Steward carried a goblet of wine and drank from it before saying, "Commander Cragrunner tells me you and your companions are surveying the damage wrought by the Noriziem. We've been lucky here, but we've heard stories and rumors of the other towns. How is it?"

Kailen sipped his own drink and swallowed a piece of pork he had been chewing. "Bad, my Lord Steward. The coast has been hit hard for the last six months, four of which were winter. The cold didn't stop the Noriziem. I worry what'll happen once summer comes."

Granitehand nibbled on a piece of cheese. His hands were skinny and large-knuckled. They held everything with a dainty, precise grip. "Do you think the Legion will send more men?"

"I hope so," Kailen said and glanced over at Zaketh and Cragrunner. The senior officer had a map of the area spread out on the table and the two spoke over it in hushed tones. "That's why Commander Darksteel is out here. If another Legion can be mustered and stationed in key points along the coast, I think it will make a difference."

"And what of the Wardens? Surely you must play a role in our protection as well. Gold from my citizens' pockets goes towards your pay as well as the Legion's," Granitehand said.

Kailen set the apple slice he was about to eat back on its tray. The musicians played a loud, bawdy piece, and the dance square was filling with men and women, some already wobbly from the ale and wine. What the Steward truly meant to say was, *Gold from my House's coffers goes towards your pay.* Every sept and high sept paid taxes to the Houses, and then the Houses paid the crown. The Legion answered only to the King, and when it was established a century-and-a-half ago the Houses effectively lost their military power. It was a fact most nobles had not forgotten, or forgiven.

He met Granitehand's gaze and chose his words carefully. "We will do what we always do, Lord Steward. Patrol the wilds, monitor the roads, go where a battalion of steel-clad soldiers cannot. There are only five hundred of us in all of Carodan, and less than half of that are here in Westlook. We do what we can."

Granitehand sipped his wine and nibbled more cheese. "I mean no offense, young warden, but I just wish to raise a point. I'm not entirely convinced the money going to the Wardens is well spent. You operate alone usually, scattered throughout the countryside. How effective are you? Wouldn't that money be better spent raising a proper legion?"

Kailen curled his right hand into a fist, keeping it behind his right leg and out of the Steward's sight. How dare he? Did he know what Kailen and the other Wardens sacrificed to keep these people safe? The sniveling little bastard had the audacity to say he meant no offense. The hilt of his father's sword hung tantalizingly close to Kailen's balled fist. "I don't make policy, Lord Steward. I merely follow orders and fight to protect the people. A few years ago, at a small homestead to the east of here, I came across a group of bandits preparing to raid the settlement. Nothing as glorious as a Noriziem war party, but they would have most likely killed the settlers, maybe raped the women, and then burned the house. I killed all four outlaws. The settlers were safe, though they never knew the danger. Correct me if I'm wrong, but I believe they would have fallen under your rule."

"They do. It sounds like the Willowind homestead. Their daughter attends temple with mine," said Granitehand. He shifted in his seat and looked to the dance square.

Kailen smirked at the man's discomfort. He drained his ale and stood. "If you'll excuse me, Lord Steward, I think I'll stroll through town."

Zaketh was still in deep conversation with Cragrunner, and

Rian had a serving girl on each knee. Nina was curled up at his feet gnawing on a side of pork. Kailen wouldn't be missed. He grabbed a fresh mug from a passing serving girl and looked once more at the Steward, who was avoiding eye contact, and wandered into the crowd. The people greeted him with polite smiles, but everyone kept their distance. Word had spread quickly of their arrival, and most of the townspeople eyed his sword as he passed by. He felt their nervousness, but told himself it didn't matter. He served to protect, and if they knew half the things he'd done, they would be more than a little scared.

Further from the town square, the press of people lessened and the air was clear and cool. Young couples were scattered here and there behind houses and in the shadows kissing and petting each other. One brave, drunken pair was in the dirt behind some barrels, bare-assed and trying to stay quiet. Kailen went far away from them, not wanting to ruin the moment. He came to the town keep and found where the children were being entertained.

Sitting cross-legged on the flagstones, they faced a small stage framed by four torches. A few mothers floated around the edges making sure good behavior was maintained. The children all held small pewter mugs filled with milk, honey, and just a bit of brandy to help them sleep. Sitting center stage, on a simple stool, was a priest. Clad in rich blue robes, his beard was long and dirty-gray, well-kept but slightly wild. His hair was wispy and almost white. Eyes green and clear twinkled in the torchlight, and he smiled wide and openly at the children. Even though he was sitting, he leaned against a wooden staff that he held with both hands. Kailen hadn't heard the Tale of The Exodus in years. He found a crate next to a storage shed and sat. He was out of the way and almost hidden by shadow.

From the folds of his robes the priest produced a small bottle and drank. The fluid inside was clear, and the priest grimaced and twitched slightly after he swallowed. Kailen chuckled. *Must be good stuff,* he thought.

Wiping his mouth on his sleeve, the priest set the bottle down and cleared his throat. "Good evening, children."

His voice was warm, and only slightly worn with age. Well-trained after years of bi-weekly temple lessons, the children responded in unison. "Good evening, Father Frostwind."

Kailen remembered his first Kelebra de'al Verdan. He had

been sitting in a group of children just like this, Carra next to him. Her hair had been a mess of golden curls then. Holding his hand she had sat close, scared of the other boys sitting around her. He imagined her tucked into the nook of his arm, sitting here with him. Maybe a child of their own would be in the group before them.

Father Frostwind cleared his throat again and said, "I'm glad to see you here tonight. Are you having fun?"

The children nodded yes, some smiling toothless grins and others wanting to tell the Father of how they'd almost won the apple-bobbing contest. With a smile he quieted them. "I'm glad you're enjoying the night. I have a story to tell. Do you want to hear it?"

The children nodded in unison.

"I want to tell you a story of long ago, when Cardanans lived far across the sea. Before even your grandparents were born. It was a time when our people clung to the shores of the Old World, making their life from the deep ocean."

Kailen leaned against the shed, stretched his legs out, and crossed them. The Father's voice was still low, almost a whisper. The children leaned closer. "It was a time when we called ourselves Clan Carothak. We had been part of a great empire called Norizaad that stretched over all of Granikar." Father Frostwind's eyes wandered onto the horizon, and he spread his arms wide. "It was an empire so mighty, none dared challenge it. The blond-haired tribes of the north, the yellow-skinned men of the south, and even the forest-dwelling savages of the far-east bowed to its will. Being the clan of the sea, we built Norizaad's great ships and crewed them with our sailor-born men. It was a time when all the different dragons were worshipped as one."

Father Frostwind tamped his staff against the oak planks, and the sapphire set into its crest glowed faintly. The evening mist that hovered here and there was drawn towards Frostwind. Shifting clouds swirled around his head, forming six different clusters, each one taking on a different color. Red, Blue, Gold, Black, White, and Green. They formed the shapes of dragons, with twisting necks and stretched wings. The children gasped. The dragons intertwined, dancing and dodging over the young faces. Kailen started when someone pressed in next to him and he gripped his sword. It was the blonde serving girl. Even though there was no room on the crate, she had somehow sat next to him. He started to speak, but she held a finger to his lips. She looped her arm around his and leaned against his shoulder. Kailen shifted his legs, ready to stand, knowing he should be as far away from this as possible. But her arms felt warm against his, and her head fit snuggly into his shoulder. He relaxed and leaned back, placing his right hand around her upper arm. She didn't look at him or smile. The young woman simply sat there and rested against him.

Father Frostwind stood, his voice gaining volume. "For a thousand years the Empire stood, but like all great things, it ended. A plague, brought home from the east by a conquering Legion, took hold. It wiped out the central capitol of Grani'Nor. Every man, woman, and child was rotted away by the disease. Their skin turned black and their blood boiled."

The children's eyes widened like little saucers. Above them, the dragons no longer danced playfully, but spun faster and faster, blurring together. Frostwind struck his staff again, and in the sky, heat lighting sparked even though the air was too cold. "The old clans fell back to their ancestral lands, walling their cities and killing any outsiders who crossed their borders. An empire that had lasted for a millennium crumbled in less than five years, and Granikar was plunged into a dark age that still holds to this day. The Pantheon was no more, the dragons were split asunder."

The swirling rings of cloud shattered into six pieces, each one flying off in a different direction. Four of them faded into the distance, leaving only the blue mist and the black. They drifted over the stage, looking like dragons again. Frostwind held his palm high in front of him, and the two dragons twisted around it, trying to get at each other. "Over time, the plague faded, and the clans began to venture out from their lands. In the Western Peninsula of Granikar five clans had maintained their strength. Carothak was one of them, and we came to worship Antaunna, for her realm is the sea, and it was because of the sea we had survived."

The blue mist moved to Frostwind's staff, dancing around the glowing gem. The black cloud went over his head, spreading its faint wings wide. "However, the other four clans, Thent, Lobrenth, Nathikan, and Wathiem, fell into cruelty and came to worship Galantaegan."

One little girl in the front cried, cringing at the Black Dragon's name. Her brother, who had been making a great show of having nothing to do with her all evening, wrapped his arm around her and held her close. Even Kailen felt gooseflesh prickle the back of his neck, and the serving girl pressed a little closer. Frostwind paced the length of the stage now, his staff thumping with each step. "Galantaegan is Chaos. Where our beloved Antaunna embodies Balance, and ordains that for everything taken there is something given, Galantaegan spreads anger, hatred, and devastation. He is not happy unless war burns the land and blood fills the rivers. He is Ash, and in the Old World stands the Galen-Tor, a blasted mountain that spews black clouds and molten rock. It his lair, and from its peak he lords over the Noriziem.

"The four northern clans tried to convert Carothak to their twisted beliefs. The five clans shared the bonds of being the birth people of Norizaad, and they wanted us to be reunited in glory. But, we would not falter. Antaunna had always been kind to us. Even when a ship was swallowed by the sea, or a storm pounded our coast, we always received food from her depths and water from her sky. We would never follow the Black One."

Frostwind slammed his staff again and the torches burned higher and brighter. The black shape hovering over him reared its head, and Kailen felt the roar in his very bones. The priest raised a clenched fist, his lips curled with anger. "The four clans rallied their armies and marched for the lands of Carothak. We were strong, but against their combined might we could not stand. Khan Carotag ordered our entire populace to take to our ships. Several small armies stayed on land, delaying the attackers. They were men in their prime, grandfathers bent by too many winters, and young boys barely strong enough to lift a sword. They volunteered to stay so the rest of their people could survive."

The torches died down, the flames a normal height now. However, their smoke drifted down instead of up, collecting just over the heads of the children. It formed into a moving panorama of wind-swept waves and the shadows of ancient sea vessels. The ships were small against the vast smoky sea. Frostwind stared at his creation. "Every single man who stayed on shore died. They were cut down and then burned, an offering to Galantaegan. They gave the others the time they needed. Thousands of ships gathered in the Bay of Carothak and then sailed west, into the empty reaches of the Ebon Sea. They didn't know what they would find, only that they had to leave Granikar."

The shadow of Galantaegan left Frostwind and hovered over the image of the Cardanan ships. Again, its wings spread wide and a bellowing roar shook Frostwind's audience. On the far edge of the smoky sea, behind the fleeing ships, a fleet of longships appeared. Galantaegan flew over them, guiding their way. They drew near the fleeing Cardanans and Frostwind said, "The other clans followed, determined to wipe away our blasphemy. They closed in on our vessels. Then, the sea came to life."

On either side of the pursuing longships tall waves crested and crashed down, swallowing the vessels whole into a roiling maelstrom. From the smoky depths of the ocean the blue form of Antaunna burst. Rising above Galantaegan, it challenged him with a piercing scream. He roared back, but she would not falter. His little ships sunk, Galantaegan turned back to Granikar, and Antaunna slipped below the water, following the refugee fleet all the way to their new home.

"For two months we sailed, surviving off the ocean as we always had. Hope was almost lost, but then seabirds gathered overhead. Such birds are never seen far from land."

Frostwind waved his hand, and the misty images melted away. The children's faces were painted with frightened, excited awe. Kailen looked down at the serving girl. She watched the children, a little smile on her lips that reminded him of Carra. He looked away before she noticed and returned his attention to Frostwind. The priest had sat down and was taking another swig from his bottle. He cleared his throat, looking very tired. "A week later, our ships sailed into what we now call Sanctuary Bay. We set foot upon Abinar this very day of spring, over three hundred years ago. Since then, every spring, on the third day of the third moon, we celebrate Kelebra de'al Verdan. We will never forget where we came from, or what it cost to survive.

"Now, children, raise your glasses with me. Let us thank Antaunna for all she has given us, and pray that she continues to watch over us."

Kailen raised his own mug with the children and drank. The priest then led them in the same prayer, the Blessing of Antaunna, he and Carra had shared only a few weeks ago. He and the serving girl recited it too. Her voice was low and sweet, and she closed her eyes as she asked for Antaunna to help her stand through the darkness tall. The girl had her own mug which she drained after the prayer. Kailen was impressed. He was going to ask her name but was interrupted when the priest stood and said, "Well, my children, the hour is late, and your mothers will want to settle you into bed. Sleep well, little ones, dream of the Blue Lady, and I'll see you tomorrow at Temple lessons."

"Goodnight, Father Frostwind," the children said in unison. The waiting mothers swooped in and gathered whoever belonged to them. The priest stayed seated, waving goodbye and smiling to the children who continued to say farewell to him even over the shoulders of their mothers. All the children gone, he used his staff to help him stand. Before stepping off the stage he noticed Kailen. He nodded at the young warden and smiled, then limped out of the courtyard. Before he disappeared between the shadowed buildings, Frostwind raised the bottle to his lips again. Thinking the priest had the right idea, Kailen lifted his mug, but found it already empty. "I hate it when that happens."

The girl raised her head from his arm and said, "Losing track of yer beer, are ye'? I didn't think I gave ye' that much."

"Neither did I. I'll have to find another."

"There's plenty about."

She laid a hand on his leg and trailed her nails up along his thigh. Slender fingers danced lightly over his privates and then firmly cupped his crotch. Kailen repressed a shudder of excitement. Slowing his breath, he grabbed her hand, and slid it back towards his knee. The hurt in her eyes bothered Kailen more than he wanted to admit. "I'm sorry, m'lady, but I have someone back home. I love her very much. It'd be a lie if I said I wasn't interested in you, but she deserves better than that. I'm sorry."

She kissed him on the cheek, stood, and rested her hands on cocked hips. "Ye're sweet, but ye' don't know what ye'll be missing."

She turned away and walked towards the town square, swaying her bottom side to side. Kailen looked down into his empty mug and thought, *Oh, yes I do. Time for more beer.*

He headed back to the center of town. Many people were still there, but their faces were flushed and their speech slurred.

He didn't see Rian or his two girls. Nina was still at the foot of his seat, gnawing on more discarded joints of meat. Zaketh had also left, but Cragrunner was still there drinking with his officers and sharing old war stories. Kailen snagged two mugs of beer off a nearby tray and left the square. All that remained there now were idiots and temptation.

He decided to climb the ramparts of the town wall and look upon the forest. The moon was full and he always felt balanced when in the presence of trees. Ascending the wooden stairs to the wall, he passed only a few guards. The soldiers all knew of the wardens and legion commander who had come into town and none challenged him. On top of the wall a cool breeze carried in the scent of the woods. Torches mounted to the battlements sputtered in the wind, and aside from a few guards, Kailen thought he was alone on the parapet. Then he noticed Zaketh several yards away leaning against the crenellations. His greatsword still hung from his back, and in the sputtering glow of the torches, its polished blade danced with orange light. Kailen thought about moving down the other way, but instead he leaned into the crenel next to Zaketh and offered him a mug. It may as well have been a cup of boiling oil. Kailen sighed and pushed the mug closer to Zaketh. "It's Kelebra de'al Verdan, you should have at least one drink."

Zaketh took the mug, sipped, and set it upon the granite battlement. He looked at it the way he would an enemy, measuring its ability to hurt him. He picked the mug up and took another sip, setting it down a little further from him on the ledge. Kailen, keeping his tone carefully relaxed, said, "See, that's not so bad. It's good for you even. We'll make a man of you yet."

Zaketh snorted, "My father used to say that."

Kailen enjoyed his own ale. The bittersweet liquid was finally starting to tickle his eyeballs. It was too damned hard to get drunk anymore. He swallowed again and asked Zaketh, "Did you learn anything from Commander Cragrunner?"

"The town is secure. He's been here for months with his men, and they've filled the time by stocking supplies, building a trebuchet, and training both the regulars and the militia. We can move on in a day or two. There's no need to stay here. What's the next town on our route?"

"Twistreed. It's a small settlement on the very western border, right next to the Grenfel Marshes. There isn't much there, but it does sit along a major trade route that connects the coast to Everwatch."

"Ever been there before?"

"Only once."

"And?"

Kailen shrugged. "It's very small."

The silence that followed wasn't necessarily comfortable, but the two men sipped their drinks. Unexpectedly, Zaketh broke the silence. "There's one thing I've not yet deciphered. Why are the Noriziem attacking? They hold no land, the supplies they take can't benefit them that much. It makes no tactical sense. They strike, then fade away. Almost like the old Grenar War."

"I don't think they put that much thought into it. They hate us, so they kill us. I'm happy to return the favor," Kailen said. "With all the infighting that takes place between the clans we are most likely spared heavier attacks."

"What happens if they stop fighting each other?"

Kailen drained his mug. "That's something I don't like thinking about. What will you recommend to King Ironheart?"

"My recommendation to the king will be to raise two new legions and have them stationed along the coast of Westlook. Then we'll build heavier fortifications. We'll bleed the Noriziem too greatly for their attacks to be worth the cost."

The two fell into silence again. Quiet had settled over the town. Most of the revelers had either passed out or taken a companion to bed.

The sound of the northern gate groaning open disturbed the still air and surprised both men. Shouting and the heavy running of soldiers followed. Kailen and Zaketh left their drinks on the battlements and jogged along the wall. At the gate they found a group of soldiers clustered around a sweaty and steaming horse whose snorts punctuated the din of voices and clattering metal with a tired panic. Commander Cragrunner was there, trying to hide the teeter in his step and wipe the blur from his eyes. Kailen and Zaketh descended from the ramparts. Cragrunner gestured towards a man who had been laid out on the cobblestones. He was soaked with perspiration and blood, dried mixed with fresh, stained his left shoulder. The soldiers dressed the wound and gave the man fresh water. "A scout from the northern shore.

Noriziem are landing."

Zaketh was unimpressed. "A raiding party should pose no threat to the town. With the four hundred men available, we can march out and smash them. I would be happy to accompany you."

Cragrunner spit on the cobblestones and looked at Zaketh. "Let me finish, Line Commander, before making battle plans. Before he was found he counted thirty longships, each holding thirty Noriziem."

Kailen's eyes widened. Nine hundred? Zaketh held steady, not letting his mouth betray his surprise. It was his eyes that gave him away.

"Thirty ships?" asked Zaketh, "How did a fleet that big get past our coastal patrols?"

It was Cragrunner's turn to snort. "That was all he had a chance to count. There are probably more. A fleet that size doesn't have to get past our patrols, it goes through them. The damned navy is spread too thin. By the time the Noriziem rally on the coast and begin marching they'll be here in two days, especially if they push on through the night."

Zaketh stroked his chin and asked, "How can you be so sure they're coming directly here?"

"The Trade Road connects us directly to that beach. We're built around a mine full of precious ore. Where would you go?"

"Very well," said Zaketh, "We should rouse the town tonight, get everyone prepared."

"No," said Cragrunner.

Zaketh tilted his head ever so slightly to the side, and as if he were talking to a child asked, "Why?"

"Waking the town will do no good. Most of them are drunk anyways. With the day to prepare tomorrow we'll have more than enough time. I'll muster all my regular troops tonight, and they'll begin readying the defenses."

Cragrunner turned his back to Zaketh and looked at the town he'd been assigned to protect. "Tonight is our celebration of spring, of the Landing. Let them enjoy it before chaos descends."

"You're drunk yourself, sir," Kailen said with a half-smile.

Cragrunner rubbed his face and nodded. "On that, son, you are correct. I'm having the kitchens brew us all khona to clear our heads. There will be no sleep for us."

Kailen fingered the pommel of his sword and looked over at Zaketh. "I'm going for my armor and bow."

Zaketh nodded absently, already arranging battle lines and supply routes in his head. Kailen jogged for the barracks, his legs numb and his gut churning. He wasn't afraid to fight, but nine hundred? The town had good walls, and well-trained soldiers to man them. They would endure this. Cardanans knew how to fight. Their whole history had been spent fighting. Would there ever be a time they weren't fighting? Would he live to see it? Entering the town square again, now strewn with empty mugs and dropped food, he spotted a fountain carved in the image of Antaunna. The blue granite almost glowed in the moonlight. He changed course and went to it, dipping a hand into the basin. A jet of water spouted from Antaunna's mouth, her head and one claw thrown back reaching for the sky.

What if he never saw Carra again? Every man's life ends. What if this was his time? A small, smooth-skinned palm covered the top of the hand he'd braced against the fountain lip. He felt the heat from the serving girl's body, and couldn't help smiling when he looked at her. The top of her bodice was unlaced and gently she bit her lower lip. Kailen said, "I'm surprised you're still up. You could have had any man here."

"I wanted you."

Kailen bent down and kissed her, cupping the back of her head with his still wet hand. When they parted lips she asked, "What changed your mind?"

"Life can be short."

Chapter 11
. . . AND A PATH LAY BEFORE ME

Skal Rend'arr, son of Chief Skal Reelan, watched the Noriziem army storm the Cardanan shore. The Grenar hid behind the rocky dunes that lined the beach. He had laid his halberd at the base of the sandy hill. Its two-foot blade would easily reflect the light from the Noriziem bonfires lining the shore.

A short while ago, he had been waiting outside the human town, comfortably hidden in a grove of willows. The unrelenting need to follow the Cardanan Warden had not left him. His dream persisted, and he had been studying the town and wondering if he'd be able sneak in and observe the Cardanans' town life. However, only a short while ago, a Cardanan scout had thundered past on horseback not far from Rend'arr's hiding place. The man had smelled of blood and fear mixed with sea mist. Never able to ignore his curiosity, the Grenar decided to visit the coast. His grandfather's warning of inquisitiveness leading to premature death echoed again. Rend'arr had never been able to disagree with him.

Hundreds of Noriziem mustered on the beach. Supply depots and cook tents stretched beyond Rend'arr's sight. Longships cut through the surf and came close to grounding on the beach. Dozens of men jumped from the rails and waded ashore carrying gear and supplies. Even in the dim light of early morning Rend'arr saw clearly, and from the stern of each longship, flags emblazoned with a black dragon's silhouette snapped in the sea breeze. It was the same flag he saw every night in the dream.

The dream was clear and constant now. The land burned, the mixed blood of Cardanan and Grenar stained the ground, and then, through the flames, walked the Warden. His presence pushed back the destruction and breathed new life into the land. Bowing before Rend'arr, who stood surveying the destruction wounded and weaponless, the Warden would then offer his hand. The dream never changed. It was the same night after night. Was he witnessing the realization of this dream?

The Noriziem battalions formed up. A long, ordered line of soldiers snaked from the shore to the cart road that connected the beach to the Cardanan town. There was not much left to the night. The eastern sky turned a wasted grey. If the soldiers started now it would take them two days to reach the town at a marching pace. He didn't have much time.

But time to do what? He slid down the dune and into the depression that ran behind it. He picked his halberd off the ground, sat, and balanced it across his knees. The leather-wrapped haft was smooth and worn to his grip. With ragged fingernails he traced the ever-curving lines of the binding. What could he do? Why should he do anything? The war with the Cardanans had been long and vicious. It had started when a Cardanan explorer, heading a small expedition, had insulted the honor of a Grenar war party that had offered to trade with the small, pale-skinned foreigners. The expedition had been wiped out, but when the Cardanans discovered what happened, the war was ignited. Rend'arr thought about the atrocities committed upon his people. Villages burned. Children hung from the trees. Cardanan soldiers heating the blades of their swords until they were red hot and shoving them into Grenar women.

However, he knew what his people had done to them in return. Cardanans torn apart limb from limb and scattered across the field of battle. Their young skinned and left piled in town courtyards to be found by the soldiers who came too late to answer the calls for help. Entire villages utterly wiped from existence. It had only ended when the Cardanans came in such force that they expelled the Grenar from the very land that had given birth to them. Rend'arr had learned the tales when he was only a boy. His grandfather, very old and near death, told him of the swarms of metal-clad men. They marched in perfect time, held their lines with stalwart precision, and cut through the Grenar armies. Individually, the Grenar were stronger than the Cardanans, but they did not fight as a unit and as such were outmatched by the Cardanans' organization and cooperation. Defeated, they had been pushed across the great river in the west and forced to survive in the Wilds.

So, why should he worry about helping them? Didn't they deserve this? Rend'arr ran his finger along the blade of the halberd. He had crafted the weapon himself, the last test of his Rite. What was his role in all of this? The Great Spirit had chosen him for some reason. It was not normal to dream the same thing every night. Most Grenar did not even dream. It was considered the realm of shamans and medicine women. He was a warrior, and while spiritual, did not claim to know the mysteries of what lay beyond the normal world. This was not even where he was supposed to be right now. He had wandered across the border on impulse; when he should have instead joined with Skal Toba's war party. The Grenar warriors were braving the mire of the Grenfel Marshes to destroy a nest of Bog Reapers. The nightmarish beasts had attacked a new Grenar settlement recently built on the edge of the swamp. Skal Toba... If he left now, and ran the entire way, he could reach her by nightfall of the oncoming day. The party was large, two hundred Grenar. They could cover the distance back to the Cardanan town in slightly less than two days. If the Cardanans held the Noriziem off long enough, they would be back in time to help.

But again, why? He had watched the Warden and his companions for some time now, and his respect had grown. They fought well, seemed to conduct themselves with honor, and did not behave in ways that differed all that much from his own people. However, there was no reason any of the other Grenar would know this. He had been the first, to his knowledge, to cross the river back into the Homeland since their defeat. They only knew the Cardanans as conquerors and destroyers: a bitter enemy that seized their homeland. His grandfather had spoken of the lines of Cardanan soldiers advancing on his village with implacable calm and precision. The village had burned, and any Grenar that could not escape was killed. He had never seen his grandfather's eyes cast so far down.

A stone scraped and bounced down the dune to his right. His head snapped around and he heard footsteps. Silently, he rose and dashed over the next set of dunes. Hidden in the dead sea-grass, he watched a patrol of two Noriziem navigate the first line of dunes. They walked over the spot where he had first been hiding. It was too dark for their human eyes to notice the depression he had left in the sand. They continued past, talking in low, guttural tones. On their cloaks, in rough stitch work, was the silhouette of the Black Dragon.

He had no good reason for trying to save the Cardanans other than a dream and a feeling that the Warden was somehow important to the future of both their people. His mother had always told him dreams reveal genuine truth and that ignoring instincts and feelings was unwise. She had been a great medicine woman until the bite of a slate viper, a serpent found only in The Wild, stole her from both him and his father.

Even if he made it to Skal Toba's party in time, the War Leader had no reason to believe him. She would most likely think Rend'arr insane, and in truth Rend'arr wondered if he were. Being the son of Chief Reela, he had the power to challenge Toba for command of the war party, but if he did that Toba had the right to request a Morash Ton'ga. One of them might end up dead if that happened, and Rend'arr knew Toba. The fight would not be done until one of them bled the ground black.

He sighed and thought of his hut back in the Vale. Tucked away high on the mountain side it was warm and hard to find. He enjoyed the quiet and the peace it allowed him. There he could find time to work on his carvings. The best nights were when Vereessa visited. He knew she was the one for him, but he had not yet attained a high enough reputation to ask for her vow of devotion or offer his. Still, she enjoyed his company and the warm bed they made together. Why couldn't he be there right now? Why did he dream of this scrawny Warden instead of her?

A steady, deep drum beat rose over the washing song of the waves. Rend'arr scanned the dunes and did not see the patrol returning. He climbed back to his original vantage point. Noriziem commanders called orders to the lines of soldiers. Organized into rectangular groups they looked impressive, but Rend'arr could see their movements were not perfectly matched or practiced. They were not used to moving in formation. The drumbeat quickened and a horn blew, echoing across the beach. Skal Rend'arr watched them step as one and move down the cart road. They marched toward the Cardanan town, the banner of the Black Dragon high over their ranks.

Chapter 12
ALONG THE WATCHTOWER

"Incoming!"

Kailen ducked behind the ramparts as a volley of scorpion bolts soared over the wall. The over-sized arrows caromed off stone, shattered shields, and skewered several soldiers who were standing in exactly the wrong place at the worst time. Kailen hugged the stone of the wall, squeezing as close to its cold surface as possible. He wished he were small enough to fit into the cracks lining the rain-worn masonry. There was no defense against what came next, and his absolute helplessness was terrifying. He felt like a child all over again. The volley of bolts was followed by several catapult-hurled stones, each covered in pitch and set aflame. One sailed directly over Kailen, the heat almost baking him. It smashed into a house beyond him, scattering timbers and roof thatch. He heard screams from the family hiding inside as the building ignited.

Another stone smashed into the ramparts to the left of him, demolishing the battlements and spraying flaming slivers of rock. Three soldiers, huddling in the same manner as Kailen, disappeared in a cloud of dust and blood. Kailen forced himself to his feet and peered through the crenellations. He saw only Noriziem, lines of them holding shield and sword, axes and spears. He saw their catapults and scorpions being reloaded. He saw over a thousand faces, each one looking to kill him. From atop the tower to his left Rian barked, "Fire!"

The legionnaire archers atop the wall let loose with their longbows, forcing the Noriziem behind their shields. Those without shields were cut down. Noriziem arrows responded, bouncing off the stone around Kailen. He ducked again, then heard a hollow thunk against the stone in front of him. He looked up and saw two wooden poles sticking over the top of the battlements. "Dammit, not again."

He stood and peered over the wall. Several Noriziem were already climbing and four others braced the bottom of the ladder. He wouldn't be able to push it over. He yelled to the soldiers at his right, "Timmon, Randall, form up here!"

The two men jogged over, their feet thumping against the stone under the weight of their armor. Lines, dark and purple, curved beneath their eyes and their arms trembled as they hefted their tower shields. "What is it, sir?" asked Randall.

Kailen pointed at the ladder, "Company."

"Damned bastards, don't they know we don't like them?" asked Timmon.

"Must be that pretty face of yours. I always said you have the look of a barmaid," Randall said.

"Fuck you."

The two soldiers stood at an angle to the ladder, to the right of it, shoulder to shoulder, with shields in front of them and swords at the ready. They moved in unison, planting their left foot in front and their right foot behind. The trembling in their arms stopped, and their faces hardened into tired defiance. Kailen moved to the left of the ladder, taking a deep breath and raising his own sword. It was the sixth time he had done this since noon the previous day.

The first Noriziem poked his head over the rampart, and Kailen stuck his sword into the invader's right eye. He fell off, screaming until he slapped against the ground thirty feet below. Kailen pulled his sword back for another blow, but the second Noriziem was faster, and as he came over the rampart he threw a dagger at Kailen. The aim was off, but it forced Kailen to duck aside. The Noriziem was on the wall. Two more followed. The first one was on Kailen, swinging a curved axe in one hand and a spiked mace in the other. Kailen parried the strikes, one up high and one aimed at his waist, wondering how the man had climbed holding two weapons. The Noriziem was bigger than he, and stronger. Kailen's arms stung every time he diverted a blow. Wielding his father's sword two-handed, he used every bit of strength to keep the Noriziem at bay. He waited for an opening, hoping the blond-bearded brute would make a mistake, but his attacks were flawless. He couldn't see Timmon and Randall, but he heard the clang of steel and the impact of blade against wooden shield.

Another volley of scorpion bolts sailed over the wall, followed by the flaming stones. He didn't hear the command to return fire. The wall had been scaled in numerous places and the archers had taken up sword. It was odd. All he could see was the man in front of him, trying to kill him, but he could hear everything. He heard the screams of impaled men, he heard an officer barking orders to hold the line, and he heard the town's lone trebuchet groaning as it returned fire.

The Noriziem pushed him to the edge of the wall. Kailen felt the empty air behind him. He leaned into the Noriziem, bringing his sword overhand towards the man's head. It was easily parried, but it stopped the Noriziem's momentum. Kailen followed with a side cut to the waist and a thrust to the chest. The invader was off balance now, trying to keep Kailen's three-foot blade away from his body. He swung wide with his axe, leaving his side open. Kailen slipped his sword in, pushing it through the boiled leather, then the skin, then the muscle, then the organs. The Noriziem went slack, grunting his surprise. Kailen pulled his sword out, smashed the Noriziem in the temple with his pommel, and pushed him over the side into the dirt thirty feet below. Kailen's ninth kill since sunrise. He had totaled twenty-three the previous day.

Timmon and Randall had cut down the two facing them, but three fresh Noriziem replaced them. Kailen stabbed one in the back. Ten. He almost didn't duck the sword of another. He chopped, he sliced, he didn't even feel his arms any more. Every move was automatic, a survival response. He was tiring, though, as were the two legionnaires. Eventually, the Noriziem would get through. One would land a blow that would send him to his parents and Antaunna. Kailen wondered if that would be so bad.

His lungs burned and his heart ached, but his sword kept moving. He smashed a gap-toothed fellow in the face with the crossbar of his sword. The man dropped his dagger and grasped at the blood gushing from his nose, as if that would stop the pain. Kailen disemboweled him. Eleven.

Another Noriziem faced Kailen. He used his axe to pin Kailen's sword against the ramparts and punched the warden in the face. Kailen fell back, tasting iron and seeing stars. His head slammed into the stone, and he stared stupidly as the Noriziem raised his axe, aiming to bury it in Kailen's skull. The warden couldn't move. All his training meant nothing. No matter how he tried, his body was numb, his limbs unresponsive.

The Noriziem tensed, his knuckles white around the haft of his weapon. His eyes locked on Kailen's. The surprise on his face matched Kailen's when a greatsword pierced the Noriziem's heart. It punched clear though his rusted chainmail and didn't stop until the wicked point protruded from his back. The axe fell from his grip, chipping the stone next to Kailen's left ear. The sword was withdrawn and the disbelief on the Noriziem's face was almost comical as the sword came in again, a swing to the right side of the body. Kailen flinched as the gore splattered him. The Noriziem was gone, the pieces of him fallen to the dirt below. A mail-clad hand looped under Kailen's arm and pulled him to his feet.

"In one piece?" asked Zaketh.

"I think so," said Kailen.

"Good, now help me kill the rest of these bastards."

Kailen shook the spots from his eyes and stood next to Zaketh, thrusting and stabbing in the wake of Darksteel's greatsword. With every swing Zaketh brought a Noriziem down. If they parried, their weapon was knocked aside. If they blocked with shield, it was splintered. Kailen followed in the wake of this destruction with automatic grace. A quick jab caught one man in the throat. A short overhand buried his sword in another Noriziem's unarmored skull. He had to brace his foot on the man's shoulder to get it out. With Zaketh leading the way the Cardanans pushed the Noriziem off the wall. A long pole with a hooked blade had been brought up, and with Kailen, Zaketh, and several others pushing, they knocked that ladder down for the third time. Kailen heard the screams of the Noriziem as they were crushed under their own construct and smiled. Zaketh handed the pole to a soldier and turned to Kailen. "We're bringing in the second squads. Go down to the relief hut. It will be some time before they try to scale here again."

"I'm not going anywhere. My place is here."

Kailen thought Zaketh almost smiled. The commander faced

Kailen fully and said, "Your skin is waxen, your eyes drawn. Your sword is shaking in your hand."

Kailen's eyes darted to his right hand. Sure enough, he couldn't keep his blade still, no matter how hard he tried.

"And," continued Zaketh, "you're bleeding all over your armor. Go get that patched up."

Kailen followed Zaketh's eyes to his upper left arm. A three-inch gash had been torn out of his chain mail, and the wound beneath was an ugly, seeping red. "When did that happen?"

"Doesn't matter. Get sewn up and rest. We'll need you again," said Zaketh. He then turned away from Kailen and repeated his orders to Timmon and Randall. They didn't argue. Kailen followed them down the carved steps and made for the tents erected in a courtyard not far from the northern gate. Townspeople ran past him, carrying buckets of water to fires that still burned. A squad of soldiers marched past in perfect formation, heading for the wall and wearing armor already dented and spattered with blood. Their rest was over.

At the courtyard, Kailen found the cluster of tents surrounded by groups of bodies. Some were clad in steel; others were not. Some moaned and flailed. Others were silent and always would be. Death's sweet stink invaded Kailen's nostrils. Bile momentarily tickled the back of his throat, but he forced it down. He went to the tent that was least crowded. As he entered, he heard the trebuchet fling another stone into the masses of Noriziem. Their catapults responded, sending more fire into the town. Kailen wondered what would happen if one of those stones landed in the courtyard.

Under the tent, he sat on a weather-worn bench. Someone came to his side faster than he expected. It was Father Frostwind. Kailen bowed his head and spoke the way he and Carra had when they were still attending Temple Lessons. "Father, you need not tend to me. There are others in more desperate need than I."

Frostwind, already looking at the wound on Kailen's arm, snorted and said, "Most of the others are beyond my help. I can get you back into the fight, but if you keep talking to me like that I'll take you out of it permanently. You'd think I was the bloody High Father."

"Sorry, Father, habit. It's not often I speak to clergy."

Frostwind dabbed the jagged cut with a cloth soaked in

yellow, pungent fluid. Kailen's fingernails cut into his palms and whistled breath raced through clenched teeth. His arm hurt worse after the cleaning than it did before. He almost didn't hear the priest say, "Today, don't think of me as clergy, but your healer. And call me Cranden. I'm fairly certain I'm not your father."

"Of course, Fath ... Cranden. During Kelebra de'al Verdan I watched your recitation of the Exodus. One of the best I've ever seen. The children loved it."

Cranden snorted and motioned for Kailen to remove his hauberk. He inspected the wound one more time and wrapped a linen bandage around Kailen's arm. He snorted again and helped Kailen put the hauberk back on. "I should hope so. I've done it enough times. You should see the one I tell about the lonely merchant and the bored milk wench. Now that's impressive."

Kailen laughed, but he wasn't sure if he was pleasantly surprised or shocked by Frostwind's behavior. It was definitely not how most clergy spoke. Frostwind was still poking at his arm. The bandage felt tight and clean. Kailen flexed his arm. It would do for now. Frostwind handed him a drinking skin and a platter from the table behind them. Kailen took the skin and poured it into his mouth. Expecting water, his eyes widened as he tasted hops and sweet malt. It was warm, somewhat bitter, but still smooth and strong. It was the best beer he'd ever had. "Cranden, you're my savior. I thought I'd have to settle for water."

"Hrrmph! Water is needed to fight the fires, everyone gets ale, so don't thank me too quick. Eat some food. Last thing I want is you swinging a sword while clouded by drink."

Kailen obeyed, devouring the dried meat, crusty loaves of bread, and slightly green cheese. He washed it down with the remainder of the ale. His head was clear and his limbs felt like flesh again, not lead. Cranden stood in front of him, grabbed him by the chin, and moved his face first to the left and then the right. "The color is coming back to your skin, and your breathing has steadied. Wait here a few minutes more for your stomach to settle. Then you can head back to the wall."

"Thank you, Cranden, I appreciate it."

"You can thank me by keeping those damned, filthy heathens out of my town. Ignorant, brutish simpletons, killing my people..."

Kailen didn't hear the rest as Frostwind left him for a soldier whose comrades carried him into the neighboring tent. A scorpion bolt protruded from the young man's shoulder. When Kailen was sure Frostwind wasn't paying him any attention, he left the tent. He wasn't doing any good here. On the cobblestones outside the tent was a half-empty water skin, dropped by someone. Kailen picked it up, sure enough, it was ale. He drained the last of it in one swallow and headed back to the wall.

***

Rian had not left his tower since battle commenced the previous day. He was coordinating the archers along the northern and western walls, using signal flags and runners. When either of those didn't seem to work, he employed his surprisingly loud voice. His own bow had found the weak spot in many a Noriziem's armor, but there were always more taking the place of those felled. He was running out of arrows.

The Noriziem had pulled back for now. Their assault a failure, it appeared they were restocking ammunition for their siege weapons. He wondered what their next move would be. The Noriziem had set up tents far in their rear positions, most likely for supplies and wounded. The middle position was a series of trenches they had dug overnight, and now hid in between attacks. The forward line of the Noriziem was a long row of heavily armored men holding over-sized shields. Behind them were archers who constantly harassed the Cardanans on the wall. In all his years fighting the Noriziem, Rian had never seen them this organized, this efficient. It truly was an army they faced, not a large, uncontrolled raiding party. In spite of all his prayers to Antaunna, he wasn't certain they would win this.

A moist, black nose nudged his left leg. Nina stayed in the tower with him. She never left him. He sat, resting his head on the rough stone that had kept him safe. He scratched Nina behind the ears, her yellow eyes open and accepting. "Life is too good to end this way, don't you think girl? I'd always thought I'd die an old man in bed with three women. A smile on my face."

Nina cocked her head to one side, moving her neck forward just enough so Rian could scratch her in the right spot. "I haven't thought about dying for years. Since I was in that cave. But you wouldn't know about that, would you? You weren't even born yet."

Nina yowled a little and pushed her muzzle into Rian's neck and licked his face. "Wish you had been there though. Things may have gone different."

He grabbed her on each side of the neck and rubbed hard, thinking he should stand and keep an eye on the Noriziem, but it was nice right here with his dog.

The snap of firing catapults triggered a quiver along his spine. He waited for the crash of stone against timber, but instead heard pottery shattering, followed by the roar of fire. "What in Antaunna's name..."

He stood and looked between the crenellations. The section of wall over the northern gate was engulfed in flame. Soldiers ran out of the inferno covered in fire. They jumped off the wall, either side of it, just looking for escape from the conflagration. Catapults sounded again, and Rian watched large clay pots, flames trailing from a hole in their top, arc perfectly though the air and smash atop other sections of the northern wall. Soldiers all along its length were forced from their positions. Commotion among the Noriziem caught Rian's attention. Their front lines parted and a group of Noriziem charged the gate carrying an iron-capped log. Rian moved to the eastern side of the tower and spotted Zaketh below and not far from the base of the tower. He was trying to smother the flames eating a soldier. Rian hollered, "Zak! Battering ram!"

***

Kailen stared at the north wall, frightened by the curtain of flames that rose from the very stone. The roar of the fire mixed with the screams of dying men to form a ghastly chorus. One hundred paces away, the heat was blistering. If he had come back from the tents a few minutes earlier, he would have been on the wall, right over the gate. He stood rooted, not sure where to go. Most of the ramparts of the northern wall were engulfed. He heard someone holler from the northwest tower, but he couldn't understand what was said.

WHUMPF!

Kailen jumped. What was that sound? Soldiers stationed around the gate scrambled and officers barked orders. He jogged towards the gate. It seemed the only place to go.

WHUMPF!

The gates shook. Years-old dirt and grit puffed from the seams between the timbers. Some of the soldiers braced beams against the gate and Kailen understood. They were coming through. The inferno still raged above the gate. No one could get up there to fire upon the Noriziem.

WHUMPF!

Kailen stood before the gates, not sure what to do. He wasn't made for this type of fighting. The trees were his protection, not stone walls. His strengths were speed and stealth, not discipline and organization. Some soldiers braced the door. Others stood together in loose formation, holding their swords tight and their shields tighter. Others ran. Kailen knew someone had to establish order, but he was no field officer. It was not his place to command men.

WHUMPF!

The groups of soldiers jumped, visibly shaken. They glanced at the door and then up at the fire that still burned strong. They shuffled backwards as a group, looking at each other, seeing what the others would do. The Legion was cracking.

"Squads, form the line! I want all men with spears or pole arms to form the first rank."

Zaketh Darksteel strode into the gate courtyard, his greatsword slung over his shoulder. Kailen was startled by his appearance. Darksteel's plate armor did not shine anymore. It was spattered with blood and oily soot. The right side of Darksteel's face was crimson, and Kailen saw small blisters forming on the commander's cheek.

WHUMPF!

Everyone except Darksteel jumped at the impact. Most of the soldiers had fallen into line, but a few groups still hung back. Kailen saw them still looking back towards the inner town. Darksteel noticed. "I said form the line! Do you cunnies have a problem with that? Now fucking move! Tidespinner, with me."

Kailen went to Zaketh's side, impressed with the Commander's rally. The soldiers had fallen into a line, three men deep, that stretched from one side of the road to the other. Fear still colored their faces, but they now had purpose and direction. Zaketh looked at Kailen and said, "You'll want to find a shield."

"From where?"

"There are plenty lying on the ground."

WHUMPF!

The protest of cracking wood followed that impact. Zaketh was right. Dead soldiers lay in the street, some still burning, their shields strapped to their arms. Kailen found one lying on the cobblestones, probably dropped by a fleeing soldier. It was heavy and felt awkward on his left arm. He hadn't used one of these since his initial legion training.

WHUMPF!

Zaketh had found a shield too, and he took his spot in the line, in the second rank, with Kailen to his right. The commander stood at absolute attention, every inch of his body rigid marshal perfection. His granite stance spread to those around him, Kailen included. In his baritone voice, Darksteel commanded the men. "First rank, form spear wall!"

The front row kneeled in unison. They planted their shields in the cracks between the pave stones and couched their spears into notches cut into the right side of their shields, all at the same height. They became a wall of wood, armor, and steel.

WHUMPF!

The wood cracked louder, and the beams that braced the gates shifted and fell over.

"Second rank, battle stance!"

Kailen hadn't stood in the line for years, but he found the motions came naturally. With the rest of the second line he placed his left foot forward, bracing his right behind him. He brought the shield up square with his chest and held his sword parallel to his body. If any Noriziem made it past the spear tips he could thrust over the head of the man in front of him and into the face of anyone trying to get past the shield wall.

WHUMPF!

The brackets that held the locking beam across the gate pulled out of the wood, and the whole door flexed inwards.

"Third rank, discard shields, heft spears!"

The final row of soldiers dropped their shields behind them and held their spears above their shoulders, two handed. They could now either throw their spears into the oncoming Noriziem, or thrust past the first two ranks and stab anyone who made it into the line.

WHUMPF!

"Where is Cragrunner? Shouldn't he be here?" asked Kailen.

"Last I knew he was on the western wall. The Noriziem had put up six ladders and he was coordinating the defense. I was the closest officer to the gate," said Zaketh.

"You did well. What's that stuff on the wall? It still burns."

"I've never seen anything like it. It's not oil, not like any I've ever seen. It's a thick, sticky paste that doesn't go out no matter what you put on it. I dumped a whole bucket of water on one man. The flames did not die."

WHUMPF!

Kailen's arms shook. Fatigue wanted to pull them down, and the battle-rush alone held them up. His chest was light with the frantic pounding of his heart. If he kept talking he didn't dwell on the bile surging in his stomach. "This should be interesting. I haven't fought in the line for ages, and even then it was only practice."

"It will come back to you, trust me. I've been fighting border skirmishes, mostly on horseback, for the last five years. I haven't held a line since the academy."

WHUMPF!

"I'd feel better with archer support."

"Look to the rooftops."

Groups of archers perched atop many of the houses and now waited with arrow and longbow in hand.

"Did you do that?" asked Kailen.

"I didn't. I think we owe Rian thanks."

Kailen looked closer and, sure enough, Rian was on one of the roofs, his own bow ready.

"Guess we couldn't keep him away from the fight, I owe him an ale and a woman after this," said Kailen.

"Just one?"

"Well, maybe two."

"Ale or woman?"

Kailen laughed, and Zaketh actually cracked a smile. The quick release of the laughter helped settle Kailen. His jitters subsided.

WHUMPF!

The gate was almost gone. Catapults fired again, and the flaming stones returned, arcing over the wall and crashing into several homes. One landed behind the line, showering the street with fiery debris. Kailen hoped one didn't land right on them.

This fancy line of theirs wouldn't mean a damned thing.

WHHUMMPPFFF!

The cross-beam snapped and the doors pushed open. Noriziem poured in, calling to Galantaegan, and charged directly for the line. Kailen braced himself, holding his father's sword even tighter. Bow strings hummed. A volley of arrows mowed down the front ranks for the Noriziem, but there were more behind them. Another volley, more Noriziem cut down, but still they came.

The line shook as Noriziem collided against Cardanan. Many were skewered by the spears, but others made it past and pushed into the shield wall. They tried to stab down at the first rank and break apart the defensive formation, leaving them open to attack from the second rank. Kailen thrust forward and caught one Noriziem in the throat. The man fell back, tripping the Noriziem behind him. Twelve. The soldier in front of Kailen tried to shake a Noriziem off the end of his spear. The invader was stuck and the Cardanan couldn't bring the spear to bear on another enemy until it was freed. Kailen watched, grossly fascinated by the puppet show, as the Noriziem jerked about on the end of the spear. Another Noriziem was in front of Kailen. He stabbed and cut the man's cheek open. The Noriziem screamed, but before Kailen could pull back for another attempt the soldier to his right pierced the man's chest. Kailen liked the soldier's speed, but was annoyed. That still counted as thirteen.

All along the Cardanan formation Noriziem tried to breach the lines and failed. The Legion held. Archers fired volley after volley into the rear ranks of the Noriziem, sapping their numbers and wearing down their morale. Kailen felt the press lightening. There were fewer Noriziem stepping up to feel his blade.

More Noriziem came through the gate. These were all large men, heavily muscled and wearing black plate armor. They carried no shields, only big, ugly two-handed swords. They charged into the line, giving no thought to their own defense. Kailen almost laughed at their recklessness until they burst through the first rank. Their heavy armor turned all but the most determined blows, and their momentum knocked down the shield wall.

The man in front of Kailen was trampled beneath two of these brutes, and Kailen tried to put his shield between him and them.

The spearman behind Kailen stabbed one of them in the face with a well aimed jab, but the other tackled Kailen to the ground. The Noriziem punched him in the face. Dazed, Kailen watched the ugly sword rise high for the killing blow. The situation was uncomfortably familiar.

The Noriziem's head disappeared from his shoulders. Zaketh's greatsword blurred by. Kailen forced himself to his feet, trying to shake away the dizziness. The line had collapsed. Men were fighting to save themselves, desperately trying to keep these huge Noriziem from killing them.

Another berserker stepped before Kailen. This time he dodged the first attack and came in with a cut to the man's thigh, where the armor looked weak. He cut through, slicing deep into the Noriziem's leg. The man didn't cry out, but his balance was ruined and Kailen rushed forward, sliding his sword through the Noriziem's throat. Fourteen.

The legionnaire to Kailen's right was crushed under the weight of a warhammer. Kailen stabbed that Noriziem in the side. Fifteen. A berserker tried to come in on Zaketh's back while the Commander was engaged with another Noriziem. Kailen hit him on the kneecap with his sword. The man fell back, screaming. Kailen brought his shield down on the Noriziem's windpipe. Sixteen.

The Cardanans were pushed back steadily. They managed to form a loose skirmish line, but could not hold ground. Noriziem began to slip past. First, just one here and there, but then whole groups broke away. They disappeared down side streets and into buildings. Kailen saw one group rush into a house where he thought women and children were hiding. He stepped towards the house, but was blocked by a Noriziem with an axe in one hand and a dagger in the other. Seventeen.

Another was in front of him, this one swinging a flail and wearing dented armor covered in Cardanan blood. Eighteen. Kailen swung, parried, and dodged without thought. Hesitation and worry were discarded, he fell into his training and instincts, hoping it would keep him one step ahead of his attackers. He moved a few steps closer to the house. Screams echoed from inside. He needed to get in there. He couldn't let it happen. Nineteen; a scrawny, scraggly wretch with armor that flopped loudly when he hit the ground.

Cardanans were in his way now. The skirmish line had been pushed back. He couldn't get to the house. The legionnaires were bunched into a group in front of it and didn't pay any attention the noises coming from inside. Noriziem were coming hard at him, at all of them, and he had no choice but to face them.

Fresh Cardanan troops came up the street from the town center, pulled off the walls not under attack. They reinforced the skirmish line and the assault lost some momentum. The Noriziem still rushed the soldiers, but were not getting through as often. Kailen stabbed a berserker through the throat, but not before the Noriziem almost broke his left arm with the haft of his axe. Twenty.

Kailen stepped back from the line, clutching his forearm. His vambrace had deflected most of the blow, but his hand was tingling and the bones felt bruised. He looked over at the house. It was quiet now, and flames danced in the windows.

The tip of his sword dropped to the street. He was tired and just wanted to lie down. There didn't seem any point to it. No matter how hard he fought, innocents were dying around him, and he couldn't do a damn thing to stop it. He turned his back to the fight and froze in place. Walking down the middle of the street, calmly and alone, was Father Frostwind. He carried a boy in his arms. The child didn't move. As Frostwind drew closer, Kailen saw blood covering the boy's head like a crimson wax seal. It stained the priest's cloak and beard, turning the chest of his blue robe purple. Over the din of battle, Kailen heard the iron foot cap of Frostwind's staff striking against the cobblestones. The sapphire set into the top glowed. The air around Kailen tingled and crawled with a lightning-like charge. Frostwind walked past him, looking straight ahead, his eyes empty and his face stone.

He reached the battle line. Men parted before him. Cardanans looked at him in awe, Noriziem in disbelief. None dared lift a blade against him. All were frozen in place. Frostwind spoke, his voice cracked and tired. "I've had enough of you. Leave my town."

Kailen could barely hear him, but his heart broke at the beaten tone of the old man's voice. One of the Noriziem laughed. He pointed at the old man, taunted him in Norzaat, and hefted his sword, walking straight at the priest. Frostwind lifted his staff, and his voice found its strength. He called, *"Kren kine Shenken!"*

He slammed the butt of his staff into the stone and a wave of force rolled down the street. It expanded like a ripple, moving in all directions from the priest. Every Noriziem hit by it dropped dead, the life ripped from their bodies. It rolled over Kailen, exerting the angry pressure of a breaking wave, and then swept down the street and through buildings, passing through wood as if it weren't there, but not destroying it. It washed over a group of Cardanan soldiers who had been cut off and trapped further down the street. They remained standing while the Noriziem they were fighting dropped like bags of stone. The wave went all the way to the wall and just beyond the gate, where it finally disappeared into wisps of writhing energy.

Frostwind fell to his knees, dropping his staff as he struggled to hold the child. He was pale and his breathing ragged. Kailen and Zaketh both rushed to his side. The priest looked at them with a slack jaw and drooping eyes, managing to reach up and wipe the spittle away from the corner of his mouth. It was tinted pink. "I've cleared the road, Commander. Now, if you don't mind, would you secure the damned gate?"

Zaketh nodded and stood. He pointed to a pair of militia, grey in hair and awkward in their armor. "You two, get him back to the relief tent and get food and water into him. Take the young one too."

"But, sir," said one militiaman, "the child is dead."

"Take him, or you'll join him."

The two men did as they were told, lifting the priest and his dead charge, and headed back into town. Zaketh jogged towards the gate ordering, "Legion, move forward! I want a defensive line at the gate. Archers, up on the wall. The fires have gone out."

Kailen jogged beside Zaketh and saw he was right. The top of the wall was charred black, and smoke still hung close over it, but the flames had died. Kailen ran up the steps to the wall, wanting to see the Noriziem positions beyond. The ramparts were slick with char and blackened bodies littered the way. He chose his footing carefully. Zaketh was behind him. The afternoon sun was high, and it cast a strong, yellow light on the field before them.

The confused shouts of the Noriziem echoed across their entrenchments. They knew something had just happened to the men pouring into Littletop, but did not understand what that something was. He watched commanders moving between the lines, trying to calm their soldiers. There were still many Noriziem in the field, and coming down the road from the coast was another column of fresh troops, the black standard of Galantaegan held high in their front rank. He hung his head, saying to Zaketh, "There are more than a thousand of them."

"Maybe twice that amount. They'll be coming again. I'll have the men build a barricade along the gate. We can fight from behind it with spear and halberd."

"I'll stay up here with my bow. Pick a few off before they get to you."

Zaketh's eyes bore into him. "I saw you step away from the line back there. Can I count on you?"

"You can."

"You've never seen battle like this, have you?"

Kailen turned his back to the Noriziem. He sat down, his back braced against the ramparts. He took a deep breath and said, "I'm thirsty."

Zaketh knelt next to him. He handed Kailen the skin from his belt. "It's only water, I'm afraid."

"That's fine," said Kailen, "Thank you."

"Different, isn't it?" asked Zaketh.

"What?"

"The combat. Different than anything you've ever seen."

"Thought I'd be ready for it. I've been fighting for years."

"You've done well. We'll still be standing at the end of the day."

Kailen forced a grin and nodded. "I'll be fine. Where are Timmon and Randall? Won't be the same up here without them."

"They made it back to the wall before you did. They were over the gate when the first fire rounds hit."

"Oh."

Kailen held the mask in place, kept his face stone, but all he wanted to do was hang his head and cry. Two more gone, and for what? His head pounded. He rubbed his temples and took a deep breath. The smoke and ash burned his lungs. He opened his eyes and wished he hadn't. The town stretched before him, smashed, torn, and burning. Townsfolk still fought the fires, but in several places they raged out of control. Entire clusters of homes burned, and no one could do anything about it. He saw soldiers, some fresh and others bandaged, coming to the gate from the relief tents. He watched one man, with a strip of cloth over a missing eye, stumble up to the line. The man set his helm, which he had been carrying, gingerly over his head. He then drew his sword, hefted his shield, and stood in formation. Kailen stood, pushed his weakness away, and thought of all the people still alive in the town. His head still pounded and all he wanted was an ale.

"What is that?" asked Zaketh as he stared over the field

Kailen shook his head and forgot about beer. There was in fact a steady, deep drumming coming from the direction of the Noriziem. It wasn't in his head. Kailen could see no drummers though, and in watching the Noriziem he saw they too looked about in confusion.

"Where is it coming from?" asked Kailen.

"The forest, behind the Noriziem, and on either side of them."

He was right. The drums pounding on the left were a deep, slow beat. The drums from the right were higher and faster, slamming out a more complex rhythm. Kailen heard something else. "Is that, voices?"

They were faint at first, but grew louder. From the trees to the right came a chorus of voices, chanting. Kailen strained to hear it.

Ka matie Ka matei
Kay ora
Ka matie Ka matei
Kay ora
Oora Oora

Another chorus answered from the trees on the left side.

Kolotash ka' Mo tai
Kolotash ka' Mo tai
Kol ta Kol ta
Koh

The voices were deep and strong. The chant was repeated and then Kailen heard scores of feet stomping the ground in unison, in time with the chant. Kailen's fist clenched around his sword, his chest swelled, and blood pounded through his limbs. The chant scared him, but he felt alive, acute. He noticed the men along the wall, Zaketh included, stood taller with their shoulders held broad.

The chant roared a third time. The Noriziem scrambled to face the woods, trying to fall into formation. They were too slow.

The tree line exploded in a rush of moving bodies. They flowed down the hillside, smashing into the Noriziem lines. Kailen squinted, trying to recognize the attackers. Had the Legion come to rescue them? The attackers were organized, coming down on the Noriziem from two directions in tight wedges that cut into the Noriziem positions. They moved fast, Kailen thought. They ran while on the attack, and there even seemed to be some who leapt over whole groups of Noriziem to attack them from the rear. This wasn't the Legion. No man moved like that. Kailen looked to Zaketh, and saw the same confusion on his face. "Who is it?"

"I don't know. They're not wearing heavy armor, and moving very fast. It could be my eyes, but they look big. Very big."

"If they're not wearing armor, why do they look covered in iron?" asked Kailen.

The two wedges joined, merged together, and drove through the center of the Noriziem, directly towards the town. The Noriziem tried to rally. Troops close to the town rushed back to meet the onslaught. They formed shield walls with sword and spear held before them. None broke ranks and they met the grey tide standing firm. Like sand castles made by children they were swept over. The screams of dying Noriziem cut the air. Kailen smiled.

The rolling wave of death was halfway through the Noriziem position now, and Kailen discerned more detail. The attackers were tall, standing at least a head over the Noriziem. They wielded huge weapons: greatswords, battleaxes, and halberds. Kailen squinted. Their faces were heavily boned, and when they opened their mouths to roar he saw large canines. He realized they actually roared. The iron grey he had assumed was armor was their skin color. A steel-cold fist squeezed his stomach. He couldn't feel his fingers, icy and useless. He couldn't breathe. He heard Zaketh swear. He closed his eyes, thinking maybe he'd see something different when he opened them. It couldn't be.

"Grenar."

Had he said that, or Zaketh? It didn't matter. He stood, rooted to the stone. Zaketh would burst into action and tell them what to do like he had before. Wouldn't he? He waited for him to call orders to the stunned men. It didn't come. Zaketh, hands braced against the ramparts, seemed frozen. Fear and wonder battled across his face. Kailen felt the same, but thought maybe he should take over, rally the men. Someone had to act, but he could only watch the destruction in awe.

The Grenar were beautiful in their movements. Their formation never faltered. They mowed the Noriziem down, calling out their war chant and leaving none alive. They came to the line of catapults, which the Grenar set aflame using the Noriziem's own torches. They tore apart the unguarded archers. A third group of Grenar charged out of the woods and headed into the Noriziems' supply train and encampment. They went unchallenged, and soon everything burned.

The Noriziem ran now. The survivors broke the line, trying to get away. The Grenar outdistanced them easily. Kailen focused on two Noriziem heading for the western woods. One of the brutes loped behind them, taking the head off one with his axe and then burying it in the shoulder of the other. The man fell screaming. The Grenar wrenched his axe free, reached down with his other hand, and snapped the Noriziem's neck.

The Noriziem were all dead in less than half an hour. The Grenar regrouped, forming a massive rectangle in the center of the Noriziem's former position. Bodies and fire surrounded them. They were covered in blood and bile. The smell of death poisoned the air. They stood stock still, facing Littletop. Behind them, some of Galantaegan's standards still flew.

Kailen asked Zaketh, "What now, Commander?"

"I don't know."

"Archers? Should we barricade the gate?"

Very quietly, so that only Kailen could hear him, Zaketh said, "What does it matter? They cut through the Noriziem without effort. We're tired, bloodied, and weak. We won't stand a chance."

Kailen wanted to argue. He looked for the strength to rally himself and Zaketh. It wasn't there. He could only stand and watch the Grenar. It was like he was seven again, small and useless.

The Grenar still didn't move, a solid block of muscle, steel, and quiet fury.

One Grenar stepped out from the front line. He was taller than the rest, with long, raven-black hair hanging over his shoulders. He carried a halberd, a monstrous thing with a two-foot blade of tempered steel. He walked towards the ruined gates, his weapon held in one hand and at his waist, swinging gently with his gait. He came within one hundred paces of the wall. Some men found the presence to ready their bows.

The Grenar set his halberd on the ground. He kneeled, crossed his arms over his chest, and rocked back and forth. He chanted quietly.

Lightning ripped the sky. Thunder shook the stone works. A sky that was blue filled with clouds that rolled in much too fast. The air became as grey as the Grenar, and Kailen felt it thicken with force. It weighed on his chest and deadened his limbs. It pushed harder and harder, and Kailen was sure it would crush him.

Rain drifted down. The pressure was gone, and the soft, warm drops on Kailen's face reminded him of Carra's fingertips. Warmth returned to his hands and his feet didn't feel iron-shod. The rain fell harder, and Kailen heard the hiss of steam behind him. He turned to the fire-riddled town and watched the rain beat down on the flames, sending up plumes of white steam. It soaked the wood and thatch that had not yet caught a spark.

Kailen looked back to the field. The Grenar was still kneeling and rocking. The brutes behind him also chanted, their voices one with his. After a few minutes, the lone Grenar stopped his swaying. He stood, stretched his arms wide, and let the rain wash over him. He shook his head, his black hair spraying water and blood.

He lowered his arms and motioned to the formation behind him. The front lines parted and two Grenar marched out carrying something between them. They threw it down before the raven-haired one. It was a Noriziem clad in silver plate, embossed with onyx dragon heads and golden leaf. The man flopped into the mud and laid still. The two Grenar returned to their ranks.

The raven-haired one picked up his halberd, flipped the blade down, and drove it into the ground, right next to the Noriziem's head. He stood by it, both hands held behind his back. He barked a single word. *"Hrolta!"*

The formation of Grenar split down the middle, one side headed into the east woods, the other to the west. They ran as fast as they had during their attack, and were gone from the field in minutes. Hundreds of the beasts melted away. The lone Grenar still stood next to his halberd. He scanned the ramparts, his head moving from side to side in a calm, easy arc. The only sound was rain. Kailen watched him, the cold no longer clutching his insides. He was soaked, but it felt good, clean. The Grenar's eyes passed over him, then came back. Kailen shook his head, thinking he was imagining it, but the brute's gaze became fixed on him. Kailen stared back, trying to read the savage's granite face. The Grenar unfolded his arms, held his right fist over his chest and bowed deep. When he stood tall again he pulled his halberd out of the ground, turned his back to the Cardanans, jogged across the field, and disappeared into the forest. The Noriziem lay in the muck, moving only a little.

Chapter 13
FOR ALL HER LIFE

"Are you sure you want another, Al? How many fingers am I holding up?" asked Carra.

"Three, and I most certainly want another. The sun hasn't even set."

She patted his bearded cheek and carried his mug back to the kegs lined up behind her bar. "Did you want the Western Brown, the Eastern Amber, or the Southern Wheat?"

Alphonse Seadancer tugged at his beard and chewed his lower lip. "I'll take another Amber. The brewers gave this batch a nice, crisp bite."

Carra turned the tap and watched ale foam into the mug. The fingers of her right hand trembled. She shook them out and tried to remember if Kailen had drunk this brew. He liked reds. She slid the filled mug across the bar to Al, whose bear-paw hands cupped it without spilling a drop. He raised the mug and clacked it against those of his two friends, Eddard and Tomlin, whose own beers were still half-full.

They were the only patrons in the tavern. The fishing fleet had not yet moored, and it would be another hour before the merchants closed shop. Every day, when the sun painted the western cliffs, the three men would come in. Bald, silver-whiskered, and softened by age, they told anyone who would listen the same stories of the sea and fishing when it really was fishing. The spasm in her fingers wasn't getting better. She held her hand behind her and alternated between stretching her fingers and balling them into a fist. The shakes were coming more often.

Al drank deep from his mug, slammed it on the bar, threw his arms into the air, and shouted, "WHOOSH!"

Carra loved this one.

"And there it was before me, a leviathan with mottled grey flesh, black eyes, and razor teeth."

"Aye, and skin of steel and bladed fins, I'm sure," said Tomlin. Al blew through his whiskers and rolled his eyes, a small smile teasing the corners of his mouth. Carra put her elbows on the bar and rested against it. Her fingers were calming down. At least she'd made it through the last several days without coughing up blood. The kitchen sounds of girls banging pots and yelling at each other faded.

"It may as well have," said Al, "I, only eighteen, and out in my father's boat by myself, just a net, my line, and a fish spear. No one else around. Siren's Point is as lonely as they say. My grandfather spoke of huge sea bass living between the shoals, but none of the fleet went because of the rocks and current. I wanted to come home with a string of them, to prove he was right, and my father wrong."

"He didn't think there were bass up there?" asked Eddard.

"No, he thought I couldn't fish. That's not important." He paused to sip his beer, "The beast circled my boat. I had speared several bass and clouded the water with their blood. It was hungry and smelled the fish in my boat, which was only half as long as it. One flip of its nose, and I would be in the water."

Carra rubbed her nose, pretending it itched, trying to hide her smile. Last time the shark had been the same length of the boat, but twice as wide. And black. The trembling returned and she hid her hand behind the bar.

Another gulp of beer and Al continued. "So, I grabbed my only weapon, the spear. The shaft was only this thick around."

He stuck out his middle finger and grabbed it with his other hand, shaking it firmly. "The blade was bronze, not even steel. My father didn't trust me with those. If I hit the brute in the wrong place the blade would bend."

"I'd heard that happened when your brother tried to drive it into your head one night," said Eddard.

"You're confused, old man, that's what happened on your wedding night when you tried to bed Anna for the first time," said Alphonse.

Carra laughed. Al blushed. He was proud of his joke, but a little embarrassed he had made it in front of her. She saw Tomlin's drink was low and refilled it. She had to hold the mug in her left hand.

"As I was saying, if my spear hit the wrong spot, it would be useless. So, I stood on the gunwale, steadied the spear, and watched the beast circle me."

Alphonse held his left arm in front of him, as straight as the gout would allow, and pretended to track the moving shark. Carra poured herself a goblet of wine.

"The beast raised its head out of the water and smiled four rows of teeth. It turned towards the boat, meaning to knock me in the water."

His friends had shut up. It wasn't the first time they'd heard this story, nor would it be the last, but this part always quieted them. Al's barrel chest, softened by years of ale, tensed as he threw the spear with his right hand.

"My aim was true, and the bronze tip drove into its eye. It swerved, spewing blood and roaring in agony."

"Sharks don't roar," Tomlin said.

"This one did," Alphonse said. "It roared so loud, and so desperately, it chilled me to the core. Then it disappeared into the black water. I unfurled the sail and headed home. I've never gone back there, and I never told my grandda or my father about what happened."

Alphonse stared into his beer, swished the remnants around, then drained them. Carra refilled the mug. Her fingers steady for the moment, she ran her hand along his smooth, sun-polished head. His eyes were distant, his skin a few shades whiter than usual. She believed that part of the story, every time.

"I don't know how you did it, Al. All those years, going out on the waves. I hate the ocean. Kailen can never get me to swim beyond the surf."

"I'd be careful what you say, lass, that's the home of the Blue Lady," Eddard said. She knew he attended Temple twice a week. When was the last time she'd gone?

"It is, and I pray to Her every night and morning and thank her for everything she gives us," Carra said, "but I hate sharks, and they live there too."

After burping and thumping his fist into the middle of his chest several times, Alphonse said, "Speaking of Kailen, how is the boy?"

"No word for over a fortnight. He went out with Direpaw and some Legion commander. Almost two months, he told me, before he'd be home," Carra answered. She sipped her wine and stepped away from the men.

"Ye' miss him, don't ye' lass?" asked Alphonse, his coastal brogue thicker from drink.

She took another sip, this one deeper, and crossed her arms. Now her left hand was starting to misbehave.

"Just remember, he's out there fighting for you. He wants to keep ye' safe. The lad's a good man," said Alphonse as he leaned over the bar and patted her shoulder.

Carra nodded.

"Your father may not have liked him when he was young, but he would now. The lad has a strong heart and good sense. He'd never hurt ye'."

Finished, Carra set her goblet down and walked to the far end of the bar, checking the perfect rows of goblets and mugs beneath. Now Eddard told a story. She kept her back to them. Her lips trembled no matter how hard she squeezed them. The powder would stop the tremors, but she refused to take it this early.

The sunlight shifted to a deep, subdued orange, casting fire-colored pools on the tavern's floor. Fishermen, smelling of chum, sea, and sweat came in groups at a time. The merchants, all from the dock district, tended to arrive one at a time. The fishermen sat around the bar and at the tables close to the door. The merchants congregated around the back, sitting near the fire and close to the bard Carra had hired for the night. Playing a soothing melody on his flute, the scraggly boy looked even skinnier compared to the thick-armed fishermen and full-bellied merchants. Later, after ale clouded the room, his pipes would fill the tavern with their merry wail. She was looking forward to the pipes. Her father used to play them.

She stayed behind the bar, keeping the drink flowing and counting silver coins. Her girls carried the food out to the tables. Tonight was haddock and flat bread with boiled cabbage and carrots. She would have preferred to serve beef, or even mutton.

Everyone here ate fish all the time, so red meat was a treat, but the supplies in town were too low for her to turn a profit at the price.

Still, the men enjoyed their meal, and Carra counted more coins. Tonight looked to be a good one. The girls would earn extra. She was inspecting silvers from Wheat Scythe, a design she did not see often, when a warm, deep voice drifted over the bar. The shakes had subsided for the present.

"You might be the best looking thing I've seen all night."

Her throat filled. It sounded like something Kailen would say. Carra turned. A man with sandy-blond hair, green eyes, and chiseled, clean-shaven features leaned against the bar. His clothes were simple but clean, his teeth - straight and mostly white.

"Paedar Swiftstream, what brings you here?"

"You."

Carra smiled. The boy just wouldn't give up. At least he was handsome, something not all her suitors could say. She poured him a beer, handed it to him, and rested her elbows on the bar. She pressed her arms against her breasts. He had trouble maintaining eye contact.

"You're daft, boy. I'm four years older than you and taken."

"I see no ring on your finger, and I see no man next to you."

"Who ever said I needed one?"

Carra patted his cheek and walked away, swinging her hips just a little. It was only a game, but it kept her mind off Kailen. She'd heard rumors of a serious Noriziem attack to the west. Only rumors, but she tasted bile whenever she thought about it. She stopped to fill a goblet with wine. The cup almost slipped from her hands. Her fingers were numb, and she felt the shakes starting in her legs. She couldn't wait any longer.

Back in to the kitchens she stepped. The two cooking hearths danced with stoked fires. The sweet aroma of bread and fish thickened the air with flavor. Her cooks, Tilda, Rayna, and Korri, maintained a chaotic control over the scene. Carra kept her distance. She didn't want to distract them. Beth rushed by, carrying two trays of fresh bread. She smiled at Carra, but paid her little other attention. Behind some cupboards, she went to a small chest that sat tucked in a corner. She glanced behind her. The girls were all busy.

From the folds of her sash she produced a key, struggled to fit it into the rust-stained lock, and turned. Trying not to disturb the dust, she raised the cover gently. Inside was a tarnished silver and sapphire brooch, a black clay pipe inscribed with the compass rose of Carodan and the glyph of Antaunna, and a gold phial, no thicker than Carra's index finger. The sigil of the Nightsong sept, twin crescent moons riding over intertwined musical notes, had been deftly engraved into the surface of the vessel decades ago by some long-dead artisan.

She pulled out the stopper, the cork popping louder than she liked. She concentrated on steadying her hands and held the phial over her goblet, tapping it three times. A grey powder fluttered down into the wine, dissolving into little bubbles against the liquid's surface. Thinking a little more wouldn't hurt, she tapped again and set the goblet down. She secured the phial, pressing the stopper tight, locked the chest, and stood, stirring the wine with her finger. She sipped and frowned at its bitterness. The first taste was always the worst, but the shakes subsided immediately.

Back to the front, she found the tavern full. The musician had switched to the pipes, which blared loud and true. The men laughed and drank, each group trying to out-shout and out-show the next. Pipe-smoke clung to the ceiling beams. Carra drank from her cup, the sting of it slipping down her throat. She breathed deeply, loving the sweet pipe leaf smell and thinking of her father. Her limbs were light, as if filled with air, and she felt an almost urgent need to smile. Papa would be proud of how busy it was, and he would have loved the music.

A full and foaming mug in front of him, Alphonse sat alone at the bar. Eddard and Tomlin had probably gone home for the night. Al wasn't drinking and wasn't talking to the men on either side of his stool. With hunched shoulders he slouched there, his eyes unfocused. Her girls had everything under control, so Carra went over to him, leaned close, and whispered, "No crying in my bar."

Alphonse looked up, his eyes lagging a moment behind the movement of his head. He sniffed and said, "I wassana crying yet, lassie. Don't ya' worry, I'll be fine."

"What's on your mind?"

"Gretchen."

Carra laid hands on either side of Al's head and kissed his

brow. She wanted to say something to make the pain go away. The words never came. All she could think of was, "I know, dear."

She brought him a plate of haddock and bread, telling him to eat it so the beer wouldn't make him sick. He picked at the food and gulped his beer. It was best to let him be. She drank more from her cup and decided to walk through the tavern and talk with the guests.

Every step was an exercise in concentration. Her left foot followed the right. Her right foot followed the left. Each one wanted to go its own direction, and neither actually felt the floor. As the room tipped a little to the left, Carra had to close her eyes and tell herself it was not tilting.

She laughed with the patrons, traded dirty jokes with them, and flashed each one a smile. They would wrap an arm around her waist, she'd trail her fingers along their shoulder, and move on to the next table. The men would stumble over their stools to stand as she approached, and offer a beer-soaked seat. She'd decline, smile, and make them laugh with a witty line that she forgot the moment it passed her lips. She sensed Paedar's eyes following her the entire time.

Somehow she found her way back to the bar. She looked down into her wine glass, and it was empty. When had that happened? Her skin tingled, and when the cloth of her dress brushed against her legs a quiver traveled up her skin and directly between her thighs. Carra poured herself more wine. She thought of getting more of the powder but decided against it. She had done that once and had woken up the next morning on the bar with Kailen, splinters in her ass and drums pounding in her head.

The tavern was quiet now. At some point most had left and gone home to their wives or mothers. A few clusters of men still hovered by the fire. It seemed there was an arm wrestling contest on between the captains of two fishing vessels. She had no idea where the bard went. Had she paid him? Alphonse was still at the bar, his plate barely touched and three empty mugs in front of him. Carra went to his side and shook his shoulder. His head jerked and he blinked rapidly, his face a slate of confusion.

"Come on, Al. Let me get you to bed," said Carra.

"I can walk home lassie. Just point me in the right direction."

"Aye, and I can piss standing up. Now, stop arguing and take my arm."

Al conceded, taking her arm and sliding stiffly off his stool. His knees were frozen with gout. Sitting too long always did this too him. He was half-a-head taller than Carra, and his chest was still broad and thick, but it was she who supported him. His face was white and clammy, his steps were a shuffle, and by the time Carra got him to an empty room on the first floor, he was gasping.

She lay him down on the bed, took off his boots, and covered him with a blanket. She retrieved a pitcher of water and a clay mug from the bar and set it on the night table. Sitting on the edge of the bed, she wiped his face with a cool cloth. His breathing calmed, Alphonse muttered, "I'll pay ye' for the room in the mornin'."

"No, ye' won't. The beer, fine, but the room is on me. I'm not letting you walk home like this."

"We'll discuss it when the room isn't spinning."

Carra laughed, wanting to tell him that for her the room swayed side-to-side, and the candles all seemed like miniature suns, burning stubborn spots into her vision. Instead, she kissed him again on the forehead and started to stand. He gently grasped her forearm.

"You're a good lass. Kailen's lucky. Hold on to him. Hold on to each other. Ye' remind me of Gretchen and I, when we were younger."

"The two of us remind you of you? We're not wed, and he's a Warden. You were always here with Gretchen."

"He has duty and the forest, I had the ocean and my ship. Not as different as ye'd think. I left her many a morn' waiting on the shore, wondering if I'd ever be back. She'd cry, she'd rage, she'd beg for me to stop. But she never gave up on me, nor I on her."

"You were lucky to have each other. You made her happy."

"I pray so. I just wish I could have said goodbye. With the fresh sun I kissed her farewell and came home that night to find her sitting in her chair, cold and still."

Alphonse cried. Carra kissed him on the forehead, yet again looked for words that weren't there, and left the room. The door closed behind her, she leaned against it. The pressure on her back felt good, and it sent more jolts throughout her body. Churning and turning, her stomach wasn't happy though. Bile tickled her throat. She needed air.

The arm wrestlers were still at it, and another group by the door had started taking slugs of Citadel Whiskey. Carra wondered if they'd be spending the night on her floor. She giggled and then held her roiling stomach. The back door was her closest escape, and she cursed as she forced the rusted latch open. She leaned on the doorframe, the room was spinning, and if she stared long enough at a wall, it turned to liquid and slid to the floor. The sound of the ocean and its cool breeze called her. Teetering, she went out to the deck, leaving the door open behind her.

Standing at the railing, she wrapped her arms around the beam that held up the center of the deck roof. The moon was full, casting a thousand silver slivers on the black water. It reminded her of a tin mirror, warped and rippled with age. Reflected torch light mingled with the moonlight, and the dancing orange and white streaks made her forget where she was standing. She didn't even remember her name.

A creaking floorboard forced its way into her perception. A voice, deep and warm, said, "You shouldn't be out here by yourself. What if you fell in?"

"Well, young Paedar, I'd have to be extremely drunk to fall over my own banister. And, I'm not."

"Why do you hold onto the beam?"

He stepped next to her. The moon turned his hair near-white.

"Tired. Been a very long day. I'll sleep well tonight."

"Your bed will be cold."

"Are you implying I'm frigid, sir?"

Paedar stepped closer. Carra smelled the beer on his breath, but also the soap on his skin. He had bathed before coming to the Nightsong's Hearth. Her heart beat a little harder and she pressed the top of her right thigh into the beam. She stopped herself from gasping, but only barely.

"Far from it, my lady. Only that the bed would be empty."

"It will tonight, but not always."

"Too often."

He trailed a finger across her cheek, below her jaw, and down her neck. She drove her finger nails into the beam and leaned towards him. She pictured Kailen lying in her stone tub, scarred, bruised, and worn. She caught her breath and stepped away, turning her back to Paedar.

"That is none of your business. Kailen and I are a secret to no one in this town."

Everything was spinning, and their voices echoed in her head. Her fingers flexed with energy that had no place to escape. Her heart raced, and she tried to ignore the warmth between her legs. He was behind her now, gently grasping her shoulders and pressing close. He kissed her neck, and she let him. He pulled her closer, and she could feel his stiffness pressing through his breeches and against her bottom. The boy was large. Maybe bigger than Kailen.

She pulled away again. Fog crowded the edges of her vision. Her mind told her to lie down, but her legs wanted to run all the way to Everwatch. Well, that's what she told herself they wanted to do.

"What will it take to win you?"

There was no frustration in his voice. He stayed back this time, arms held behind his back. His chest was heaving and sweat beaded his forehead and neck. Carra tried, with little luck, not to look down by his waist.

"More than you have."

"When I inherit my father's fleet, I'll control a quarter of the fish market in Angler's Cove. I can give you money, silk gowns, and a house in the upper district; all the luxuries that come with being a lady of a high sept. Your bed will never be empty."

She thought of her sheets, cold and rough. Kailen's smell had faded long ago. The women from the upper district always dressed so beautifully. She imagined a gown of blue silk, trimmed in gold and ruby, fitting her body like a second skin. The bust would be elegant and flattering, the train ridiculously long.

"Why me? Many girls seek to catch your eye. I'm older than you and poor. Why chase things beneath you? Things you can't have?"

"I remember the first day I saw you. My father brought me down for my first ale in a tavern. He said yours was the best place in the entire Cove. You were behind the bar, smiling and laughing, and every man in the room was wrapped around your finger. Except him. He sat in the corner, away from everyone, with a damned pipe and a mug of ale you kept filling for him. I remember thinking, this is the perfect woman, and he doesn't even care."

Carra actually remembered that day. He had been young, but

even then Paedar was handsome enough to catch her eye. Kailen was recently returned from one of his first patrols. He had found a fishing crew washed up on the beach with their throats slit and the Mark of Galantaegan gouged into their foreheads.

"You don't know him. You don't know what he does for me. For all of us."

The fog was still in her sight, but it felt like her heart wasn't beating so hard, and the spinning was slowing. Paedar again stepped towards her.

"But what can he give you? A legion pension and a plot of overgrown land?"

The houses in the upper quarter were immaculate. The masonry and wood were always freshly sealed and the roofs newly thatched every year. The beds were like clouds, filled with so much down she imagined it was like disappearing into a fresh snow drift. The laughter of children would echo like music in the halls of such a place, and they would be raised with the money and privileges of a high sept. They'd never be cold on winter nights. Always have food. Never want for anything.

"He always stands by me. He would die for me."

"As would I. I would be the best man I could to you. I would never hurt you."

Carra saw Kailen's face twisted in rage and his white-knuckled fist ready to strike. What would it be like to have a man's arms embrace her every night? How would it feel to touch skin unscarred by blade and strife?

"Neither would he."

Paedar reached for her, she almost let his fingers touch her face, but she batted them away. How would it feel to love a man untouched by violence?

"Go home, Paedar. I'm tired."

He balled his fists, holding his arms straight and at his sides. He bit his lips, opened them to say something, and then closed them again. She realized he wanted to keep arguing.

"Go home, boy."

He rocked back, his eyes squinting. He turned and re-entered the tavern. Carra heard the front door slam. She went to the far end of the deck, where she could best see the town. The only light came from the lanterns lining the streets and the torches along the waterfront. She felt alone in it all.

Bending over the rail, she wretched as her stomach clenched and emptied. It gripped again and again, trying to cleanse her of the Hadari dream powder. When it finally stopped, her legs shook and her throat was raw. A film of blood covered her tongue. She sat on the deck and leaned her head against the beam. Tears burned her eyes.

"Kailen, where are you?"

Spinning and lurching, the world tried to pull away from her. The tears flowed unbidden, and sobs forced their way past her bloodied lips. Maybe, if she just let it go, the pain would stop. Everything would fade.

A hand gripped her shoulder. Rage cut through the disorientation. If it was Paedar she would hit him the same way she'd struck Kailen. Pushing away from the deck, which she was now somehow laying upon, she clutched at the shirt of whoever was leaning over her.

It wasn't a shirt. Instead, the lacing of a dress wrinkled under her balled fist. She forced her eyes to focus and found Beth's porcelain features darkened by weariness and concern. The young girl didn't seem fazed by Carra's grip. She loosened the fingers from her dress and placed a cup of water in Carra's hand. Still trying to determine up from down, Carra stared at the simple wooden vessel. Kailen's cousin, a girl who possessed the same piercing eyes as the Warden, guided the cup to Carra's lips and helped her drink. The cup drained, Beth helped Carra stand. Her faculties slightly restored, Carra asked, "Why are you here? Go home. Or go see your boy. Don't bother with me."

Beth slung Carra's arm over her shoulder and wrapped one of her arms around the older woman's waist. She allowed herself a small grin and said, "It's what Kailen would do."

Chapter 14
BY WORD OF LAW

"Why did it have to be Dora?" Morrikii again asked.

"I don't know, my Lord. I'm still trying to understand," Axehaft answered.

The two men stood on a hastily erected dais, in front of the great statue of Galantaegan in Cavern Centre. A crowd, dressed in dark wool and linen, stood before them. Their faces were still. The only sound came from the statue behind them, with its huge torch of a mouth burning high and strong. The four Noriziem khans had wanted to watch, but Morrikii forbade their attendance. This was a matter for House Stonestriker, no one else.

Loud enough for only General Axehaft to hear, Morrikii said, "I don't want to do this, Adeus. She's been like a mother."

"By your own word, my Lord, you must."

Morrikii couldn't meet his general's eyes. He knew the old man kept his face neutral, but those eyes, worn and gray, pitied him. Morrikii wanted an answer, not pity. Why did it have to be her?

From beyond the crowd he heard footfalls, steady and heavy with armor. The people parted, and through the center of the crowd marched six soldiers led by Jamon Brokesaw. The councilor had spent extra time slicking his hair back with oil, and his clothing and cloak were arranged just so. Morrikii thought the man still looked like a badger, just well groomed. Behind Brokesaw, and flanked by the guards, was Dora, her legs and wrists shackled. Her hair was neat, pulled back into a tight, silver bun. She held her chin high, the mouth above it a straight line. She looked Morrikii right in the eye.

Brokesaw climbed the stairs and kneeled. "Rise, Councilor," Morrikii said.

"My Lord, I present to you Dora Wooltaker, daughter of Rejerd Wooltaker and Camilla Hammersmith. She has been brought before you to answer charges of heresy and blasphemy."

"Bring forward the accused."

Morrikii bit his lower lip, forcing the lump from his throat. The guards led her up the stairs. The arthritis in her hips forced a grimace for every step. When she reached Morrikii, sweat beaded her lined face, but her eyes remained steady and her head high. He looked into those eyes, surrounded by life-earned wrinkles and again asked himself, how could she have done this?

"Councilor, the evidence please."

From the folds of his cloak Brokesaw produced a small, moth-eaten, leather-bound book and a string of prayer beads, each blue and engraved with the glyph of Antaunna. Morrikii took them and ran the beads through his hands and parted the pages of the book. Memories of evenings in Temple with his mother and father came flooding back as he glanced over the old sermons and prayers to the Blue Lady. He could still feel the cold granite against his knees as he kneeled in the great amphitheatre. Thousands of voices, in unison, called Antaunna's praises. The white stone had always looked so clean, and it caught the blue ghost-light that came from the great cistern at the temple's center the way a prism captures the sun. As the masses chanted, the priests would stand around the cistern, arms joined and praying. The sea water in the great stone vessel would churn and glow, and sometimes, if those gathered believed strong enough that day, the water would rise out of the cistern and take the shape of Antaunna. Morrikii still remembered the benevolent and loving face of the Blue Dragon.

Now, he stood in the halls of Galantaegan, surrounded by stone of onyx and black granite. Heat radiated from the statue behind him. The Black Dragon's effigy stared at his back, unblinking and teeth barred. This was the real god.

"Dora Wooltaker, are these yours?" Morrikii asked.

"Yes," she said.

The crowd, silent until now, rumbled a mix of shock and

disappointment. A group of old women, close to the foot of the dais, openly wept.

"Silence!" Morrikii barked.

Only the fire behind him dared break the quiet. Morrikii looked at the cover of the old book. It was emblazoned with the Seal of the Faith, a diamond shape with the glyph of Antaunna dominating the top half and the compass rose of Carodan taking up the lower half.

"Are they keepsakes, or do you use them?"

"I have prayed to Antaunna every morning and every night since we came to this miserable land."

Morrikii closed his eyes. His head tilted slightly to the floor. Why her?

"You spit in the faces of the people in this city. You've spat in the face of your god. You have spat in my face. Why have you committed this blasphemy?" Morrikii made sure every word was tinged with just the right amount of anger and hurt. The people needed to believe in him.

"My god is Antaunna, and always will be. I followed you to this rock because you are a good man and believe in your people. I still think you would have changed Carodan for the better, but I will never worship the Black Dragon. He stands for everything that almost destroyed our ancestors. I never meant any offense to you or the people. To him," Dora jerked her chin at the glowering statue, "I meant every offense."

Morrikii turned from her and walked to the back edge of the dais. He looked up to the ceiling, hundreds of feet above him, and asked for strength. The great columns of the hall closed in on him, hugging close and squeezing the breath from his lungs. Axehaft leaned over and whispered, "Hold fast, Morrikii."

With a flick of his wrist Morrikii threw the book and the prayer beads into the fire that roared in the stone mouth. They sizzled and hissed as they splashed into the large vat of oil hidden within the statue. He turned back to Dora and the crowd, his face a mask of righteous indignation. "You have willfully committed blasphemy and heresy in the face of Galantaegan. The only suitable punishment is death."

Dora did not blink. She didn't quaver. Her skin did not pale. She stared at the man she'd served for the last forty-six years. Even when General Axehaft drew his greatsword, she did not flinch. Morrikii took the sword from the general and asked Dora, "Do you have any final words?"

Dora nodded and kneeled. She clasped her hands and in the loudest voice her seventy-three-year-old throat would allow said, "Though I near the end of my path, my stride is certain. Though I come to the end of my days, I do so with calm."

The crowd gasped. Some had never heard Antaunna's Prayer For the Dead. For others it had been two decades. Brokesaw stepped towards her and raised his fist, ready to silence her. Morrikii gripped his shoulder. When his councilor turned a shocked face towards him, Morrikii said, "She deserves her final words."

Morrikii hefted the sword and walked behind Dora. She paid the commotion little heed and continued praying. "My journey has been blessed, and my wants few. I have stood on the edge of the world and seen grace."

Morrikii stopped on her right side. She had leaned far forward. Her head was tilted down and her scrawny neck, with its age spots and blue veins, stretched naked and open.

"I have cried, I have wailed, I have known despair. I have laughed, I have loved, I have known joy."

Morrikii spread his feet and spaced his hands on the hilt of the sword.

"The world I leave behind has been my shelter, my crèche. I now go to my new home by Her side. My time has run its course, it is time to say goodbye."

Morrikii raised the sword, holding it high over his head. In a whisper, so quiet almost he couldn't hear it, he said, "I am so sorry."

Dora whispered back, "Find peace."

The sword came down and cut through her neck in a single, smooth, blow. The crowd jumped as one. A mist of blood covered Morrikii's face. Dora's head rolled away, coming to rest at Axehaft's feet. Her body fell in a heap. Morrikii handed Axehaft the sword. He bent down, picked the head up by its bun, and walked to the edge of the dais. Bile surged up his throat, but he forced it back down. He took a deep breath and said to those gathered, "Remember, this is the fate of all who challenge the might of Galantaegan, of those who challenge me. Commit this face to your mind, and always think of how she brought this upon herself. Remember."

Morrikii turned to Dora's body and rested the head gently on the floor next to her neck. A pool, dark and crimson, was steadily spreading across the dais. "Brokesaw, clean this up."

"Me, sir?"

"Yes, you. I don't want her stink filling the hall."

"What should I do with the body?"

"Bury her outside in a marked grave."

"But, my Lord, she blasphemed!"

"Are you questioning me?"

"No, my Lord."

"Good. Axehaft, with me."

The general descended with Morrikii. In his gravel tone, Axehaft asked, "Where are we going, sir?

"Away from here."

***

Three days later, Morrikii still felt the weight of Axehaft's sword in his hand. He heard the clack of Dora's head against the stone dais. The blood still seeped from the ghastly wound. Even the cold wind and freezing sea spray of Fridinikar's coast couldn't drive the images away.

Standing on the cliff overlooking Slatewater Bay, he imagined the biting elements scouring him clean. Axehaft was with him, as well as the four Noriziem khans. All were bundled in furs and cloaks. The winds still howled down from the north, carrying a breath so chilled it would kill an unprotected man in minutes. Many said Remtagast the White, dragon of ice and death, made his home there. Morrikii believed it. The wind dug into every crack and gap in his coverings. He longed for the fire in his quarters, but endured the chill. Jenaka kept catching his eye with that look. Somehow, her company tonight didn't seem appealing.

In the bay below, scores of ships rode at anchor with sails furled and lines tight against the weather. His war galleys lay next to more Noriziem longships than he could count. This bay was where his people had first landed, over two decades ago.

"All the ships I can spare have arrived. Clan Nathikan is ready for war," said Khan Markan. He did not huddle against the cold. His furs flew about him in the wind, and his barrel chest was so inflated Morrikii thought if he pricked the khan with a dagger he'd flutter around like an air-filled bladder.

Instead, he placed his hand on Markan's shoulder. "Very good, old friend. Because of you we've hurt Carodan. Bled them. Sowed fear into their dreams. I couldn't have done it without you. General, how long until the rest of the Noriziem forces arrive?"

Morrikii knew the answer, and he enjoyed seeing the other three khans bristle that he didn't ask them directly. They needed to remember their place here. There had been no real need for them to come out here and observe the gathering fleet, but Morrikii needed to see the sky. Axehaft glanced at the khans and said, "Just over a month, my Lord. I received a courier hawk from our eastern fleet a few days ago. They met up with the Noriziem armada off The Empty Islands."

"Good. By then the chill will have lessened, and we can supply my army and yours," Morrikii nodded to the khans, "then load them back onto the ships and sail south."

"One thing troubles me, Stonestriker," said Toral.

Morrikii looked at the khan. Toral's face was blank, his eyes empty. He could never read the man. Only once had Toral shown emotion, and it had cost him his family's spear. "What is that, Khan?"

"When Ironheart exiled you here, with so many of your people, did he not ever think to send his navy to watch you? If they sail into this bay and see this, we're done."

Jenaka had asked him this same question a few nights ago, lying next to him and covered only in sweat. She always talked about war after sex. Morrikii would never admit it, but she frightened him. "There is truth to your words, Toral. For many years Cardanan war galleys visited these shores. Look to the southeast, see those buildings?"

The khans' gaze followed Morrikii's pointed finger. On a hilly slope, roughly a mile from the shore, stood the town of Stonedeep. The buildings, made of the same gray rock as the rest of the land, were squat and unadorned. A few plumes of smoke rose here and there, but otherwise the town was lifeless. Morrikii wondered if Dora's old house still stood. "My people built that town in three months. Before we found Frostwrath, before Galantaegan guided me to our home, that was all that protected us from Fridinikar and Remtagast's Breath." As if to punctuate his words, the wind gusted. "Now, the Cardanans never knew about Frostwrath, but if we had all simply disappeared from the town in a week's time, they would obviously become suspicious."

He held his hands behind his back and paced along the cliff edge. "So, over the years I kept a few garrisons of soldiers in the town. I would rotate them every month so no one had to spend too long out here. But, they made the town look alive, and when Ironheart's warships stood off our coast they saw a ramshackle town struggling to survive."

Morrikii kicked a rock off the cliff and watched it bounce down the rock face and skitter across the frozen beach. "They never landed to see how we fared. Never dropped supplies of food, or wood, or clothes. They were content to watch us freeze. The kindness of Antaunna."

Dora's recitation of the Prayer for the Dead echoed in his memory.

"With time, and planning, I gave them what they wanted. I kept fewer and fewer men in the town. The cook fires dwindled and the torches that lit the town at night became few. The graveyard on that hill there, to the right of the town, grew in size. The Cardanans didn't know they were just blank stones over empty patches of rock. Six years ago, when that entire hill top was covered, and the town was empty, they stopped coming. We're dead to them. Their ships will not bother us here."

Morrikii lowered his head, as if considering all the years passed. He was putting on a bit of a show, as he had when first meeting with all four khans, but Noriziem were temperamental. They needed to be convinced there was no unforeseen danger, and he was fairly sure there wasn't. Fairly.

Morrikii straightened, shook his head, and said, "Well, the past is the past. We're here for the future of all our peoples. Come, let us return to Frostwrath. The journey back is long."

They walked down the hill to a narrow road. Whoever had built Frostwrath had also paved a path from the beach to the mountain. It had taken his people some time to discover it, so covered by dirt, snow, and rocks it was, but now the way was clear. It was the artery between his city and the staging grounds. Two carriages awaited them, and as Morrikii climbed into his, with Axehaft, Jenaka, and Markan, he could only think of how much warmer Whitebreak was this time of year.

***

It was comfortable in his chambers. He sat by the hearth, at his desk with its piles of maps, battle plans, and supply requisitions. His third goblet of wine sat empty in his hand. He'd had to pour them himself. Margo was sick today and Dora, well... He stared into the fire, telling himself it had to be done. The people's belief in his iron will could not be compromised. The Noriziem needed to be convinced he had Galantaegan's favor. It was the only reason they had committed to the invasion. He was grateful to the Black Dragon. Galantaegan had guided them here, given them shelter, and taught Morrikii not only how to survive, but to thrive in this arctic wasteland. He could never repay their new god.

Morrikii couldn't remember when last he'd prayed. Perhaps today he should. Rising from the chair, Morrikii grunted as his back cramped in protest. Ignoring the lances of pain, he knelt before the fire and scooped some of the ash into his hands. He pressed his palms together and let the ash slip between his fingers as he recited the first Black Prayer he had ever learned.

Questions, confusion, and doubt
Surrounded by change and shifting
The only constant is pain, loss

The world brings pain
But I will strike first
If it brings me despair, I bring it death

Let those who wrong me be harmed
Let those who help me be blessed
Let those with questions never find answers

In the darkness there is truth
In ash there is simplicity
In me there is strength

He stood, feeling stronger. His regret over Dora's death would lessen. It was what was needed for his people. In half-a-year's time all of them would be returned to Carodan where the grass was green not bone-yellow, and the sky was blue not slate.

Morrikii walked to the table, raised the decanter, and poured another glass of wine. He hadn't been up to see Mella yet. What would he say about Dora? She had been Mella's favorite. His glass emptied quickly. No use in putting it off longer.

He heard her shallow breathing as he ascended the stairs. The room was quiet and cool as usual, only a few candles burning. Pulling aside the curtains that hung over the bed, he peered in. She was asleep. Her brittle hair spread around her, and her cheekbones were sharp as blades. Veins, purple and twisting, snaked beneath her paper skin. She'd been sick for so long, he often wondered if death would be better for her.

She opened her eyes and struggled to smile. "'Kii, I didn't think I'd see you today."

Morrikii sat on the edge of the bed and took her hand in his. "My work is done for now. We've stockpiled most of our supplies. We're just waiting for the Noriziem to arrive in full force. After that, I take you home."

He was glad she recognized him. She hadn't yesterday.

"I wonder if Whitebreak looks the same. It's been so long since I've seen it. I still remember the white towers reaching like fingers towards the sun. I can see the columns and amphitheatre of the Temple, the walls of the palace."

"Well," said Morrikii, "if it has changed, I'll put it back to exactly the way you want it. And I'll build us a cottage on the bluff overlooking the bay, in our spot. That way you can always look at the city when you want to."

"I'd like that."

He stroked the side of her face. It was ice cold. "Would you like any tea or something else hot?"

"No, but thank you, 'Kii. I haven't seen Dora lately. Where is she?"

Morrikii took a breath. He ran his tongue against the back of his lower lip and said, "Dora died seven days ago, Mella. It was in her sleep. The clerics think her heart failed."

"Why didn't you tell me sooner?"

The surprise and betrayal that cracked her voice cut Morrikii to the heart. "I wanted to, but you were in the middle of an episode. You weren't -- yourself. I couldn't reach you."

Mella opened her mouth, then closed it. She bit her lips, which were so dry they bled. She cried, her sobs weak and ragged. Morrikii didn't know what to say. He looked for words, something to make it better. Instead, he slid his boots off and lay under the covers. He smelled her sweat and what he thought may have been urine. He gently slid his arm under her and placed her head on his chest. She wrapped her fingers in the cloth of his tunic and pulled it tight as she cried.

He wanted to tell her the truth, wanted to tell her of how he hated himself for killing Dora. Would she understand it had to be by his hand and by no one else's? Would she know it was for the good of his people? Their people. He ran his fingers through her hair, gently untangling the knots. Maybe she would. She'd always been there for him before.

"Did her family bury her yet?" Mella asked.

"They did. She's in the graveyard on the northern slope, with her sister and niece."

"Before we leave, will you take me to see her? I want to say goodbye."

"I will."

"Promise?"

"I promise."

"I'm so tired, 'Kii. I wish I'd never become sick. I hate this bed. I hate this room. I hate this place. I want to go home."

"I know, Mella. If it means my death, I'll bring you home."

He lay with her for an hour. When her cries subsided and she had drifted back to sleep, Morrikii slipped his arm out from under her and left the bed. He poured her a fresh glass of water and made sure that the blankets covered her neatly and entirely. He'd have the servants change the bed with fresh linens tomorrow, and they'd give her a hot bath. She'd like that, assuming she recognized them tomorrow.

Morrikii went back to his study and looked at the papers piled on his desk. There were requisitions and deployment plans he needed to review, but his desire to do so was noticeably lacking. Instead, he went to the bookcase on the far side of the room, by the door to his bedchamber. He pulled a tall, brown leather journal from the top shelf. He sat down on the bench next to the fire and flipped through it. The first pages were sketches he had done of Sanctuary Bay during the dawn, when the shipping lanes were quiet and the city of Whitebreak sat on the southern shore, still sleeping. The middle pages were mostly drawings of weapons he had copied from books of history. The swords of the early Norizaad Empire had always fascinated him. The end pages of the book he'd filled after meeting Mella. He had used charcoal, ink, and umber to do these. Her red hair had always been the hardest thing for him to draw. He had done one sketch of her sitting by a pond, skirt hiked up to her knees and her feet dangling in the water. Another was of her before one of his father's galas. He had made her stand still for twenty minutes while he tried to capture every detail of the gown she wore. Never had he seen anything more beautiful.

His favorite sketch was the last one. It had been her idea. They had been on the bluff overlooking Sanctuary Bay, and she'd slipped off her dress. She stood on the edge of the cliff, her arms wrapped around her stomach and her chin tilted down and to the right. He had drawn it from behind, her form silhouetted against the bay and the afternoon. He'd always wanted to turn it into a painting but could never seem to find the time, and he was more gifted with charcoal than the brush. Maybe he'd hire a painter after he conquered Carodan. There had been a young artist who had lived in Wheat Scythe and was coming to prominence just as Morrikii launched his rebellion against the Ironheart Throne. He would not be so young now. What was his name? Oh yes, Iatoli Deepgrass. If the man was still alive, and if he survived the invasion, Morrikii would have him paint Mella's picture.

Chapter 15

EVERYTHING ONE DESERVES

Zaketh's steel-clad hand slammed into the Noriziem's jaw. Kailen flinched as the wet crunch snapped though the air and against his ears. Blood splattered over the table. Wet flecks overlaid dried streaks from this morning. Kailen had lost his temper and driven the man's face into the rough tabletop.

Five days they had done this. The Noriziem captain, left to them by the Grenar, had refused to speak. First, they had kept him in the legion dungeon without food and water. Then, they had stripped him naked and left him tied to a post in the courtyard. Still he didn't speak, not even revealing his name. Last night they had brought him here, into the heart of the legion barracks. There were no windows. The only light came from four torches mounted to the bare stone walls. The floor was cold slabs of granite, and the table and chairs were unfinished pine. Kailen, Rian, and Zaketh had stood all night and day circling the prisoner. Zak had been the first to hit him.

Kailen couldn't remember what the Noriziem's face used to look like. All cuts and blood now, his nose was smashed, his lips split wide, and his skin purpled. The gauntlets Zaketh wore, made of lobstered steel, were red, sticky, and dented. Half the man's teeth lay on the floor.

"Again, why did you attack? Who is your commander? What is your name?" Zaketh asked.

The Noriziem lifted his head. He blinked several times, visibly forcing his eyes to focus on Zak. The prisoner licked his lips, loosening some of the dried blood. He worked his jaw and cleared his throat. Kailen straightened, wondering if he would finally talk.

The Noriziem spit on Zaketh's face. Zak wiped the blood and saliva off with the back of his sleeve. "You don't learn, do you?"

Zaketh drove his right fist into the man's stomach. The Noriziem's breath blew past his ruined lips. Zaketh placed his left hand on the back of the man's head and rocked it back and forth. The ridges of the plate mail ground into the man's scalp. Kailen turned away. Since slamming the man's head into the table this morning Kailen hadn't touched him. Watching the Noriziem spit out his front teeth had bothered the warden more than he'd shown. Rian hadn't laid a hand on the Noriziem, but he'd come close. When the Noriziem was first brought in, Rian had Nina waiting for him. She had stood her front legs on the Noriziem's lap, her muzzle inches from his face, and her fangs barred. The man never flinched. Rian had then taken out one of his kukaran knives and sharpened it while sitting across the table. The Noriziem had watched the whet stone trace along the edge of the wicked, curved blade, but still did not speak. Angry, Rian had grabbed the man by the front of his tunic, brought his knife a hair's breadth from the Noriziem's throat, and screamed like a madman. Nothing. After Zaketh had hit the man Rian withdrew. He lent his presence to the proceedings, but little else.

Kailen didn't know how to act either. He often looked away, thinking no man should be treated this way. Fighting with a weapon in your hand was one thing. You could defend yourself and be on equal terms, but when tied to a chair and stripped down to his woolen hose, the blood of the Noriziem was less satisfying somehow. Whenever he looked at the Noriziem he felt pity.

When he felt that pity, he would think of the burned homes, the dead soldiers, and the slaughtered townspeople. He would look at the Noriziem and smile whenever Zaketh hit him. He deserved this. Of course he did.

Zaketh stepped back. He flexed his hands, took a deep breath, and said, "This isn't working. Let's try something else. Guard! Bring in the prisoner's belongings."

A legionnaire entered, carrying a small leather satchel. Zaketh gathered it from him and dismissed the soldier. There were three items in the bag, and Zak laid each on the table, one-by-one. First, was a small obsidian statue of Galantaegan. Second, a small book bound in soft, black leather. Third, a small square of embroidered cloth. Kailen looked at it, seeing both lilacs and thistles stitched across it with an expert hand. The Noriziem's eyes lingered longest on this last piece. Zaketh picked the items up. He handed Rian the book, he gave Kailen the kerchief, and kept the statue for himself. He held the statue up to the torch light. The fire danced across the carved obsidian, covering it with a thousand tiny flames. The dragon's head was reared back, its front claws stretched before it, grasping at the air. The wings were folded in tight against the body. Zaketh nodded his head appreciatively. "Beautiful craftsmanship. Whoever made this has great talent, but there is a problem."

Zaketh kneeled in front of the Noriziem. "Galantaegan is an abomination. To worship chaos and vengeance is barbaric. Ignorant really. It amazes me that you as a people still exist after centuries of worshipping this demon. Here, on Cardanan soil, such effigies are forbidden. I'm required to destroy this."

The Noriziem pinched his mouth shut. He looked down at the floor and refused to meet Zaketh's eyes. He flexed his hands, tied to the chair behind him, but still they did not budge or find any slack.

"Of course," said Zaketh, "I might be convinced to let this survive if you told us why you attacked with such a large force and who sent you."

The Noriziem did not look up. He remained locked on a seam in the floor and did not move his gaze. Zaketh sighed. "Very well, your choice."

He stood and went to a large gap in the wall where the settling and shifting of the stones had pulled apart the masonry. The head of the statue fit the gap easily, sliding all the way in to the shoulders. Zak pulled quickly to the right, and the snap of breaking volcanic glass echoed in Kailen's ears. The Noriziem's shoulders twitched, but he did not raise his eyes. Zaketh took the two pieces of the statue and went to a corner of the room. There sat a chamber pot the three of them had used that morning. The pieces plunked into the urine and settled on the bottom. Zaketh pointed at Rian. "Warden Direpaw, what's in that book?"

The Noriziem glanced at the book then resumed staring at that seam on the floor. Rian, who had been fingering through the book, said, "I think it's a journal. I understand bits and pieces, but it looks like dated entries, logs of a sea voyage, verses from their scripture, and even a few sketches. There's even one in here of a black mountain with a gate carved into its base. Don't know what to make of that."

"But it looks important?" asked Zaketh.

"If it were mine, I'd say yes."

"How about it, Noriziem? Will you save this?"

The beaten man closed his eyes. Kailen could see a tear trace its way down his cut cheek, but he did not raise his head.

"Burn it," said Zaketh.

"Are you sure that's wise? The information may be important," said Rian.

"Nothing matters but breaking him. Burn it." Zaketh's tone brooked no argument.

Rian flipped through the pages once more. He looked at the Noriziem, swallowed, and stepped to the nearest torch. He held the top edge of the book in the flame. It took some time to catch, but when it did he set it on the floor in front of the Noriziem. The flames, reflected in the Noriziem's empty stare, slowly and surely ate away the journal. After the flames died, Zaketh scooped up the black flakes and said, "Ash, how appropriate. This is the symbol of the Black One, is it not? I wouldn't want you to be without your god. Here is Galantaegan's essence."

Zaketh held his palm out flat and blew the ash into the Noriziem's face. The prisoner closed his eyes but gave no other reaction. Zaketh pointed to Kailen. "What about that sorry rag in his hands? It looks like some little, ignorant bitch from the old world stitched that for you. Is she your wife? Your lover? Your whore?"

The Noriziem shook. His knuckles were white and his forearms corded as he tried to stretch his bonds. He grit his teeth. Zaketh chuckled. "Well, that answers one question. You do understand Cardanan. You're just being uncooperative. So unwise."

Zak punched the Noriziem in the face. Kailen closed his eyes as the man spat more blood-covered teeth. He thought of the dead soldiers. The dead men and women. The dead children. He looked down at the piece of cloth. It was lovely work. He pictured the Noriziem standing on some dock, halfway across the world on the shores of Granikar, and saying goodbye to his woman. Was she blonde? Brunette? Fire-topped? Maybe she was thin, with small breasts and narrow hips. Kailen looked at the Noriziem and decided not. He looked like a man who preferred a woman with curves. Kailen pictured long, rich brown hair, full breasts, and hips curved just right to embrace a man. He thought of Carra and her touch. He tried not to think of the girl from the night of the festival. He still didn't know her fate after the battle.

"Tidespinner. Tidespinner!"

Kailen shook his head. Zaketh glared at him, anger creasing his face. Kailen's insides chilled. Darksteel's face was so hard, his eyes so focused and cold, he could have been made from the granite surrounding them. There was no remorse or conflict evident upon his features, only calculated, controlled rage. "Yes, Commander?"

"I gave our friend here a choice. He can either speak, or you cut that little rag to shreds."

"Of course, Commander."

Kailen pulled a dagger from his boot. He hadn't used it during the battle so it was still sharp. He draped the cloth over the tip of the blade and held the edges with his free hand. A quick push and the blade would cut through the center. Kailen knew the Noriziem watched him.

"How about it, friend? Speak and you keep this one last trinket. Remain silent, and I'll have him cut it to shreds and throw the pieces into the chamber pot."

The Noriziem said nothing. He stared at Kailen, anger, desperation, and longing all flicking across his face. He opened his mouth, took a breath, but then closed his mouth and looked down to the charred spot on the floor. Zaketh nodded to Kailen.

The tip of his dagger sliced through the linen as easily as he thought it would. He drew the kerchief halfway down the blade and then pulled it away from his body. The tearing of the cloth seemed loud and rude in the small room. The Noriziem wept, making no attempt to hide the tears.

Kailen focused his attention on the kerchief. The threads frayed and snapped. The lilacs and thistles twisted and distorted as he cut the cloth into more pieces. With every rip he tried not think about the hands that made this. He thought of the people being buried right now, of his own parents beneath their cold tombstones. If it hadn't been for the Noriziem they would still be with him.

The kerchief was shredded. Kailen walked over to the chamber pot and dropped in the remnants. The strips of fabric floated on the yellow liquid. Beneath them the broken statue of Galantaegan looked up at him. The eyes appeared angry and alive, but Kailen just told himself it was a trick of the torchlight playing across the surface of the piss.

He looked at the Noriziem as he walked back to his spot across the table. Kailen didn't think the man would break. Zaketh was pacing behind the prisoner, rubbing his chin. He called to the sentry. "Guard, see if Father Frostwind is available. Tell him I need his services after all."

Kailen wondered what that meant. He'd no idea Zaketh had even spoken to the priest. Last Kailen had heard, the Father was still recovering from the spell he'd cast at the battle. It was rare for anyone to cast magic like that. Kailen was unfamiliar with the manifestation of Antaunna's Power, but from what little he did know it took huge amounts of will and energy for a person to do what Father Frostwind had. The man was lucky he was still alive. What services could he possibly offer?

Several minutes passed. Kailen avoided eye contact with Rian and Zak. He kept looking at the chamber pot where the pieces of the kerchief, stained yellow, had settled to the bottom. He thought of all they had put the prisoner through and wondered if he could be as strong as the foreigner. Would he have broken? What would it take for him to betray his people? Was it right what they were doing?

Of course it was, he told himself. They had to stop the Noriziem from doing this again. They had hurt Carodan badly. Too many people were dead. They had to do whatever they could to gather information. Even this.

Kailen heard soft foot-falls approaching. The door creaked open and Father Frostwind shuffled in. His face was drawn, his skin pale even in the orange torch-light. He hadn't combed his hair. He held a worn book under his left arm and carried a large bowl of water with both hands. He nodded to Kailen as he passed, setting the bowl on the table and lowering himself into a chair. Frostwind sighed as he took the weight off. A thin film of sweat beaded the priest's forehead. He dabbed it with a cloth produced from the sleeve of his robe and said, "So, Commander, there had better be a damned good reason you disturbed my rest. Turning the tide of your battles is exhausting."

Zaketh bowed his head just slightly. "I'm sure it is, Father, and for your efforts we are grateful. If it weren't for you, the town would be lost. But, I'm afraid our guest here will not speak with us. It's crucial he does."

The Noriziem sneered at Frostwind. He recognized the man as a priest of Antaunna, Kailen realized. The prisoner's eyes darted between Frostwind and the bowl of water. The priest stroked his beard and said, "He's been treated harshly. Perhaps all he needs is the caress of our beloved Lady."

As Frostwind pulled the book from the crook of his arm and started flipping though its yellowed, cracking pages, Kailen wondered what he could mean. He jumped when Frostwind said, "Ah ha! Here we go. It's been a long time since I've done this, but I think it will serve."

Frostwind laid the book on the table, pressing the spine flat. He lowered his head and clasped his hands. Through half-opened eyes Frostwind read from the book. Kailen realized, with no small amount of shock, that it wasn't an ancient spell the priest was reciting, but it was the same prayer said in temple when the congregation tried to summon the shape of Antaunna from the Holy Cistern. The air temperature dropped, and Kailen shivered. Goose pimples covered his skin. The water in the bowl boiled and swirled even though no flame was near.

As Kailen watched, the water flowed over the edge of the bowl, but it didn't spill. Tendrils of the clear fluid weaved around the bowl and across the table. They twisted and melted into each other until Kailen saw a leg here, a wing there, and from the top of it all, a head on a long, slender neck. In temple the water column, at most, only resembled Antaunna. But now, before his very eyes, was a small, perfect dragon made of water. It stretched its neck and back. It flapped its wings which made a surging, sloshing noise as they beat against the air. The torchlight caught every ripple and pulse on the dragon's surface. It was a creature of water, shadow, and fleeting light.

Frostwind opened his eyes and said, "Ahh, yes. Master Noriziem, I would like you to meet a very small part of our Goddess."

The priest flicked the fingers on his right hand, and the dragon floated across the table, gently climbed the Noriziem's chest, and began to circle his neck. Kailen noticed the small, wet paw prints it left on the front of the Noriziem's tunic. Its movements were hypnotic. It moved so gently, caressed the prisoner's skin so perfectly, that he actually closed his eyes and smiled. The dragon flowed over his face, washing away the blood and grime. Kailen could see the clouds of crimson flow through the body of the dragon as more and more of the Noriziem was cleansed.

Frostwind leaned forward and whispered, "Do you feel her touch? I still remember when I was a boy and first taken into the Monastery. The High Priests summoned something very much like this. I had never felt such love, such understanding. It all made sense. This is what we can offer you. Have you ever felt that with the anger and chaos of Galantaegan?"

The Noriziem's head tilted back. His eyes were closed and he rocked in his chair. The relief and pleasure on his face was impossible to misunderstand. Kailen thought maybe this would be it. Maybe they had tried to break him the wrong way.

The Noriziem pulled his head straight. He opened his eyes and blinked rapidly. Looking at Kailen, he seemed to remember where he was. He sneered and the hatred painted across that ruined face forced Kailen to take a step back. As the dragon passed by the Noriziem's mouth he actually pressed his lips to it and drew in. The dragon twisted and pulled until it broke free from the Noriziem and fluttered down to the table. It seemed a little smaller to Kailen. The Noriziem looked at Father Frostwind and sprayed the mouthful of bloody water in his face.

Frostwind produced his kerchief and dabbed the water off his face and out of his beard. Zaketh stepped forward, his steel-clad fists raised. The priest waved him back. He put away his kerchief, looked the Noriziem in the eye and said, "That was unwise."

He waved his fingers again and the dragon arched its back, spread its wings, and with speed that only water possesses, flew from the table at the Noriziem's face. The dragon narrowed, becoming a single tendril of water. It flowed up the Noriziem's nostrils. The prisoner's face stretched with panic as his lungs filled with water. He coughed, or tried to. His chest heaved and convulsed. No matter how hard he wrenched his muscles he could not push the water out of his lungs.

Kailen felt sick. No man deserved this. He looked to Rian. His friend was bone-white and still. The senior warden stood with clenched fists, trying not to shake. Kailen looked to Zaketh. The commander stood still, unflappable and calm. The objectivity and interest in his eyes scared Kailen more than the water filling the Noriziem's lungs. Kailen looked to Frostwind. The priest's mouth was pressed into a grim line, his eyes cold flecks of slate. Kailen felt the hatred and pain emanating from the priest. What was happening? Is this what they had become? Was this the type of man his father would have wanted him to be?

Frostwind flicked his fingers again and the water forced its way out past the Noriziem's lips. It reformed into the dragon and poured onto his chest, clinging to the prisoner's tunic, spreading its wings and hissing. Frostwind leaned towards the Noriziem and said, "I can hold this spell for an hour. After some rest, I can do it again. I will fill you with the gentle touch of our Goddess until you break. And I will break you. Tell us what we want to know."

The Noriziem's ragged, stuttered breathing rasped against the stone walls. The room was hot with soot and body heat. Kailen prayed the man would break. What was worth tolerating so much pain? The Noriziem coughed blood all over the water-dragon. He worked hard to steady his breathing. He opened his mouth and said, "Nenqa."

"What does that mean?" asked Zaketh.

"Never," said Frostwind.

Kailen closed his eyes. Would this ever end? Frostwind sent the dragon back into the Noriziem. It went in slow this time, oozing up his nose and forcing its way through the pressed crack of his mouth. The man gulped for air, but Kailen knew all he felt was the water. He remembered when he was a boy, playing with Carra in the surf at Angler's Cove. A big wave had broke on them, knocking him down. Panicking, he'd tried to scream underwater. The cold saltwater had filled and burned his lungs. He remembered his body shaking and pushing the same way as the Noriziem's. Identical desperation had surged through his body. It had been Carra, half his size and laughing, who had pulled him up and helped him find his footing again. Kailen watched the Noriziem and knew this man's savior was half-a-world away.

The water dragon surged from the Noriziem's mouth. This time it wrapped itself around his neck and squeezed. Not so tight as to stop breathing, but enough to keep the panic in the Noriziem's eyes. He sobbed. His shoulders slumped and his mouth was so slack that the dragon would be able to hold its shape the next time it entered him. Kailen wanted to say something to stop this, but what? This man had led soldiers that decimated Littletop. He deserved this. But, Kailen thought as he looked at the Noriziem, he is a man as well. A brave one. Kailen admired him for not breaking, but what could he do? If he asked them to stop, Darksteel and Frostwind would look at him as weak. He could appeal to Rian, and maybe the two of them could stop this, but he knew what the senior warden would say. This was necessary for the safety of their country. So, Kailen stood silent.

"Will you talk?" asked Frostwind.

"Nenqa."

The Noriziem closed his eyes and breathed deep. Muscles in the prisoner's arms tightened and corded. He wrenched his right arm and pulled it loose of the bindings. Tendons popped like snapped bowstrings under the strain. The Noriziem reached across the table and grabbed Frostwind around the neck and squeezed. Through ruined lips he whispered, "He comes for you."

Kailen moved without thought. Looking back, days later, he didn't know how his dagger ended up in his hand. Had he never put it away? Had he drawn it on the move? He had no idea. But, with clean aim he drove that dagger under the Noriziem's jaw, through Antaunna's image, and up into his brain. In the shortest second Kailen ever experienced, his glance met the Noriziem's, and he saw only thanks in those beaten, tired eyes.

The Noriziem's grip on Frostwind loosened, and he slumped onto the table and then slid to the floor. The water dragon thrashed and squirmed, losing cohesion. It ran over the Noriziem, soaking his shirt and staining the floor. The water ran into rivulets through the seams of the flagstones. Some of it followed the slant of the floor and collected around the chamber pot. Frostwind rubbed his throat, coughing. Zaketh was frozen in mid-step, his arms outstretched and ready to tear the Noriziem off Frostwind. Kailen was glad he had been faster. Zaketh wouldn't have killed the Noriziem, only prolonged his torment. The young warden wanted no more to do with it. He was glad he'd killed the man. Rian left the room, his skin pale and tinted green. Kailen heard him vomit in the corridor. His own stomach was a pit of unrest, and it would empty if he wasn't cautious. He had never seen Rian this unsettled. He left the room, wiping the dagger on his cloak and refusing to acknowledge Darksteel or Frostwind. His duty was fulfilled.

***

Frostwind rubbed his throat. It would bruise. His body did not need the abuse. Every joint ached and every muscle screamed exhaustion. The spell he'd cast during the battle had drained most of his strength. It had almost killed him, really. Remtagast's chill grip had not been far away that following evening, Frostwind knew. How his soul found the resolve to resist the White Dragon's call he did not know, but he almost wished it hadn't. His role was that of a healer, a spiritual guide and teacher. He prayed with the people. Led them in worship. Healed their wounds. He'd just tortured the dead man who now lay slumped before him, and did so using the image of their god. It went against everything he stood for.

And he didn't even care. Kailen and Rian had already left. Zaketh pulled back the dead Noriziem's head, snorted, and let it fall forward again. He muttered something about sending the guards in to clean the mess and nodded his farewell to the priest. Frostwind acknowledged with an absent wave, but was unable to break his stare from the dead man.

That's what he was. A man. No different than himself or Zaketh or Kailen. But the pain he'd brought upon Littletop made him easy to hate. A blind, searing, undiscerning hate. Frostwind never knew himself capable of such emotion. It felt foreign and dirty. It felt satisfying. The pain was so great it burned through his chest. Sobs threatened to push their way up his throat, but he clamped them back. He had not the energy to cry.

Life in the frontier was fraught with inherent danger. Townspeople had died under his care before. Whether it was a mining accident, an animal attack, or a drowning, death was unavoidable. Sometimes a body sustained too much damage to be saved, even by the healing powers of Antaunna. In the past, that sadness had always been tempered by joy. From the simple pleasure of chatting with parents after the children's Temple Lessons to the wonder of birth, those moments counterbalanced the shadowed instances of life. He still remembered delivering a son to the Stonehew family. A strong lad, it was their first boy. Their oldest daughter, Natasha, was a red-haired firebrand who stirred up trouble with all the young men in Littletop. Frostwind would never forget the way she hugged him after he delivered her brother. Her kiss on his cheek lingered just slightly too long and her fingers trailed across his back as she released her embrace.

He'd only laughed at himself that evening. An imagined attraction. What could a stunning woman like her see in a tired old man? Besides, being a priest, he was sworn to celibacy. A sacred vow. Almost as sacred as the oath not to use Antaunna's power to harm others.

Collecting his things, he stood and shuffled out of the claustrophobic room. Sleep is what he needed, and nothing would keep him away from his bed. A now empty and cold bed. He would pray first. Maybe there would be absolution in the words of Antaunna. Some passage of transcendent text that placed the events of the last several days in a context that made sense. The holy words were a source of guidance and strength. They gave light in the darkness. Every Cardanan was taught this from birth.

The books. The Temple. He'd tried his best to forget their fate, but reality flooded his struggling spirit. A few of the townspeople, those tending him during his recovery, had described what happened to the Temple. The stained-glass windows were shattered. The Noriziem had overturned the Holy Cistern and set flame to anything that would burn. The tapestries, libraries, and roof were turned to ash. All that remained were the stone walls and floors. There was hope in that the Noriziem did not have time to damage the integrity of the structure. Rebuilding the Temple was possible. They just needed the time to heal and the resolve to press on. Antaunna would hold them through the darkness. They would stand tall and endure as always. Cardanans were a people tempered by struggle. From this destruction a new strength would emerge.

Frostwind stopped in a quiet corner of the stone corridor. He leaned against a wall and caught his breath. A Legion banner, with its proud compass rose, stared at him. A new strength?

The only thing he saw in people's eyes and felt in his heart was despair. He chided himself for foolish hope. He let the anger in. Let the hate dwell in his core. It numbed the pain and muted the sorrow. How could man visit such horrors upon others? How could such senseless killing exist? How could Natasha be gone?

Chapter 16
WHAT DOES A NAME MATTER?

"How are you?" asked Kailen.

They were outside the legion barracks. Rian wiped the corners of his mouth and spit bile onto the cobblestone. Wax-white, his skin shimmered with cold sweat, and his eyes wandered without focus. Nina, who'd waited for them outside the barracks, ran to her master's side. Rian kneeled down and hugged the wolf, burying his face in the thick fur of her neck.

His fingers digging in behind Nina's ears, Rian said, "I'll be fine. Just not feeling well."

"I don't believe you," Kailen said. Rian's skin was still deathly white.

Rian stood, cracked his knuckles, and scratched Nina behind the ear. Pressing into his knee, and still whining, Nina didn't seem to believe Rian either. He cuffed her behind the ears and waved her away. With lowered head and ears, she lay in a corner.

"It's not your place to question me, Warden."

In all the years they'd served together, Rian hardly ever acknowledged the rank difference between them. Nodding, Kailen let it go. This was unusual for his friend, and he wasn't sure what to say. He was unsure of his own feelings. The Noriziem's blood still stained his gloves.

Turning to what remained of the town, they left the barrack's courtyard. Fires still smoldered and a dirty, brown haze hung low over the shattered rooftops. Ruined walls and debris clogged the alleyways. They walked across the main street and had to circle a catapult stone. Most of its pitch was burned away, but it was ringed by the blackened remains of the cart it had obliterated. Around them, soldiers and unwounded townsmen worked to clean the roads and gather bodies. Following the main road, they arrived at the square where Kelebra de'al Verdan had been held just a few nights ago. Now it was home to the dead. Laid out in neat rows, they waited for someone to identify and collect them. If they lay there too long they were put into a mass grave on the eastern border of the town. They couldn't be allowed to rot.

Kailen wasn't sure he wanted to go further. He had not seen the serving girl since before the battle. The interrogation had occupied most of his time, but even when he'd left the Noriziem alone, he'd stayed in the barracks. What if she were here? With every woman he passed in the street, he searched for her. Hoping to spot those blue eyes, blonde hair, and delicate face, he prayed for her safety. Ignoring the desire to remove his armor, lie down, and sleep for as long as he could get away with, he turned back to Rian. "Get some rest. You look terrible. I have something I need to take care of."

"I'll help you find her."

"You met her only once," Kailen said.

"By met, you mean I found you two in bed. Right?"

"You could have knocked."

"I'm glad I didn't. She was gorgeous," Rian said and shrugged. "What makes you think she's here?"

"I hope she's not. Come on, let's start."

"You don't need to trouble yourself, and some sleep might do you good."

"It's fine. Besides, dreams are the last thing I want."

Death hung sweet and thick in the air. The clouds of flies were inescapable. If Kailen breathed through his mouth to lessen the stench, he swallowed flies. If he breathed through his nose, his innards clenched. Scores of people lay in rows upon the flagstones. When possible, they were covered with a sheet, but most lay with only a shred of their own clothing over their face. Maybe he had killed the Noriziem too soon. He glanced at Rian. Instead of white the senior warden's face was tinged green.

Scanning the bodies, Kailen asked, "Why did the interrogation trouble you so much?"

"Interrogation? That was torture, my friend. I'll cut anyone's head off in a fair fight, but a man deserves to stand with honor and defend himself."

"But look at what they've done," Kailen said, pointing to the sea of still Cardanans, "He was one of the commanders. Perhaps he deserved it?"

Rian fiddled with the pommel of one of his kukaran knives, working a piece of grime out of the decorative grooves. "Not long after I'd joined the Legion, but before I became a Warden, I was on patrol in the southern reaches of Westlook, among the foothills of the Forlorn Ramparts. A group of outlaws had made the place their home and were preying on the new settlements in the area."

The two men stopped. People pushed past them, paying their weapons and armor no heed. They too were scanning the dead, trying to find a husband or a wife. A daughter or a son. A brother or sister. A lover. Rian chewed his lower lip, the bristles of his ragged beard scrapping against his lips. His gray eyes drifted away, looking back more then ten years. "My century was ambushed in a ravine. The line commander was an idiot, fresh from the Academera Militarium. Our sergeant told him not to go in there, but what did he know? Only I survived."

The smell of rotting flesh tightened Kailen's stomach. He swallowed, forcing it to calm. Unsure of why Rian had decided to open up, he remained quiet. His mother once said the best listeners rarely spoke. He swatted away a swirling ball of gnats.

"They took me to this series of caves, the main base we'd been searching for. There were more of them than we'd thought. At least six score. They wanted to know how many legionnaires were in the region and how we were deployed. I wouldn't talk."

Rian forced the grime from the pommel, but his broken fingernail still worked the spot. "First, they dunked my head into a bucket of water, holding me down a little longer each time. Then they hung me by my arms from a rack. If I'm not careful my left shoulder still pops out of the socket. Then, they took slivers of iron, heated white, and slid then under my fingernails."

"By Antaunna."

"That wasn't the worse though. A young girl was brought before me. They'd snatched her from the edges of her sept's settlement. If I spoke, she lived. Duty kept me silent. The dagger cut her so easily."

Again Kailen wondered if he had that same strength. A

few nights ago he was unable to resist the temptation of flesh. And why? Because he was scared he'd never feel the touch of a woman again? Because he might not live through the following day? Because he'd never see Carra? She deserved better than he. Someone with greater strength. "What happened next?"

"A few minutes later a silver horn sounded. The mighty Legion arrived. Finally finding the caves, they stormed in, rounded up the bandits, freed me, and brought the girl's body home to her parents. If they had been there just a little earlier, we could have saved her. If I had broken I might have saved her. But she died, and no matter how much I want to go back and save her, I can't."

"No one deserves that. I am sorry, my friend."

"Exactly."

Kailen thought of the relief on the Noriziem's face as his dagger had pierced the man's brain. Part of him was satisfied with ending the Noriziem's suffering. He rubbed his face, not knowing what to think anymore. It was easier when the man had just been "the enemy" and not a man. He needed Carra. Looking at the lines of bodies, he prayed to Antaunna the serving girl wasn't here.

They walked further, heading to the courtyard's center. Teams of men picked up the more decayed bodies, and here or there people cried over someone who couldn't hear them. Rian saw her first.

"Oh, Kailen."

His friend's tone left no need for question. He followed Rian's eyes to the edge of the courtyard. Maybe he was mistaken, it could be someone different. There were many blonde girls in the world.

It was her. Navigating between the bodies, they reached the girl's corpse. Her eyes stared open, blue and clouded, and the yellow-green of decay tainted her skin. Much longer and the grave detail would have taken her. Jagged and wide, the wound on her stomach was crusted with dried blood.

"It doesn't make any sense," Kailen said.

"It rarely does," said Rian, "What was her name?"

"She never told me."

"Someone must know," Rian said.

An old woman, bent with age and wearing a torn cloth over her face, hobbled past. Kailen gently grabbed her shoulder.

"Excuse me, ma'am. Do you know this girl? We're trying to," he paused, "find her family."

The woman raised an eyebrow, looked down at the girl, and said, "She doesn't have family here. She'd been in town only a few weeks. A refugee from Shark Bay I think. I heard all her family died there. She came here to start her own life."

"Do you know her name?" asked Kailen.

"No, she kept to herself. Lived over the Miner's Inn," the old woman said and pointed to a part of town that had burned to the ground, "Now, if you'll excuse me, I have to find my son. He was a legionnaire. Maybe you know him. His name is Randall."

Kailen paused, opened his mouth, and then closed it. He could tell her he had never heard of Randall. Maybe he'd tell her to check over by the gate. Why should he be the one to tell her? Enough pain had been delivered this day. He licked his lips and said, "I fought beside Randall on the wall. He was a great soldier. The Noriziem's fire burned him when they breached the gate. I am so sorry."

The woman said nothing. She turned away, her shoulders a little lower, the hunch in her back a little greater. There were no words of comfort.

He looked back to the girl. She had been beautiful. Gentle, warm, and receptive, Kailen knew she'd possessed a generous soul. He had thought about Carra the next morning, but it didn't seem to matter much. He'd been so sure he was going to die. "I'm tired."

Rian scratched his crooked nose. "I'll help you bury her. We'll give her a private spot."

"I am so tired of fighting to save people, and failing. She left Shark Bay. A town decimated and she survived. She came here for a better life and found more death. We fought to protect them Rian, and we failed."

"We didn't fail. Most of the townspeople lived and will rebuild."

"We did fail. If it hadn't been for the Grenar, we' d all be dead."

Rian did not respond. No one understood why the Grenar had intervened. Talk of it was conveniently avoided as well. An unknown, it brought more fear to people's minds than comfort, and the efforts to clear the town and bury the dead provided a ready distraction from the Grenars' actions.

"You may be right," said Rian, "but we are still here. Our duty is to carry on. Remember the dead. Honor them. Don't let them haunt you."

"Easily said."

"Aye."

Kailen looked again at the girl. "What do we put on her gravestone?"

Rian kneeled next to her. "Here lies a daughter of Antaunna. May she find peace and watch over us all."

"I like that."

"It seems right. I'll have a mason from the barracks carve it into some stone."

"Where will we bury her?"

Rian stood. "If I remember right there is a clearing not far to the south. It'll be a good spot. I camped there once a few years ago. I believe it even has a little pond."

"I think she'd like that."

Kailen looked at her face, distorted by death, and wondered why Antaunna allowed this to happen. Rian moved next to Kailen, grabbed his shoulder, and asked, "How are you?"

"I just wish I knew her name."

***

The next day, in the early afternoon, Rian and Kailen stood in the clearing. Rian was glad his memory of the spot was accurate. It could have been the inspiration for an Iatoli Deepgrass painting. The artist apparently loved the Westlook landscape. He'd once seen a few of the man's works adorning the walls of Legion Command in Citadel. They were the prize possessions of the Lord Commander, an arrogant blowhard that had never even set foot in Westlook.

The girl's grave was a simple mound of tightly packed soil lined with stone Kailen had collected from the pond. The small headstone was well-shaped, with the epithet carved clearly. It was crafted beautifully in the short time available to the mason, and Rian had rewarded him well. The artisan had lost his home in the battle, but his family survived. Rian hoped the extra coin would help them rebuild.

Their horses snorted from the edge of the clearing. Tied to the trees they dug the ground for fresh shoots. Kailen's was uncomfortable with the small cart strapped to its harness.

They bowed their heads with hands held across their chests. "I feel like we should say a prayer," Kailen said.

"Which one?" Rian asked.

"What about the Mother's Embrace? My mother always liked that."

"It's been awhile, but I think I remember it," Rian said. It had been his mother's favorite as well, but after his father's death she never recited it again.

The two kneeled and together recited the prayer. Rian dug deep into neglected memories. He did not pray often.

When the winter presses close
When the cold holds all down
When the night is too heavy
Her touch will keep me safe.

In the raging storm
In the angry river
In the burning fire
Her arms will hold me high.

Through temptation
Through sin
Through evil
Her love will keep me strong

I know love
I know peace
I know my place
In the Mother's Embrace

The two touched their hands to their foreheads, leaned forward and touched their heads to the ground, and then stood. Kailen walked to the head of the grave, kissed his hand, and touched it to the gravestone. "You deserved more life. I'm sorry I couldn't give you that, and I hope you have peace. I'll always remember you."

The two turned away and walked to the horses. Forcing a little bit of his old grin Rian said, "Well, at least she has a happy memory to take with her. You're a fine man."

"I'm not sure. For her to have that memory, I betrayed another."

"I won't judge you."

"Someone should."

Rian shrugged. He was certainly no one to pass sentence. "That's Antaunna's place, not mine. I'm your friend."

Rian felt sorry for Kailen, but he kept that hidden. He knew the lad well enough. Pity would be ill-received. The young warden wasn't looking for a friend. He didn't know how to reconcile his actions. He wanted someone to scold him, to wag an accusing finger. Instead, he was being praised for his valor during the battle and forgiven for his indiscretions on its eve. Ten years Kailen's senior, Rian still remembered the conflicted morals that youth engendered. The boy was thinking his defense of Littletop did not excuse his betrayal of Carra. He was wondering why no one understood that. Kailen fought for duty, or said he did, but it really was his revenge. It was all of theirs. Revenge for different indiscretions suffered during their lives. Kailen was still too pure to admit that. Never to Carra, never to Rian, and most certainly never to Zaketh. The boy still had hope. He didn't think this desperate existence pardoned him from all other consequences. Out here though, amongst the dead and the angry, it did. You couldn't tell someone that. It was learned. Commoners wouldn't understand it. Young warriors wouldn't understand it. They were still trying to save the world. Only old soldiers really understood. Rian missed the innocence. If he had remained on the vineyard, perhaps he would still possess it. He liked to think he was a better man for having not stayed. To compromise, and live among those murderers, would have insulted the memory of his father. The only regret that plagued him was knowing his mother felt abandoned. She would never say it, but it was always there beneath the surface of her words when he visited home.

They guided their horses down the rough, narrow path. Rian hoped the girl would rest well here. It was all she had left. Kailen looked at Rian and said, "Do you know where Darksteel is? I figure we should find out what's next."

"I'd heard he was going up to the coast to survey the Noriziem landing site. Try there."

"Want to come with me?"

"No. Remember those two girls from Kelebra de'al Verdan?"

"I do."

"They lived. I saw them this morning, before I picked up the gravestone. I'm going to see if they're available. A woman's touch sounds fantastic."

Kailen nodded. He was imagining Carra's arms wrapped around him and the way her head fit perfectly into the nook between his shoulder and chest. Rian would have bet money on it. He knew that look, had even once been with a girl who made him feel the same way. He'd caught her in bed with a grunt from the 4th Legion. Never again. Well, almost once more, but that girl had been of such kind spirit that he had stayed clear. Aleaxa was her name, and she deserved better than him. He liked to remember her smile though. It had been years since he'd last seen her, and it was one of his favorite memories. Rian hoped Kailen would remember the blonde girl fit well in his arms too, and at least cherish her memory. Rian said, "There are few things better than a soft hand and a gentle kiss."

"Agreed," Kailen said, even though his drawn face betrayed otherwise. Not at this moment at least. They left the blonde girl behind.

The breeze blew past them and stirred the dirt at the crest of the girl's grave. A clump of soil shifted and slid. The leaves whispered their constant, sad song. A shadow fell over the grave, tall and wide.

***

Rend'arr lay his halberd on the ground and kneeled. He wondered who the human woman had been. Why had she been so important to the Warden? Watching the town for the last several days, he'd seen many humans thrown into pits and buried without ceremony. It was no way to treat one's dead, but the Warden had taken special care with this woman. What of the red-haired woman the Warden had been with at the other Cardanan town? Were the two connected?

He had watched them bury the girl. Wrapped in a thin gossamer sheet, she seemed so small and harmless. Who was she? Her relationship to the warden was unknown to him, but still he grieved. Not a warrior who chose to die on the field, she was an innocent caught in the fire. They had honored her well by burying her here, Rend'arr thought.

Reaching into a pouch at his hip, the Grenar produced a handful of fine, yellow powder. He sprinkled it over the grave, and in his deep voice chanted, "*Tokara Can. Loknai oul tou.*"

With his nail, black and sharp, he traced several patterns into the grave mound. Facing the sun, he touched his hand to his forehead, and stood. The blessing offered protection on her journey to the Spirit World, and prevented any scavengers from disturbing her. She could sleep without worry.

Rend'arr picked up his halberd and jogged to the side of the clearing where the wardens had departed. He slipped into the woods, shadowing the path.

***

Kailen guided his horse along the North Road. Noriziem reinforcements and their supplies littered the ground, making footing for the animal treacherous. The Grenar had attacked here too, and as on the field outside of Littletop, they had wiped out their opponents. Kailen surveyed the carnage, still not understanding. No one in Carodan had seen or heard anything from the savages in eighty years. Why had they appeared now? Why had they attacked the Noriziem and not the Cardanans? Why had they saved the people that had defeated them after a brutal, unforgiving war? No matter how he approached the question, he had no answer.

It was enjoyable to finally be alone, as even on horseback the trip to the coast had taken him a day and a half. Rian had found his girls in the town hall courtyard and parted company with a wink. Kailen let him go without a word. The more he thought about it, the less convinced he was the immediate gratification of the women's touch would assuage the pain awakened in Rian by the Noriziem's interrogation. It wasn't his place to judge, though.

The quiet was nice, but the sickly sweet smell of decaying Noriziem did set his stomach to burbling. He would assign a grave detail to burn the bodies. The road cut through a series of hills and dunes, and sandy banks rose steep on either side of it. The Noriziem had been hit from above with no avenue of escape, and the road was fast becoming a trough of pestilence.

The ocean's rhythm oscillated in Kailen's bones and salt flavored the air. That odd coastal overcast, the type that hurt one's eyes greater than a noonday sun, blanketed the sky. Roaring waves replaced the ambient sounds of wilderness. Kailen exited the road and was on the beach.

He'd made camp here once, about three years ago. It wasn't a sheltered beach, wide open to the winds and waves. More pebbles and rock than sand, it had been clean and untouched. War was an unknown here.

Kailen rode past charred wagons and overturned supply crates. Smashed Noriziem supply depots burned all along the coast. Dozens of Noriziem bodies floated back and forth in the surf. Fragile fingers of smoke floated up to join the haze. Would the ocean wash away this taint?

Kailen tied his horse to an over-turned wagon. The beast was skittish and he didn't want it bolting into the waves. The sea breeze blew away the stench of decay, mostly, and the horse calmed. Kailen patted its neck and slipped the feedbag over the horse's mouth.

He went to the water. Faces, puffed and rotted, stared at him. Shattered hulks and burnt hulls littered the surf. He counted scores of ships. Somehow, the Grenar had destroyed the vessels as well. They floated lifeless and broken in Antaunna's touch. It was a large fleet, bigger than reported. For the first time in decades, Carodan had been truly invaded.

Kailen turned away from the carnage and walked east along the beach, trying to find Darksteel. In the distance, by a group of boulders where several supply carts were clustered, he spotted movement. Weaving through the detritus, he closed the distance and discerned Zaketh using one of his arms to hold something against a cart. In the commander's other hand was a hammer. Zaketh raised the hammer and struck four times. It sounded like he was driving a nail. The corner of the cart was in the way, and Kailen couldn't see what was against its side.

Thinking it unwise to surprise the warrior, Kailen hollered while still fifty paces away. "Zak!"

The commander looked back at him, waved with his hammer, and drove another nail. Kailen blinked. Was that a pair of legs hanging below the cart's edge? They were. Zaketh had nailed a Noriziem, stripped of armor and clothes, to the sideboards of the cart. He nodded to Kailen, and then drove a long, thick nail through the Noriziem's forehead, tacking his head to the cart.

"So, it's true," said Kailen.

"What?"

"That you do this."

"Never said it wasn't," Zaketh said. He tugged at the Noriziem. The corpse held firm. Kailen looked at the other carts. Stripped soldiers, nailed with arms spread wide and head tacked back, decorated every single one. Each had a square of parchment glued to their chests. Kailen couldn't read what they said. It was a single phrase, written in thick, solid characters that looked vaguely familiar. "Is that Norzaat?"

"Aye. Father Frostwind knows the language and penned them for me."

Kailen scanned the beach, paying close attention this time, and saw more Noriziem nailed to crates, half-constructed siege engines, and wagons. How had he missed them? All had the parchment stuck to their chest. "What do they say?"

Zaketh set his hammer on the edge of the cart, picked a water skin off the ground and swallowed half of it. Unarmored for the first time in days, he wiped his beard with the back of his sleeve and tossed the skin to Kailen. Ale would have been better, but the water did ease his drying throat. Zaketh turned to the ocean and put his hands on his lower back, stretching. "Fuck off, you bastards."

"I'm sorry?"

"That's what they say. Fuck off, you bastards."

Kailen stared at Zaketh. For an instant, just a brief instant, he thought he saw the man's eyes crinkle with a smile.

"It was Frostwind's idea. Since he was kind enough to make them for me I didn't argue."

"Fuck off, you bastards?"

"I think it loses something in the translation."

Kailen shook his head and sat down on a split barrel. The waves washed the shore. He focused on them, imagining them scrubbing the beach clean if given enough time. The destruction and ruin were on his periphery, something to be blocked out and ignored. Zaketh sat next to him on the sand. Two weeks ago Kailen would have been appalled at the commander's actions. One week ago even. Now, thinking about what the Noriziem had done, he found he had no good reason to protest. What did that mean for him? Giving in to curiosity, he asked, "So, why do you do it? A warning?"

"Something like that. I've dedicated my life to defending Carodan. As long as there is breath in my lungs I will do all I can to protect its people. Too many Cardanans died at Littletop. I couldn't change that. The only power I had was to keep fighting. This," he pointed back at the stapled Noriziem, "is my way of telling our enemies I'll never stop fighting. They brought violence against my country. I bring violence to them, even after they're dead. They hurt us. I violate them."

"Ever wonder if you're losing a bit of yourself with every person you kill?" While that thought had long lurked in the shadow of his thoughts, he'd never voiced it. The events of the last week made it harder to ignore. Would Carra recognize him when he went home?

"In service, in duty, there is no room for regret. I have sworn to serve Carodan, and that's all that matters. That's all there is. It is me."

"You once implied I fought because of scars to my soul. You bear your own scars."

"Who doesn't? Each man lives as he sees fit."

"Do the scars define us?"

Zaketh reached for a crumpled sack by his feet. He produced a long-necked bottle made of clear glass and half-full with amber fluid. Zaketh pulled out the stopper and handed it to Kailen. Sniffing it, raising an eyebrow, he swallowed deep. Warm and smooth, it burned all the way to the bottom of his guts. Tears peaked at the corners of his eyes, and he tried not to cough or twitch. He handed it to Zaketh, who also drank. The carefully held lines of his face never wavered. His eyes didn't water.

"I thought you didn't drink," said Kailen.

"Only on certain occasions."

Zaketh pulled another swig and stood. The hammer had never left his grip.

"You said no one benefits when you do."

Zaketh nodded to the hanging Noriziem. "I didn't lie. I have a few more to do. Want to help?"

Kailen stood, brushed off his bottom, and looked at the dead Noriziem. He didn't understand the Grenars' actions, but he was grateful for them. Hundreds of Noriziem lay dead, and all of them had come with the goal of hurting his country. His people.

The hammer in Zaketh's hand spoke of violent satisfaction. The pile of sharpened nails promised retribution. He could play a part in the macabre message left to any Noriziem who might land at this beach in the future. He thought of Carra's sea-green eyes.

"Not today," said Kailen. Turning away from Zaketh he returned to his horse.

The dead beach swallowed the sound of his footsteps.

***

Three hundred paces away, lying in the dune grass, Rend'arr watched the warden leave the legionnaire. Never had a word been exchanged between him and the human, but relief flooded him as the warden walked away from the hammer-wielding soldier. Desecrating a body, even that of your enemy, disturbed the Grenar. He knew the tales of his own people doing so during the war with the Cardanans. It was a part of their history he'd rather forget. Didn't the dead deserve greater dignity? It seemed the variations of compassion and savageries were not dissimilar between Grenar and Cardanan.

Toba's forces were safe across the border by now. Her death would haunt him until his own. The disbelief over his request had not surprised him. The honor challenge of Morash Ton'ga was also expected. Her life spilling across his face and into his eyes seemed unreal. They'd grown together as younglings. For her life to end in his hands... The Grenar soldiers had followed him, but only because he'd won the right through bloodshed. Only the Great Spirit knew what awaited him when he finally returned home. Why did he keep following this human? Because of that damned dream. Even after his attack against the Noriziem it had not abated. It compelled him.

Rend'arr slid down the dune's back and nestled against a large piece of driftwood left by some storm. From the satchel at his belt he produced a book with torn pages and faded binding, holding it delicately. Reverently. Six glyphs scored its cover. Two he recognized; one that the Cardanans displayed constantly and the other he'd seen on the Noriziems' banners, often next to the silhouette of the black dragon. He opened to where he'd earmarked the book. Trying to remember the lessons from his mother and the other tribal shamans, he wrapped his tongue and lips around foreign syllables. Saying the first sentence on the page required the same concentration as battle training. “And the nation shall be ruled by those who are chosen by the people. They will serve the people, and govern with the needs of the common man foremost in mind.”

Chapter 17
TRUST I SEEK

"Do you really think Stonestriker will let us have a hand in ruling Carodan? Are you really that naïve?" Toral asked.

"Keep your voice down. I still think we're being followed," Logarsh replied. The Khan of Clan Wathiem paced. He always paced. Even here, hidden among the paths of the Arboreal Cavern, he looked over his shoulder and twitched at every sound.

"I'm speaking in Norzaat, and this," he pointed to the gurgling pool of earth-heated water they stood next to, "is loud enough to cover our voices."

"You don't think he has translators? There are more than enough places to hide in here."

"Possibly," Toral said. They were tucked away on a ledge in the upper levels of the vast and labyrinthine Arboreal Cavern. On the south side of the mountain, the cave was the result of an underground river's long work. It still flowed clean, cold, and strong through the center of the chamber. The builders of this city, still a mystery to even Clan Thent's well-versed scholars, had cut gaping windows into the cavern's ceiling. Fifty feet of rock they penetrated, and then somehow set panes of thick glass into the stone. It was beyond any technique or craft that either the Cardanans or Noriziem possessed. Sunlight warmed the cavern, and with the moisture in the air from the hot pools, Stonestriker's people had managed to grow a vast number of edible plants and fruit trees. It was the only place in this forsaken continent where one could see green.

During the day the cavern was busy as crops were tended

and harvested, but come twilight it was ghostly quiet. Only the occasional young couple or introspective elder were to be found. This was Toral and Logarsh's fifth time meeting here. "I can't ignore the chance to finally destroy Carodan," Toral said, "My father, and all his fathers before him, swore an oath to punish the blasphemers. For the first time in generations it looks like we have the opportunity, but if Stonestriker is willing to betray his own people, why should we expect any different?"

Logarsh paused his pacing and rubbed his chin. Toral still did not understand how this weakling was the Khan of a great clan. Clans Thent and Wathiem were typically allies, warring with each other only occasionally. Clan Wathiem's honor on the field was well-known, but Toral could not envision Logarsh wielding a sword.

"He has brought the four clans together. Our pointless wars have halted. Stonestriker has the blessing of Galantaegan. Perhaps he will rebuild the Norizaad Empire," Logarsh said.

"You've been listening to Jenaka too much. She has delusions of grandeur, and you're blinded by the potential for wealth."

"I've heard amazing tales of Cardanan cities," Logarsh shrugged his skinny shoulders, "Whitebreak spreading around a huge bay and shining in the afternoon sun. Citadel is built of blue stone and trimmed with silver and gold. Everwatch and South Hawk guard over fertile land and trade routes. Think of what we could bring to our clans. We reap Carodan and rebuild Granikar."

Toral thought of his homeland. So much was fallow and broken from Noriziem civil war. Great cities stood in ruin, and thousands died from illness and starvation. They never stopped fighting long enough to heal themselves. Until now. Even among his own men Toral noticed an optimism, a hope, that was new and infectious. "What makes you think Stonestriker will let us take any wealth from Carodan? After he conquers and throws down House Ironheart, he will want to rebuild Carodan in his image. He can't do that if we suck the land dry."

Logarsh smiled. With rot in his teeth and the spottiness of his pale skin, the expression was unpleasant. "You are correct, and I expect Morrikii to keep a tight watch over what we do. But he can't be everywhere. It is a large country. He is smart, however, and I don't think he'd try to cross us after the invasion."

Arms folded in the cloth of his sleeves, Toral caressed the hilt of the dagger strapped to his forearm. Logarsh's turkey neck would split easily under its edge. Part of him just wanted to see the weasel bastard bleed. Being here was madness. Jenaka was a whore who rose to power by bedding men and then knifing them while they slept, her stink still on them. Markan was a brute with no finesse or subtlety. Toral had remained only because of Galantaegan. The Black Dragon's favor of Morrikii was irrefutable.

"How large is Morrikii's army?" Logarsh said, "Ten thousand? When the four clans have amassed their strength we will be eighty thousand. If he tries to stab us in the back, we smash him. He needs us, and he knows that. He also knows we could turn on him, and if we did he would not have the power to control Carodan and stop us at the same time. Then, there would be no one to watch over his precious country, and we could burn it from the face of K'aeran and take everything we wanted."

"What happens to us after that? Does this grand alliance among the Noriziem survive?" asked Toral. He turned to the pool and looked at his distorted reflection. Evening was fast approaching and the sky's gray light filtered weakly through the massive windows. His face was pale and ghostly on the water. Perhaps he was seeing his face after death.

"Probably not," Logarsh said and shrugged again.

Toral raised an eyebrow and studied his counterpart. "Are you already planning where to put the knife in my back?"

"Oh, no. Trust me, I would prefer the alliance to stand, but our people never change. We've fought for so long we know nothing else. After we defeat Carodan, and I am sure we will, who do we fight after that? Maybe Morrikii can hold us together. Maybe not."

"My mother often spoke of the Noriziem will. The world looks at us as barbarians, but the constant fighting prevents us from becoming complacent."

"It also drains resources, depletes populations, and destroys homes," Logarsh said.

"The weak are culled. No one sits idle long enough to horde wealth. Carodan has stood firm for over two centuries, and I'll acknowledge the strength of that. They've grown fat though, and corrupt. A cleansing fire is long overdue."

Toral balled his hand into a fist and slipped it in the water. His skin scalded almost immediately. Men of Clan Thent took pride in their tolerance of pain and displayed it whenever possible. The image of Logarsh's throat parting under his knife was still tempting.

"So, if we do fall apart, what side will you be on Toral?" Logarsh asked.

He removed his hand from the water and held it before Logarsh's face. Bright red and already blistering, the hand would take weeks to heal. He squeezed the fist so tight blood wept from some of the blisters.

"The side that wins."

Chapter 18
HER ARMS

"Beth, if you don't hold this stool steady I'll hit *you* with the hammer."

"Sorry, Carra. The floor is uneven."

The daggers in Carra's gaze prompted the young serving girl to wrap her arms around the stool with renewed enthusiasm. *Good*, thought Carra, *I still owe her for watching after me, but at least she remembers who pays her.* Carra focused again on the lamp she was trying to hang. Some lumbering idiot, a sailor from the eastern shore of Tidal Guard, had been so drunk the previous night he thought he could do back flips. His foot knocked the lamp clean off the post and it had shattered across the floor. Only the quick thinking of some of her patrons, and several tankards of ale, had saved the Nightsong's Hearth from going up in flames. Carra threw the man out despite his claims of having no other place to sleep. Three battalions had marched into town over the last week, and a war fleet rode anchor in the harbor. The town was bursting.

Eyeballing the bracket, she hoped it was straight against the age-warped timber. Looked level enough to her. She took a nail from between her teeth, set it in place, and drove it into the wood with her father's old hammer. The second nail almost went in crooked, but her anger and frustration forced it straight. Her hands were steady today. She grabbed the bracket with her left hand and tugged. It didn't shift. "Tilda, hand me the lamp."

She took the wrought-iron monstrosity from her senior cook and slid the back hook into the bracket. Aside from gouges in the wood to the left of the lamp, there was little evidence of the damage. Even the floor had only minor scorches. Carra stepped off the stool, gave Beth a look of thanks and then nodded her off to the kitchen, and admired her handiwork.

"He was cute," Tilda said.

"Don't tell me you took the sailor home," replied Carra.

"He needed a bed. Bran wasn't home, probably out boffing Nileny. We've worked long hours since the soldiers came into town. I needed a bit of fun," Tilda said. She punctuated it with a shrug and half-frown.

"Was he good?"

"A bit clumsy, as you might imagine, but he carried a long yardarm. Put Bran to shame."

Carra shook her head, if only to hide the smile behind her auburn curls. "I did not need to hear that. Are the girls ready for tonight?"

Tilda carried the stool Carra had been standing on back to the bar. "Of course. All the legionnaires and sailors have them chattering non-stop. Between the tips and the attention they couldn't be happier."

Carra nodded. The men of the Legion and Antaunna's Grand Navy had money to blow and large appetites to fill. The tavern had done well. She might be able to get the roof freshly thatched before the summer rains. There would be enough money to pay for a competent job this time.

"I heard another column of troops came in from the west today," Tilda said. Picking at a spot of dried gravy on the bar, she didn't look at Carra and seemed wholly uninterested in doing so.

Carra studied her and then looked down to the floor. "I hadn't heard. Know how many?"

Tilda rolled her shoulders and cracked her back, her ample bosom catching even Carra's attention. Men rarely ignored it. Tilda's rich brown hair, hazel eyes, and radiant smile further drew in her prey. At times, it was a battle for Carra to ignore her jealousy whenever Kailen looked at Tilda.

"I don't, but I heard they bring word from the frontier. Everyone is talking about the attack on Littletop. They say the town was decimated."

"I've heard the story. Don't need to again," Carra said. She walked behind the bar and checked the mugs on their shelves.

All were clean and neatly lined up for the evening.

"He's fine. You don't even know if he was there," Tilda said.

"See if the girls need any help back in the kitchen. I'll watch the front."

Tilda parted her lips, ran the tip of her tongue over the lower, and then shut her mouth. She went back to the kitchen, squeezing Carra on the shoulder as she walked by. Carra checked the bottles behind the bar. Each in its place, none too low. She checked the beer kegs. Fresh and full, as always. She'd gone through a lot of ale since the influx of soldiers and sailors, and had almost run out. By chance she'd heard of a shipment arriving all the way from Wheat Scythe, meant for a tavern in the upper quarter. A large bag of coin and Tilda's batting eyes changed the trader's mind. His ship still rode anchor in the harbor, and from what Carra gathered Tilda still entertained him from time to time. He had friends who were bringing more ale soon.

The headache was starting to return. The only thing that pushed it away last night was a bit of the dream powder. She couldn't take any now. To do so during the day felt dirty, and was something she mostly avoided. A few star points of yellow and purple light danced across her vision.

She pulled a bottle of Hedge Row Red from her wine rack. She uncorked the bottle, smelled the oaky undertones, and smiled. Filling the goblet, she sipped a bit off the top and then filled it again. The bottle would remain in her private nook for the remainder of the evening. Her mouth pouted with the wine's dryness. The flashes of light stopped and her headache receded.

She wandered between the tables, looking for crumbs or any waste her girls may have missed. Everything was spotless. Carra sat down in front of the sprawling stone hearth and drank more. The stool needed to be closer to the fire. Its four legs bumped and squeaked against the floor as she lazily shifted it. She stared at the cracking, sparking logs. The flames wrapped phantom fingers around the blackened wood, and she imagined Kailen's fingers trailing up her spine. Sun-orange, the bed of embers rippled the air. She thought of Kailen's eyes, the way they could look right through her. Tenderness and hurt lingered there, but also an anger that burned hotter than this fire. She thought of his hands, callused from his sword and scarred from fighting. She'd always felt so safe when he held her with them. Her fingers brushed across her cheek.

"It's never good to drink alone."

Carra's hand froze. Her breath stuck in the back of her throat. She hadn't heard anyone come in. It had to be him. If it was only someone who sounded like him her heart would shatter. She turned around.

Kailen leaned against one of the support timbers. Well beyond scruff, his beard was thick and full. It did little to hide his drawn skin or unusually prominent cheek bones. A long tear, ringed with a brown stain, marked his left sleeve. Yellowed bandages peeked from underneath the torn fabric. He smiled, but with shadowed eyes.

Her goblet thudded against the floor, and the remainder of her wine seeped into the wood. The stain would remain forever. There was no lapse of time between her leaving the stool and being wrapped in his arms. He held her tightly. She wasn't sure he'd ever let go. She was a little embarrassed at her sobbing. It never felt right to appear weak in front of him. However, after a few moments she realized he too was sobbing. He gasped for air, his fingers tangled in the mass of her hair. The kiss was so hard she cut her lip. "I was so worried about you."

"I missed you," he said.

"I know."

His hands slid down her back and cupped her bottom. He picked her up and set her on one of the tables. Her skirt was long and flowing, and the material bunched around her knees. Kailen pushed it up as high as it would go, reached beneath the skirt, and pulled away her smallclothes. She started to undo his breeches, but put a hand on his chest, caught her breath, and said, "Not here. Let's go upstairs."

It wasn't easy to stop, but she didn't want this to be a dirty romp in the middle of the tavern. "Tilda! Come out here!"

Kailen stepped back, trying to calm his breathing. He chewed his lower lip. Tilda came out of the kitchens, concern written on her face, but she smiled and laughed when she saw the two of them, "Kailen! You're home. Thank Antaunna," she said and then noticed their panting and mussed clothing, "and I see you're wasting no time."

"Tilda, do you mind watching the bar for a while?" Carra asked.

"I'll take care of it."

"Are you sure?"

"If you come down those stairs at any point this evening I will kick your ass back up them," Tilda said.

"Thank you. Pay yourself extra tonight."

Tilda waved a hand and sniffed. "Go have fun. Kailen, treat her well."

"Always," he said.

Carra almost tripped up the creaking stairs. Her legs were all knee, and they felt air-light but leaden at the same time. At the top Kailen grabbed her around the waist and pulled her close. He kissed her neck, his lips lingering on her skin. Up to her jaw line he traced, and she turned into him, pressing her lips to his. She pulled him down the hall, keeping one eye half-open so they didn't bump into one of the wall sconces. Setting her hair on fire would not enhance the mood.

Kailen picked her up, she wrapped her legs around his waist, and he pushed her firmly, but gently, against the door to her rooms. The bronze pommel of his sword was cold against her outer thigh. He stopped kissing her, tilted his head back, and said, "I need you. More than you'll ever know."

"I'll never stop needing you."

Again he kissed her. She didn't want him to stop, and he didn't as he fumbled for the latch with one hand while somehow holding her steady with the other. Her room was dark, lit only by the sunset that pooled in through the two harbor windows. Kailen kicked the door closed.

One spot of early evening sun fell over the bed, and she squealed as he tossed her onto the feather mattress. She wiggled out of her dress, throwing it over her head and somewhere on the floor behind her. Kailen unbuckled his sword belt and hung it on a peg in the wall, next to a painting of her parents. His cloak, tunic, breeches, and boots piled on the floor. In the orange light his skin was an odd pattern of light and shadow. It threw every corded muscle on his body into wiry relief. She saw bruises, yellowed and healing, scattered across his body. The bandage on his arm was dirty and crusted. Never had he been so battered.

Carra sat up and slid to the edge of the bed. She ran her fingertips along the outside of his legs. He quivered a little, and breathed faster. His penis stood up straight before her face with tension and expectation. She gripped it with one hand and slid her lips down it. The moan from Kailen was the best thing she'd heard in two months. She didn't know what he had seen out there, could only imagine how he had received the cuts and bruises, but none of that mattered tonight. She was going to take it all away.

She moved her mouth back and forth several times before pulling all the way back and flicking her tongue against the tip. "I have little patience for foreplay right now."

"As do I. That can come later."

He bent down, wrapped her in his arms, and laid her gently on the bed, rolling her spine out along its length. He was on top of her and kissing her neck again. His tip brushed against her opening. "I love you."

"And I love you, more than I could ever tell you," he said. Restrained tears clouded his voice. She reached down and guided him in. There were no more words.

***

The night came in a blur of sweat, twisting sheets, and waves of sensation. When they finally finished, her lungs burned and labored to feed her body air. Both legs were jelly and she knew she'd be sore for two days. She had cried several times. Tears of joy, she had promised him. Mostly they were.

Now, laying on his chest and hearing his heart slam against his ribcage, she was simply glad he was here and wanted him to hold her for the rest of the night. The bar was still loud, and it sounded as if there had been several fights, but she did not care. All that mattered was his touch and the din of the tavern was easier to ignore than she would have guessed. The moon was high, casting blue light instead of orange. Everything, even Kailen, looked ghostly and pristine.

Carra smiled. She loved this spot, in the nook of his shoulder. She fit perfectly here. Kailen's breathing was rhythmic with the beginning of sleep. Her lungs steadied and matched his, expanding when his did and expelling in that same, purposefully calm way. Her eyelids were heavy, and the warm embrace of sleep seemed just moments away.

"Do you often think of your parents?" Kailen asked.

Sleep was gone, her eyes no longer weighted. "I do. I hope

my father is proud of me. I know my mother is," she replied, wondering why he had asked.

"I've been thinking of mine over the last several weeks. Thinking of how they were killed and of everything the Noriziem took away from me. I was never able to know them. My memories are few."

Carra propped her head up with her left hand and tried to see his face. The ghost-light seeping past the curtains provided just enough illumination to cast his face in silhouette. For whatever reason he had pushed away sleep and now stared at the shadow-thick ceiling. She asked him, "What are your favorite memories for each of them?"

"What do you mean?"

"Well, you can't think of only their death. There must be good memories you have. What's your favorite for each?"

He chewed his lower lip, and she watched the light shift as his eyes moved with memory. "Well, for my mother it's more a set of memories. When I was five, maybe six, I became convinced that shadow-trolls and hobgoblins lived under the floor and beneath my bed. I was terrified to go to sleep."

Carra smiled at the thought of Kailen being afraid of anything.

"Every night she'd come in and sing to me. Usually off-key and off-rhythm, but her voice was low and soothing. I'd lie on my stomach and she'd just rub my back. Very lightly, sometimes only using her fingernails. It put me to sleep every time, and she never seemed annoyed. Never rolled her eyes at me or let frustration color her voice."

"And your father?"

Kailen took a deep breath. "I'll never forget this. About a month before the Noriziem attacked, I was coming home from Temple lessons. You weren't with me that day for some reason. Two of the large boys had been picking on me for a while. It had been going on for months, but I was too proud, or maybe too scared, to tell him. One day the boys spit on me and Father saw it in my hair. After washing me, he very calmly asked how it happened. I couldn't very well lie, so I told him.

"So, about a week later I was walking home. I think it was the tail-end of winter. Most of the snow had melted, but piles of hard, dirty ice were still about. I was coming down a side street from the temple, and the two boys came up behind me and threw me into the snow."

Carra tried to read his face, but clouds had passed in front of the moon. His tone was far away and tinted with the past.

"They started laughing, then Father came around the corner at the end of the street. He wore his full militia uniform. Chain hauberk and steel helm, Legion tabard, his shield slung over his back and sword strapped to his side."

She heard Kailen's smile.

"He bristled with anger, somehow appearing twice his normal size. Maybe that's just a child's memory playing tricks. He went right up to the boys and leveled his mail-clad finger in their faces. He said, "If I ever catch you touching my boy again, I'll beat you senseless." Their faces went whiter than the snow I was sitting in. One of them stuttered something about telling his father that mine was threatening them."

"What did he say back?"

The moonlight returned and Carra saw Kailen scowl in imitation. He deepened his voice and made it graveled the way he remembered his father's voice sounding. He lifted his arm towards the ceiling, index finger extended, and waggled it in the face of the shadows. "I know your fathers, and if they found out what you were doing they would beat you even harder than I will."

Kailen laughed, rubbing his face. "They never touched me again. They survived the attack that would come, but even after my father was gone, they left me alone."

His smile had faded, and Carra, in the slightly brighter light, saw tears in the corners of his eyes. She laid her other hand, the one that wasn't starting to tingle from the pressure of her head pushing her elbow into the mattress, on his chest. Part of her wanted to say something, but she held back. She somehow knew his words would come on their own.

"They died protecting me, and after that I swore I would do the same for all those I care about. I would give my life in the service of my people if I had to, but it seems like no matter how hard I fight, people die, and I can't stop it."

"Kailen, you don't have the power to decide who lives or dies. Only the Dragons know when it's our time. Only they know the reason. Any man able to decide who lived and who died would probably be a monster. What happened out there?"

"I should be dead Carra," his voice cracked with fettered emotion, "I was at Littletop. So many who were around me are gone. People they loved have to deal with that loss and I can give them no good reason why. Some died without families. I had to bury a girl without knowing her name. Her marker sits bare except for an inscription."

"A girl?"

"One of Rian's 'friends.' He became close to her during our stay in town."

"That's terrible, Kailen. I had no idea where you were, but I couldn't shake this dread that lingered over every thought. Something just felt wrong."

"I've never seen anything like it, Carra. I've been fighting for years, but the slaughter was something from nightmare. In spite of all my commitment and skill, the town burned and so many were lost."

"I can't imagine it," Carra said. Why couldn't she think of anything better to say? This was her Kailen; why did the words come with so much difficulty? Her mind always worked better after some dream powder, but it was all the way down in the kitchen. She refused to keep it in her quarters.

"I hope you never have to. I may as well not have been there."

"But you won. If you and the other soldiers hadn't been there no one from the town would have lived."

"Carra, we didn't matter. There were too many. We were going to be crushed."

Kailen sat up quickly and flung his feet over the side of the bed, his back to her. "Something happened that I don't understand. None of us do. General Bronzehide ordered us not to speak of it."

Never had he kept anything from her, even when under orders. She pulled a blanket off the bed and got up. Wrapping herself tight, she went to the window and looked out at the nighttime world. It was a bit quieter downstairs, and along Harbor Street she watched soldiers leaving the taverns and heading up the hill to the barracks. From this angle she couldn't see people leaving her own bar, but she knew that Tilda was most likely shooing everyone out. "You've never held anything back from me," Carra said.

She heard Kailen scratch his legs and then his head.

"Anyone who breaks the edict will be charged with treason.

I can't violate this order, and I understand why. If word spread through Carodan of what happened, all of Chaos would break loose. As soon as I'm allowed, you'll be the first I tell."

She nodded, still upset but knowing that asking him to go against his duty would cause resentment. A corner of her mind asked if that were fair, but she shut that part away. Him being home and alive was all that mattered.

Kailen rose from the bedside and went to his pile of gear. One of his boots scuffed against the floor. Was he getting dressed? she wondered, but he came around the bed, still naked, carrying one of his daggers.

That distant night, the smell of vomit flooding her nostrils, his hand clamped around her throat, came rushing back. The hatred in his eyes. His knuckles slamming into her face. A blind anger that drove her to strike back. Not a detail was forgotten. If he had drawn a blade that night, her life would have covered the floor.

But there was no anger twisting his face now, and he wasn't drunk and drugged. Standing next to her, he offered the dagger hilt first. She took it and looked up at him, not sure what he intended. He saw the question on her face.

"I won't be here all the time to keep you safe, but at least keep this with you. It's killed many Noriziem and should serve you well."

"I can't take this. It was part of your Initiation when you became a Warden."

Kailen shrugged, "I have a second and rarely use both at the same time. Besides, I prefer my father's sword. Keep it. Do you remember what I taught you?"

Kailen had spent a great deal of time showing her the vulnerable spots of the body and the best way to pierce them with a blade. She owned a dagger herself, but it was not as large, or as well-made. "Thank you. I'll keep it close. Do you have a sheath?"

"I do. It's buried somewhere in my sack. I'll dig it out in the morning."

"Thank you."

"It's the least I can do. It's late. Come on you, let's get some rest."

Carra smiled and nodded, dropping the blanket on the floor

and taking his outstretched hand. Again they climbed under the covers and she fit herself perfectly against his body. She set the dagger on the bedside table. Cold and harsh, it glimmered with the last of the moonlight. She'd have to find some way to carry it. Her dresses did not really leave much room for weapons. Maybe if she strapped it to her ankle with a length of silk ribbon. That might work.

Carra succumbed to sleep, dreaming of ways to keep Kailen close to her. Right then, in the small hours of that spring night, she did not think of why he was giving her the dagger. His concern over her added protection rang no alarm.

As she slipped into the depths of sleep, images of her father and mother played across her dreamscape. Her dreams shifted to the nights with Kailen and then to one odd trip to the neighboring town of White Cliffs. She did not hear Kailen slip out of bed. He moved with a hunter's grace and did not disturb her sleeping form. He tiptoed to his gear, fumbling in the folds until he found his whetstone. Pulling his sword from the wall, he walked across the room and opened a narrow door. He closed it behind him so carefully that the rusty hinges did not squeak. In Carra's sitting room there was only a bookcase and a single cushioned bench that faced one large window. She did not hear the wood shift as Kailen's naked form sat on the dust-saturated pillows. She could not see him study the edge of his blade in the moonlight, and as she moved along sleep's gentle currents, she did not hear him running his stone over the edge of his sword again and again and again.

Chapter 19
CITADEL

Father Cranden Frostwind grasped the rail of his ship, the *Crusader*, with both hands. He still lacked much of his strength. Weakness rippled though his muscles like the whitecaps that dotted Lake Azureron, and his stomach lurched with threatening determination. Dreams of Littletop burning disturbed his sleep constantly.

"I hate sailing," he said. If it weren't for the direct summons of King Ironheart he wouldn't even be near a boat. One did not leave the king waiting.

A sailor shuffled towards him and offered a cup of water. Frostwind nodded and accepted. The sailor smiled, bowed his head, and scooted back down the deck. Why was everyone so damned nervous around him? The priest drank the water and splashed some over his face. Cooling his skin, the water offered some relief.

Almost there, he thought. When Commander Cragrunner, limping with a heavily bandaged leg and leaning on a crutch, had met Frostwind on the beach and pointed out to a waiting Cardanan war galley, the priest's inside had tightened. Even though from Tidal Guard, he'd grown up inland. His House's seat, the Frigid Manse, was set deep in the heart of the Sea Step Hills. His oldest brother had been drawn to the ocean though, and had drowned in a storm while sailing for pleasure off Cape Lone Mist many years ago. He didn't trust boats.

But the King had requested his presence as soon as possible. The Trade Road would not be an option. So, he sailed half the length of the northern coast from Littletop to Whitebreak. From there he was carted up the turbulent River Karneden on a flat-bottomed barge. A broad, serpentine belt of water, it joined Sanctuary Bay and Lake Azureron. The spring runoff turned the normally calm waters chaotic. Two weeks of travel he endured.

When they'd finally reached Lake Azureron he spent a night at Lakemouth, one of his favorite little towns. Then this very morning, when the sky first turned gray with the coming sun, he set out on this lake cutter. Small and swift, the *Crusader* was part of a fleet used by the Legion to patrol the massive lake.

"So much water. So much beauty and danger intermixed," Frostwind said to no one. He looked to the horizon where the sun hovered early in its ascent. Streams of copper and bronze tinted the pale morning sky. Frostwind focused on the sun. Fat and red with the day's newness, it warmed him. He thought of the legends, of the myth of the world's creation, and of Darogo and K'aeran. The father and mother of the dragons, these two great beings came from the heavens. It was said they sailed between the stars, their silver wings and scales shining with unrivaled brilliance. They traveled the black skies until they found a safe place for K'aeran to give birth to their children, the Six Dragons. Frostwind tried to picture it, the great behemoths floating through empty vastness without worry or concern. The stories told of how they spent their days in bliss, caring only for each other.

Until the Shadur' Wranth came. Different scholars described the monster differently, but most often it was ink-black and serpentine. The children of Darogo and K'aeran were almost consumed by the demon. Only Galantaegan was actually bitten, the Shadur' Wranth's poison seeping into his veins and forever tainting his soul. They would have all been devoured if not for K'aeran. She charged the beast and fought with the unique strength of an enraged mother. K'aeran managed to kill the Shadur' Wranth, but was mortally wounded. Before her spirit slipped away, she gave the last of her life force to a barren piece of rock that sat alone in the heavens. Life sprung there instantly and a home was formed for her children to live on safely. She became the world, a place that cradled all. Her mate, broken over the loss of his beloved, swore to shine light into the darkness forever, and burned with such rage that he became the sun. The

Six Dragons came to the world and each assumed an aspect of its foundation.

Thinking back to Littletop, and all the senseless tragedy there, the reassurance of the old myth comforted him. He told himself everything was formed for a purpose and that everything happened for a reason. It must.

"Excuse me, Father."

Frostwind frowned, turning away from the sun and his thoughts. The ship's captain, a lad of maybe twenty summers, stood behind him. His sun-hardened skin and scarred hands spoke of a life on the water. "Yes, lad?"

"I'm sorry to disturb you, but I wanted to see how you were feeling."

"I endure. How long until we reach Citadel?"

The captain nodded to the starboard bow. "Not long."

Frostwind followed his gaze and saw the edge of land creeping up from the endless line of water. "Good. My old body taxes me, and my stomach somersaults. Will it be long?"

The captain rubbed his chin. "We'll be there before mid-morning."

Frostwind again thought of Darogo. Did he see them all? What did he think of this endless conflict between his children's disciples? "Good. Good, good. I think I'll stay up here. Don't want to stray too far from the rail."

"Of course, Father. If there is anything you need, let me know."

"Not unless you have a shot of brandy and a soft woman."

"Aren't the priests supposed to be celibate?" asked the captain with a smirk.

Frostwind managed a smile and winked at the captain. "Of course we are lad. Of course we are."

The captain laughed and left him, but he seemed unsure of how seriously to take the priest. *Poor lad*, thought Frostwind. He had obeyed the Vow of Celibacy for most of his priesthood. Then he had met *her*. Those emerald eyes and flaming red hair, mixed with the raw, untamed spirit that was common in the wilderness of Westlook, shifted something within him. He realized in the beauty of that untouched land that life was too short for high-minded rules and mandates. Natasha was so full of life and had treated his old bones very gently. He wasn't able to get to her in time though, and her light was extinguished.

"Remember, Cranden," he said to himself, "there is a reason for it all. For everything lost, something is given. It is Antaunna's balance."

He leaned against the rail, watching True Tower Isle grow close. Its rocky cliffs, topped by a line of stone, grew in clarity. The Premiere Wall, made entirely of blue granite, encircled the whole island. No other structure like it existed in the rest of the kingdom. An entire legion was required to man it properly.

The cutter tacked into the wind and paralleled the coast. At the island's southernmost point, Kentar's Bluff, they bore east and plowed through energetic whitecaps.

The waters calmed as the ship turned north and headed between Kentar's Bluff and its sister point, Mist Spear Tower. The sails flapped and sagged in the sheltered waters. Vibrations tickled the bottom of Frostwind's feet as the *Crusader's* crew deployed their oars. The boat surged forward with each stroke and soon they entered Port Tenar.

Ships were everywhere. Fat-bellied cogs carrying grain from Wheat Scythe, gilded merchant galleys from Tidal Guard loaded with wine and fresh fruit, and, sitting low in the water, simple barges from Westlook carrying lumber, ore, and hides. Frostwind wondered at it all, amazed that the few lake cutters he saw here and there were able to keep everyone in their respective lanes and prevent collisions. This was the hub of Cardanan trade. The very lifeblood of the nation pumped through this harbor, each province helping to keep the others alive. If along the way someone was able to line their pockets with some of the wealth that coursed through here, well, that was just the way of things.

Frostwind's ship cut a straight path to the massive wharfs of Port Tenar. The *Crusader* slipped into a berth, was tied up quickly, and several dockhands positioned a gangway. Frostwind carried his only possessions, so he was first off the ship with little fuss. He didn't realize he'd left his staff below decks. A wave of dizziness invaded his body and he paused to let it pass. Resisting the urge to bend down and kiss the stone wharf, the priest did offer a quick prayer to Antaunna. Waiting for him, with crossed arms and puffed chest, was a legion commander. The soldier snapped to attention and saluted the priest.

"Father Cranden Frostwind. I am to escort you to Citadel

and directly to King Ironheart."

Frostwind rubbed his nose, sniffed, and looked the man over. "And, who are you, might I ask? And how did you know I'd be on this ship?"

Somehow puffing his chest out farther, and catching more sunlight on his expertly polished breastplate, he said, "I am Commander Steffan Alderhouse of the First Legion, First Battalion, First Brigade, and it is our job to know who is on what ship."

"I'm sure you are, and I'm sure it is. Fine, bring me."

"Of course, my Lord. Will you need a separate carriage for your luggage and servants?"

"I'm a priest, not a magister," he said without trying to hide his disdain. "I carry only what I need."

Alderhouse didn't pick up on Frostwind's tone. "Very good. This way, Father."

"Lead on, brave Commander."

Alderhouse, with his perfect armor and unstained tabard, turned on his heel and pushed his way through the crowded merchants and dockhands. Every man he pushed aside shot him a look of venom, but none dared speak. Legion soldiers were posted at regular intervals along the wharf. The commander almost knocked one older man, with a bent back and missing arm, into the water. Frostwind helped the man up and needed to rush to catch up to the commander. "Ass," said Frostwind.

"What was that, Father?" asked Alderhouse over his shoulder.

"Just clearing my throat."

It was going to be a long ride to Citadel.

A carriage, covered and gilded, did indeed wait for them. Shadowed by the Premiere Wall and flanked by guards, the bustling crowd gave it a wide berth. Alderhouse held the door open for Frostwind. The priest did not like being waited on, but he did not protest. Seated, he helped himself to a bottle of wine that was sitting in a rack between the two benches. His head spun and everything felt oddly distant. A drink might calm his nerves. The goblets accompanying the bottle were deep and wide. Frostwind filled one and drained it just as fast. The commander raised an eyebrow.

"Long trip," Frostwind said.

Alderhouse knocked on the panel behind him and the

carriage rattled forward. Pulling aside the curtains, Frostwind filled another glass and watched everything roll by. They passed through the engraved oak and iron doors of the Grand Gate. The strongest doors in the kingdom, they'd never been closed to an invader. The passage through the wall was long and dark, lit by only the daylight at either end. Frostwind had almost forgotten the beauty that lay on the other side.

Rolling fields of green and tree-topped hills spread before him. The road was smooth and paved with square-cut stones. Four cavaliers, their escort to Citadel, flanked the carriage. Blue banners fluttered from their lances and the Compass Rose of Carodan looked back at Frostwind with its dragon eye. The floating sensation filling his head intensified for just a moment, and his vision flashed with blurs of fire, smoke, and combat. The rolling fields were charred and the trees felled. Bodies littered the road. He shook his head and everything returned to normal. The land outside his window was still untouched by war. He drank more wine.

The road pushed through the interior of the island, and they passed the occasional cart loaded with supplies or a carriage carrying members from one of the affluent high septs that populated the island. Ironheart was the only House that lorded over these lands. It was all so perfect.

They climbed a small hill and Frostwind, craning his neck out the window, saw Citadel in the valley below. Made of the same blue granite as the Premier Wall, the city was laid out in the same lines as the Compass Rose. Its outer wall was a great, eight-pointed star that rose from the verdant fields. Towers and obelisks reached for the sky, each topped with likenesses of Antaunna or golden domes. In the center of it all was Rynar Keep, home of the Royal House and named after Rynar Ironheart, the first and greatest king. The dizziness increased again and the city was consumed by flames. He blinked repeatedly and finished his cup. The fires were gone and everything looked as it should. He refilled the goblet.

He turned to the commander, who had been mercifully quiet during the trip. "Where will the King be today?"

The commander rubbed his chin. "A class is graduating from the Academera Militarium. He'll be at the ceremony to commission them."

"Will there be a parade?"

"As always."

Frostwind drank his wine. "A military parade. How grand."

***

The drums, with their incessant beat, gave Frostwind a headache. His body screamed at him. It had few energy reserves left. After entering the city gates, and passing buildings made by generations of the best masons, they had arrived at the Parade Ground just outside the Inner Wall of Rynar's Keep. Crowds of townspeople, dressed in their finest silks and linen, circled the grounds. He and the commander had ascended an observation platform reserved only for dignitaries.

"We won't be able to see the King until after the parade. He's clear across the field."

"How long will that be?" asked Cranden.

"I think the parade is just starting."

"Of course it is."

The drum line held the center of the field. The deep and rhythmic booming shook the bones of all present. Frostwind rubbed his head again and snuck a sip of the wine he'd poured into his flask. He breathed deep. His head was still fuzzy, but not from the wine. The air in Citadel was clear and helped ease some of his tension. A breeze always blew in off the lake, and trash was not allowed to accumulate in the streets. He didn't smell shit, unlike Whitebreak, where the gutters were choking with the waste of overpopulation. Here it was channeled underground into vast cesspools. Everything was kept clean and perfect.

The crowd cheered and applause rolled across the stone-paved field. King Joël Ironheart ascended a platform in the middle of the grounds. Even at this distance the strength in his frame was apparent. A breastplate of polished adamantite covered his broad chest. A cloak of red velvet, trimmed in white fur, hung from solid shoulders. His tunic and trousers were fine black wool. Vambraces and greaves of the same adamantite steel complemented his breastplate. A sword, said to be carried by Rynar Ironheart himself, hung at his side and upon his brow rested the crown of Carodan. A band of pure silver, jeweled with sapphire and diamonds, and engraved with the old language, the pristine piece did not show its two hundred fifty years. Ironheart waved and bowed to the crowd. Everyone bowed in return, lower than he and longer. Even Frostwind, who'd known the king when he was a boy, bent low. When he straightened and looked at the king again, Ironheart was naked and covered in blood. A noose choked his face blue as he swung from the railing of his podium. Frostwind rubbed his eyes.

Ironheart placed his hand over his heart and lowered his head in appreciation. Then, motioning to an officer at the far end of the parade ground, the King initiated the proceedings. The gates to Rynar's Keep opened, discharging the Legion of Citadel. The Heavy Cavalry appeared first, trotting in perfect step. The hooves of the massive war horses punctuated each drum beat. Frostwind's observation platform shook as the combined weight of three hundred horses thundered by. Five thousand foot soldiers followed. Pikemen, swordsmen, and archers, arranged into perfect squares of steel and flesh, marched in unison. Tall, rectangular banners of deep blue, emblazoned with the Compass Rose, stood high over every regiment. The crowd cheered and hollered. Women threw flower petals over the soldiers and men looked at their sons with pride. The drums kept everything in time.

With every passing soldier Frostwind thought of the men of Littletop. Torn, bleeding, their armor crumpled like tin, they begged him to help them, yet so many were beyond his power. Only able to give them honeymilk mixed with poppy to ease the pain, he would bless them and move on. The men burned by the Noriziem's accursed fire were the worst. Even poppy did not assuage their torment. He was supposed to be a healer and a leader of faith. He had failed at the first and wasn't sure if he believed in the second anymore. The way he had used Antaunna's form on that Noriziem prisoner went against everything he'd learned while sequestered at the Antaun Monastery. If the High Order ever found out, he would be excommunicated, and when he searched his heart, he almost thought he deserved it. He was so angry. So many young men gone. All those children. Natasha.

"A fine parade. The Legion of Citadel was in perfect form."

Frostwind jerked and strained to keep his face composed. He didn't know what was wrong with him. His head still felt enveloped by fog and sweat coated his skin. Not wanting the Commander to see his weakness, he nodded, scratched his bearded chin, and said. "An exemplary display of Cardanan power. When can I see the King?"

The legion had completed one loop around the parade ground and the last ranks were now filing through the gates on the opposite end of the field and into the grounds of the Academera Militarium. Ironheart descended his platform and strode to three lines of waiting, fresh-faced officers.

"The commissioning ceremony won't take long. We should be with the king before the sun rides high."

Frostwind's knees ached. His head spun. More sweat slicked his skin. Alderhouse turned back to the ceremony. Feeling only the need to be any place but here, Frostwind descended the platform and stumbled through the crowd.

***

He didn't know this street. Frostwind was certain the Temple was in this direction. The storefronts were all wrong, and none of the signs were in the right place. The streets were becoming more crowded. Where were all the people coming from? They seemed not to see him, and more than once he was knocked aside by preoccupied citizens in fine clothing. How dare they? He was a priest of Antaunna! With a flick of his finger he could call Her wrath down upon them and make them regret sins long forgotten. He did not remember that in Citadel priest wore fine robes of blue wool and decorated themselves with exquisite silver jewelry. His simple attire was no better than a beggars, and beggars were not tolerated in Citadel.

His limbs were numb and his mind swirled and tumbled. He tripped and fell, skinning his hands on the cobblestones. A lady dressed in only the finest silks stepped on his fingers as she strolled past. She looked at him the way she would a rat and continued into the nearest shop. Frostwind pushed himself up, his stomach clenching and wanting nothing more than to empty. His vision distorted again and flames filled the streets. Bodies lay scattered, their blood pooling in the gaps of the cobblestone. Ash filled the air. A roar shook the ground and shattered windows. Frostwind looked up. Vast and night-black, Galantaegan filled the sky. His bulk blotted out the sun. He alighted upon the battlements of Rynar's Keep. A second roar pierced Frostwind's mind. The Black Dragon unleashed a stream of flame into the streets of Citadel, incinerating everything.

Frostwind pushed his way through a knot of townsmen. His eyes wild, he didn't see what lay ahead of him. The people around him started to back away, unsure of what the crazed beggar in dirty robes would do. A sound pierced Frostwind's mania. Running water.

He followed the noise instinctually. Towering and pristine, a huge fountain graced the Temple Plaza. Antaunna, carved from blue granite, stood tall. Water streamed from her mouth and fore claws, catching the afternoon sun in the pattern of a million broken diamonds.

Frostwind kneeled at the lip of the fountain. He cupped the clear water in his hands and washed it across his face. The pure liquid eased his burning skin and cleared his mind. He submerged his entire head and then withdrew it. Water ran in rivulets off his beard and soaked the front of his robes. When he opened his eyes Citadel was intact. The masonry was still perfect, the people were still beautiful, and the order of things stood firm. Frostwind cupped more of the water in his hands and drank. The cool caress spread in his stomach and eased his discomfort.

"Oh my, what a dirty, dirty man. How did he get here?"

Frostwind paused at the voice. It was a woman's. He stood and turned. The same woman who'd stepped on his fingers, she now wore a new fur shawl over her shoulders. Her attendant, a girl no older than sixteen, stood behind the lady and nodded without raising her downcast eyes. "I beg your pardon," Frostwind said.

"You dare address me, filth? I have a mind to call the city guard."

Frostwind stepped towards the woman. He pulled back the sleeve of his robe and held his hand before the woman. The silver and sapphire ring of Antaunna glinted under the sun. "That would be Father Filth to you."

The woman's eyes doubled in size and her mouth moved, but no sound came forth. Frostwind thought back to an old spell he'd learned when he was only a boy. He and the other acolytes had discovered it in a text hidden far in the corner of the Antaun Monastery's library. "*Toaria qual ishma vruul.*"

The sapphire set into his ring flashed. It was then he realized he'd forgotten his staff on the boat. He'd have to retrieve it. A ripple moved across the woman. Her clothes swelled, pulsed, and then became translucent. They writhed and shifted and before she blinked, her beautiful silk and new fur turned to water and splashed on to the plaza. Naked as the day she was born, the woman screamed and tried to cover herself with her arms. Her attendant suppressed a laugh. Frostwind smiled, but he felt the blood rushing from his head. His vision faded in a pattern of rainbow-colored stars and he vaguely felt the impact of his head against the fountain's edge.

***

"Cranden? Cranden, can you hear me?"

The baritone voice was calm and soothing. Frostwind forced open his eyes, but only the right one responded. Hovering over him, without armor or regalia, Jo'el Ironheart looked every inch a worried mother hen. "Don't you know it's better to leave an old man sleeping?" Frostwind asked.

"Thank Antaunna. That cut on your head is deep. We weren't sure if you'd wake at all," Ironheart said.

Now that the king mentioned it, Frostwind's head pulsed like a kettle drum. The priest opened his left eye and pushed himself upright. The pillows were stacked high behind him, and he was able to sit straight. His stomach wasn't happy with the movement, but he forced it calm. "How long have I been out?"

"Three days. What happened Cranden? Alderhouse almost died of panic when he realized he'd lost you."

Frostwind snorted and smiled. "I'm not sure. I haven't been myself lately. The battle at Littletop taxed me. I need rest." The admission was surprisingly liberating. He'd not acknowledged the full extent of his fatigue to anyone. Being left alone and in peace was all he wanted. It would be so much better if Natasha were here.

"Rest you will have, old friend. My solar will be yours as long as you're here."

The king's solar, an open room of balconies, book cases, and crimson curtains, was perched high on the side of Rynar's Keep. Frostwind blinked and looked closer at the bed he was in. Not normally a part of the solar's furnishings; Ironheart must have moved it here for his recovery. One of the balconies was before him, offering a stunning view of the city's streets and walls.

Beyond the stone walls were the green fields and hills of True Tower Isle. "I appreciate that, Jo'el. I accept."

"Good. You do realize you created quite a mess for me."

"I'm sorry?"

"You used Antaunna's power to strip Mirabell Hightower, daughter of Reginald Hightower, of her clothing in the middle of the Temple Plaza."

Frostwind cocked his head to the side and raised an eyebrow, but then remembered. "So that's who that was. She looked better without the dress."

Ironheart stared at Frostwind for a moment, scratched his forehead, and then started laughing. "I've missed you, Cranden. It hasn't been the same since you left."

"And I you, Jo'el. How are Anna and the boys?"

Frostwind had married the king to his queen right after the Stonestriker Rebellion. He'd been happy to give the young monarch a moment of such happiness after the bloodshed and disloyalty brought about by Morrikii Stonestriker.

"They're well. She took them to the North Beach today. If you're up to it, I know they'd love to see you when they return."

"Certainly. If I weren't celibate, I'd have stolen Anna from you."

"Ha, that would have been quite a feat, old man. Besides, if you had won her, I'm not sure you could have handled her. She'd wear those old bones to dust."

"Perhaps, but what a way to die."

They both laughed. Ironheart stood, went to a nearby table, and poured them two glasses of an amber liquid from a tall, graceful bottle. Frostwind accepted his and took a large sip. The smoky fluid warmed his insides and burned his throat. "Hadari Sun Whiskey? This stuff is illegal," Frostwind said.

"I make the laws, I can break them," Ironheart said and shrugged.

"I'm not complaining." Frostwind drank more.

"What happened out there, Cranden? The letters make no sense."

"I imagine they don't," Frostwind said. He shifted in the bed and sipped more whiskey before saying, "The Noriziem attacked with overwhelming force. If the Grenar hadn't come we would have lost."

"Even with the spell you cast?"

"The spell only delayed them. It almost killed me. They were winning."

Ironheart walked out onto the balcony and looked down at his city. "The Noriziem attacks on Westlook cannot continue. I'm shifting the Seventh Legion to Westlook and mobilizing all militia in the province. The next time the Noriziem attack, I want them eradicated."

"What of the Grenar?"

"What of them?"

"There were hundreds, Jo'el. After they wiped out the Noriziem, they could have easily destroyed Littletop. But they didn't. They helped us."

"I'm reinforcing the border along the Grenfel marshes and the Amen'Kar River. I will not permit any further incursions upon my kingdom."

Frostwind leaned forward. His head throbbed terribly. "They saved us, Jo'el. If it weren't for them, I wouldn't be here right now. We should at least talk to them."

King Ironheart turned to his old friend, finished the last of his whiskey, and said, "You can't talk to animals, Cranden."

Chapter 20
I CAST MY EYE WIDE

Kailen wore no armor. His sword hung on Carra's wall. Armed with only a dagger and his bow, he stepped quietly through the woods outside Angler's Cove. It was beautiful here. Only the songs of wind and sea filled his ears. The coastal trees were small and stunted. Sunlight flooded the forest floor. He needed this. The silence and isolation were invigorating. In town he was constantly surrounded by people with their noises and mess. Folks were nervous and on edge after the attack at Littletop, but that was something that had happened to someone else. It didn't really affect them. Besides, with all the soldiers in the area they were surely safe. Kailen wanted to shake them, punch them. He wanted to scream in their faces and call them idiots. Only Carra kept him sane. Every night Kailen prayed for Antaunna to watch over her. If it weren't for Carra he may have drunk himself dead by now. The dreams came every night. Littletop burned. Soldiers died. Innocents were slaughtered. The face of the serving girl stared at him with empty, clouded eyes. Every night.

He jumped over a dead birch, landing quietly and smoothly. There weren't many deer left in these woods, and any remaining were very skittish. The slightest scent of a man sent them running. There was no need for him to hunt. Carra fed him well and he'd enjoyed everything laid out before him, but being out here and having nothing but his own senses to rely upon was reassuring. He was still a man, still Kailen Tidespinner. Was he a man his father would be proud of? Would his mother still love him? They were senseless questions, but he couldn't shut them from his mind. Why did he still live when so many others fell?

The undergrowth rustled behind him and to the left. The hairs on his neck stood. It might be a deer, but it sounded big. To find a buck this close to town would be surprising and definitely earn him the right to boast over a few mugs of ale. He changed direction, heading for the sound and pulling an arrow from his quiver. He nocked it and tested the pull. The string was fresh and the bow newly oiled. It would strike hard and true.

Creeping around a copse of stunted trees, he picked his way behind a thicket of jade berry. Beyond was a small clearing, but it held no animal sign. Kailen checked the ground closely, but there were no droppings or even fresh prints. He stood and scanned the vegetation. The sound had certainly come from here. Gently blowing, the wind rustled the leaves and pushed his hair into his eyes.

SNAP!

Kailen whipped to the right and raised his bow, drawing it back. A wall of vegetation was his only target. No other sounds followed. When a deer walked in the woods it was noisy. Ridiculously noisy. Between the previous rustling and breaking twig there had been no other sound. Keeping his bow raised, he tried pushing through the brush. The branches were thick and close, and he had to lower the weapon and ease the string forward. After surviving a major battle, he was not going to die by shooting himself in the face with his own arrow.

The ground sloped down and he found a wide game path. He raised his bow again and followed the trail down to a bubbling, spring-fed creek. Nothing. Relaxing his bow and kneeling, he dipped his hand into the clear water. It numbed his fingers instantly. While spring had come to the trees, the water still held stubborn ghosts of winter. He scooped a handful into his mouth and sighed as the fresh liquid eased his parched throat. A water skin hung on his belt, but this was much fresher. Scanning the woods, he wondered what was out here. Was he being stalked? There were no big forest cats this far north, and there was no sign of wolves. A bear would have announced its presence long ago. Something was here though. Kailen could feel it. His neck still tingled.

Perhaps he was imagining things. Shadows seemed to linger

everywhere recently. He still didn't understand why the battle had affected him so. He'd fought and killed many times. His adult life was dedicated to the Legion, and it was a certainty he would see further fighting. One night, after too many beers, he'd asked Carra if being haunted by the battle made him weak. He wasn't sure if he even deserved to carry a sword anymore. She had taken his hand, kissed his brow, and said any man not affected by the battle had no compassion or heart. Then, teasing him, she said that even though he didn't let others see it, he was full of compassion and heart.

Something landed behind him. The ground vibrated under the impact. It was close. Every muscle in Kailen's body quivered and his breath stuck. An odd scent carried on the wind. Musky and sweet, it wasn't unpleasant but reminded him of a horse. The closeness of whatever it was pressed on Kailen's senses. If he moved too fast he might startle the creature, but if he was too slow he left himself vulnerable to attack. Figuring that if it were a predator, he'd already have teeth buried in him, he turned slowly and readjusted his bow.

A Grenar, standing with its feet apart and holding a giant halberd, towered not more than a sword's reach from him. Kailen snapped to his feet, took several steps back, and leveled his bow at the brute's face. He'd have one shot. If he didn't drop the ape-face it would close and tear him to pieces. He might be able to fend it off with his sword . . . which was hanging on Carra's wall. "Shit."

The Grenar did not move. One hand behind its back, the other resting on the massive halberd, it cocked its head to one side and regarded Kailen with a raised eyebrow. Kailen realized he should be dead by now. The thing could have skewered him as soon as it landed behind him. Where had it come from, anyways? Was it swinging through the damned trees? His arm was starting to shake, and it would be extremely easy to plant his arrow in the beast's eye, but the Grenar's calm confidence gave him pause.

Raising the halberd, it stepped forward. Kailen prepared to release, but held when the Grenar drove the halberd blade-first into the ground. That weapon, the raven-colored hair, it all seemed familiar. This was the Grenar that attacked the Noriziem. He was the one who saved Littletop. Kailen lowered his bow and removed the arrow. Not sure if he'd gone crazy or not, he set both on the ground. The Grenar nodded, reached to the small of his back, and produced a curved dagger. That too it buried point first in the rocky soil. Kailen removed the dagger from his boot and did the same.

He had no reason to trust the beast. The stories were old and familiar. The ferocity and depravity of the Grenar had terrorized the Cardanans for generations. Thousands were murdered by their hands, but this one had saved Littletop. This Grenar had saved him. It could have killed him now and with embarrassing ease, but didn't. Something was different.

The Grenar tapped its chest and in a growling, resonant voice said, "Skal Rend'arr."

Placing a hand on his own chest, the Cardanan said, "Kailen Tidespinner."

The brute nodded again and sat cross-legged by the stream, taking a moment to look at the water appreciatively. A small smile revealed its canines. Looking at Kailen, the Grenar pointed at a spot of ground in front of him. Perhaps this is a dream, Kailen thought as he sat. Surreal did not even begin to describe the moment.

The Grenar pointed at Kailen, and with visible concentration said, "You."

It tapped its own chest. "I."

The intimidating creature then motioned back and forth between Kailen and itself. "Talk."

Chapter 21
TO GO FORTH, BRAVELY

"What happened to my men?"

Morrikii Stonestriker stood by the large table in his throne room, looking down at the map of the three continents; Granikar, Fridinikar, and Abinar. His companion, Markan, was angry and had reason to be. "They sailed for Carodan two months ago. We've heard nothing."

Morrikii met the khan's glowering eyes. Markan had stormed into the throne room demanding to speak to him, and Morrikii had ordered everyone to leave. On the eve of their departure he could not risk creating doubt in the other Noriziem. "Markan, we've fought together for years now. You know we lose raiding parties. Either the weather or the Cardanans could have taken them."

"I sent two thousand men. This was no raiding party. The other khans have asked me how the attack went. I can't tell them because we don't know. I still don't understand why I sent them. The Cardanans will be on guard now."

Markan's face grew progressively redder, making his ginger beard look paler than it actually was. A vein pulsed in his neck and another on his forehead. Morrikii needed to calm him down fast. The khan had been this mad only once before, and the Noriziem's second-in-command had lost his head shortly after. Stonestriker motioned to the map. "Markan, come here."

The Noriziem stepped next to the table. Markan's battle axe was still strapped to his back, but Morrikii knew with a swift motion it could be loosed and used. He rolled and stretched his shoulders in case Sunder needed to be drawn. Pointing to Westlook, where Littletop was, he said, "By now, they'll have seen the pattern of us attacking Westlook more than anywhere else. Yes, we've struck elsewhere, but only so they don't grow suspicious. Whether or not your men were successful, a force this large will be impossible to ignore. Ironheart will reinforce Westlook, but it will still be too weak to repel the strength of your entire clan. More than likely he'll have moved a legion, maybe two, from Tidal Guard. Jo'el Ironheart is a good tactician, but not very creative. So, alive or dead, your men have aided the success of this invasion."

The vein in Markan's neck pulsed less. He smoothed the wild locks of his beard and said, "But so many wasted."

"We don't know they're dead. Maybe they were successful and have pushed farther inland, causing mayhem throughout Westlook."

"Galantaegan has not told you their fate?"

Morrikii tapped his finger against the wood, chewing his lower lip. Last night he had tried to summon the Black One, but the great statue did not stir. He still felt the dragon with him and in his thoughts, but this was the first time the Black One did not answer his call. "The God of Chaos is not concerned with our military planning minutia. Now, are your ships ready?"

Markan's gaze lingered on the map before meeting Morrikii's eyes. "Yes, fully loaded. As are Clan Thent's. In two days your ships, Clan Wathiem's, and Clan Lobrenth's should be filled."

"Good. We'll sail with the next day's first light. We're a month ahead of schedule. Make sure everything is running smoothly, and keep an eye on Toral. I need you to watch him for me." Morrikii still did not trust the Khan of Thent.

Markan bowed his head. "Of course. However, if my men are dead, the soldiers of Westlook will pay for it."

"I understand, my friend. I know you've wanted Westlook since you led your first raid. You will be its Magister. Now go. I still have much to do."

Markan bowed again and left. It was odd to see the throne room completely empty. There was always some activity. He walked up the center aisle, his footsteps echoing and mixing with the sputtering torches. The obsidian walls and columns swallowed the light. The likeness of Galantaegan lingered everywhere.

Carved, painted, or etched, the Black Dragon watched over it all. Morrikii knew that when he left here the dragon would follow. There would be no statues, no ancient, cracked murals, but that cold echo in the back of his mind was always there.

"Beautiful, isn't it?"

He hated when she did that. Her silence was uncanny. Turning to the doors behind him, Morrikii smiled at Jenaka, hiding that she'd startled him. "It is. Even Whitebreak or Citadel can't rival the stonework."

Wearing a dress of dark blue wool, finely woven and fitted, Jenaka looked a part of the decor. The long braid of her ebon hair hung over her left shoulder. Her every step was measured and her hips swayed perfectly. He knew what she wanted.

She passed him, climbed the dais to the throne, and trailed her fingers along the armrest. "Since coming here, I've wondered what it is like to sit in His presence. To be His vessel. His instrument."

"I am no one's instrument, my lady. I follow His word, and He gives me strength, but my choices are my own."

"Of course, I meant no offense, but to be the channel of Galantaegan's power must be exhilarating," she said and sat in the throne, crossing her legs. Her fingers still traced the carved stone.

"It can have its benefits," Morrikii said and climbed the steps to his throne. Some days it seemed more burden than benefit. Dora's head, bloody and decaying, still flashed through his dreams. It skittered over the marble floor again and again. The same expression of anger mixed with pity frozen in place. He did what was necessary. His choice allowed his people to live, and now he was bringing them home. All costs were inconsequential.

Jenaka's company was enjoyable, but sometimes she overstepped her bounds. Even though he planned to never set foot in this great hall ever again, it bothered him that she sat in his throne. Her allure was dangerous though, and he stared at the curve of her hips and breasts. Mella deserved better than him, but it had been so long since he'd held her close. The Noriziem whore was a decent substitute. "You're in my chair."

"Perhaps you'd like to join me," she purred.

He grabbed her shoulders and pulled her to him. Violent and bruising, they kissed. Picking her up, he turned and sat on the throne. She wrapped her legs around him. With Sunder still strapped to his back he needed to sit ramrod straight. It wasn't quite comfortable, but the way Jenaka rocked her hips against him took his mind off the inconvenience. He hiked her skirts up and found no underclothes, something not unexpected. She undid the front of his trousers, pushing aside the segments of his chain hauberk that hung below his belt. Pulling him out and giving it a single squeeze, she grinned wickedly and slid onto him. Morrikii shuddered at her warmth. It was tempting to release right there and let go of all control. Maybe it was her youth, maybe it was his inability to relinquish control, but he restrained himself and pushed against her with slow, steady thrusts.

For the warrior leader of her clan, she made the smallest, most-womanly noises during sex. She leaned into him, gasping, and whispered in his ear, "Doing this here, in the hall of our God, would be called blaspheming by most."

"I think He'll forgive us this one trespass. We are about to carry out his divine will and wipe Carodan, and the worship of Antaunna, off the map."

Jenaka sighed with pleasure and Morrikii closed his eyes, pretending it was Mella.

***

First light in Fridinikar broke clear and cool. With the onset of spring the outside air had lost some of its bite, but not much. Morrikii's breath still bellowed around his face, and his toes tingled against his boots. On the deck of his ship, the *Black Lord*, he surveyed the harbor. Slatewater Bay was vast, but his armada filled it. The combined strength of the Noriziem and House Stonestriker equaled two thousand vessels, and roughly one hundred thousand soldiers. Twenty-five years of planning had granted Stonestriker the largest army to walk the world since the height of the Norizaad Empire. It was intoxicating. He curled his lips momentarily, flashing his teeth like a wolf, and breathed deep. The cold didn't hurt so badly today.

From the high afterdeck of *Black Lord*, the harbor mouth ahead of him and his fleet behind him, he barked the order. "General, signal the fleet to make way. We sail south for Carodan!"

Adaes Axehaft, looking greener than normal, nodded and barked to his men on the ship's forecastle. Twelve archers, six to port and six to starboard, loaded flaming arrows and aimed for the sky. They released in unison, and the men on the *Black Lord* cheered as the arrows streaked high into the sky. The uproar spread across the fleet and to the shore, where the women, children, and those too old to fight watched. It worried him to leave them behind, but they'd be safer here until he secured Carodan. Within a year he'd give them a new home.

A stuttering groan floated over the harbor as every ship slipped their oars. The cheering intensified as the fleet took motion. Something unexpected happened. The raucous calls became unified and soon every man in the fleet chanted the same thing.

"Stonestriker! Stonestriker! Stonestriker! Stonestriker!"

He fought to maintain his reserve. A ruler needed to be calm and collected at all times. The cheering continued and he couldn't ignore the pride welling in his chest. His heart beat faster and he smiled openly. On the *Black Lord*, Axehaft led the cheer. The general's age-worn eyes crinkled shut with joy and his cracked, yellowed teeth, usually hidden behind his beard, were barred in a smile that rivaled Morrikii's.

The ships cleared the harbor, and the oars were stowed and sails unfurled. Remtagast's Breath, blowing hard off of Fridinikar's coast, filled the canvases, surging the ships forward. The vessels spread out, forming a great V that cut through the water like a titanic spearhead. Once they passed the Tol Archipelago, the fleet would split. The ships of Clan of Nathikan would make for the coast of Westlook where they were well-versed with the terrain. The rest of the fleet, the main thrust of the assault, would land just east of Sanctuary Bay and Whitebreak.

Morrikii moved to the bow. The winds generated swells upon the ocean, and a cold spray showered the deck whenever the ship cut through one. He withstood it though. Part of being a leader was showing your men you weren't afraid to get cold and wet. Axehaft joined him. The two men stood in silence, looking at the gray and endless expanse ahead. The general cleared his throat and spit into the water. "Does it make you nervous we're sailing to invade our homeland, a country whose god's domain is the ocean?

Morrikii chuckled. "It does not. Aside from legends and the magic tricks of priests, when was the last time Antaunna actually used her power to help Carodan?"

Axehaft nodded but said, "This is a fleet worthy of legend. It might be a good time for her to step back into things."

"She could, but fortune does not favor the meek. We'll have no trouble. Galantaegan watches over us."

Axehaft opened his mouth and then closed it, his grey eyes darting side to side. Whatever he was going to say he thought better of it. "Of course, my Lord. I'm going to see to the men."

Morrikii turned from the rail. "I'm headed below for a short while. I want to check on Mella."

"Of course."

"I'll see you for dinner?"

"Yes, my Lord."

Morrikii descended the narrow ladder to the second deck. Careful not to bump his head on the crossbeams, he squeezed his shoulders through the passage. Squinting to see in the dark, he came to a simple door at the end and pushed it open. His cabin held a wardrobe, small table, a desk, and bed. There was room for little else. The chill was thick down here, and the only light came from two candles held in thick iron mounts and protected by glass bowls. Propped up on several pillows, Mella lay on the bed beneath a pile of blankets.

Morrikii sat on the stool beside the bed and placed his hand on her forehead. It was cool and dry. He was worried the stress of the move would put her into a fit, or worse, bring on a fever. His advisors and her nurses all warned against her making the trip now, but he would not leave her in Fridinikar. Looking at her, trying to see her face in the dim light, he thought of how the sun and green fields of Tidal Guard would bring back her health. When he reclaimed his House's lands and rebuilt their stronghold, the Basalt Tor, he'd dedicate an entire wing to her. She could rest and recover there while he pushed his army south to Citadel.

The ship crested an especially violent swell and Morrikii fought to maintain his balance. Mella moaned and shifted. The dreamwine kept her asleep, but the motion of the ship seemed to disturb her. Morrikii caressed her forehead but she remained unsettled. He didn't want to give her more wine. Too much and she might never wake up. In their youth she always enjoyed his singing, but years had passed since last he sang. Often since she became sick, he would sit on the edge of her bed and think of singing. The words were never there though, and the melody was flat.

Today, though, he was bringing her home and giving her everything he promised. He thought back to when he was a boy and to what his mother sang whenever she sat on the terrace and did needlework. He didn't understand the song's meaning back then, but it was about a man who feared losing the love of his life. He was fated to roam the world, often very distant from his home and family, but would return whenever possible. It was her love that held back the darkness. Her touch that kept him sane. Her smile that made life whole.

Sitting in the dark, rocked by the waves of the North Ebon Sea and set upon a southerly course, Morrikii sang.

The Story Continues In:

The Paths We Choose

THROUGH DARKNESS TALL

VOLUME II

To delve deeper into the
World of K'aeran visit:

DWCRAIGIE.COM

PHOTOGRAPH BY JEANETTE WILSON

ABOUT THE AUTHOR

A New Hampshirite, born and raised, D.W. Craigie hails from the North Country. Reading and writing is a life-long passion of this mountain boy, and he believes the written word is the soul and cornerstone of any society.

Without words of inquiry our minds stagnate. Without stories of hope and loss our hearts grow shallow.

To the best of his ability he has tried to convey that passion for writing in this, his first novel.

CPSIA information can be obtained at www.ICGtesting.com
Printed in the USA
LVOW13s1141020314

375723LV00001B/43/P